More praise for Neal Barrett, Jr.....

"PINK VODKA BLUES"...

"For all the miles and laughs he racks up on the road, Mr. Barrett finds his best inspiration in bars and dry-out farms, places where he can size up the clientele and crack bitter jokes, the kind that leave bloody tracks behind."

-THE NEW YORK TIMES BOOK REVIEW

"Really a romp...reminiscent of several Hitchcock movies... Barrett has a wonderful way with words and has created a very funny crime story."

-MYSTERY NEWS

"DEAD DOG BLUES"...

"(Barrett) has peopled his town with crazies, but they're crazies we recognize...a detective novel with humor, excitement and suspense."

-DALLAS MORNING NEWS

"Following Barrett's success with 'Pink Vodka Blues' comes a wacky mystery in which Jack Track tries to solve the case of the barking dead dog in a millionaire's backyard, a dead *electric* dog...And that's just the beginning of this Texas mayhem."

-BOOKNEWS, THE POISONED PEN

"SKINNY ANNIE BLUES"...

"'Skinny Annie Blues' is one more example of a gonzo style that makes Kinky Friedman's work look sane..."

-HOUSTON CHRONICLE

"'Skinny Annie Blues' is in many ways, his best off-beat, outrageous yet...Barrett is not your typical tough-guy mystery writer...But when it comes to what he does, he's the best there is...think about Robert Parker and Elmore Leonard spiked with cheap margaritas and truck driver jokes...or just read the first page of this book, or any of Barrett's novels. You'll get the picture..."

-AUSTIN CHRONICLE

INTERSTATE DREAMS

Neal Barrett, Jr.

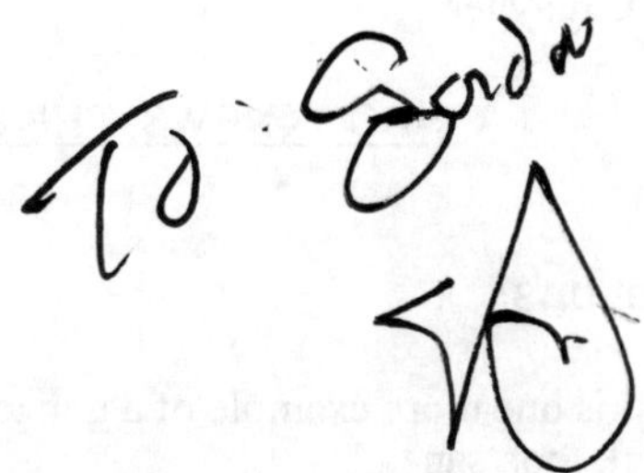

Dripping Springs, Texas

This is a work of fiction. All the characters, incidents, and dialogue, except for incidental references to public figures, products, or services, are imaginary and are not intended to refer to any living persons or to disparage any company's products or services.

Published by Mojo Press,

P.O. Box 1215, Dripping Springs, Texas 78620
www.mojo.com

Book Design by Ben Ostrander

Printed in the United States of America

ISBN 1-885418-22-1
Interstate Dreams
Neal Barrett, Jr.

For

TOM GARNER

It would be real hard to find
a better friend.
I don't guess I'll even try.

INTERSTATE DREAMS

PART ONE

MINNOWS,

GUPPIES,

and

SHARKS

INTERSTATE DREAMS

In the burgundy-colored van, the white man smoked and sorted colors in his head. Waited for a neat chromatic fix that might reveal the facts of life. Why cats don't seem to give a shit. Why girls don't like to fish. These would be good things to know, things that might lead to a better life for all.

The black man drove and watched the road. Didn't just *drive* like an ordinary man, like a man going down to the 7-Eleven store. Junior Lewis drove with heart, drove with his soul linked directly to the road. Driving was the second best thing he liked to do.

Dreamer didn't like to drive. He lacked dedication to the wheel, but he understood another man's needs. He liked to sit back and put his feet on the dash and watch Junior Lewis drive. Junior thought stopping off for gas was a pure aggravation, a precious waste of time. He didn't like to stop he liked to go. If a car didn't have to stop for gas, he'd drive straight through past Houston, Kansas and Fargo, North Dakota, up across the polar ice. Down the other side into Coldass, Russia, tires down to nothing, out of beer and barbecue. Rosy-cheeked girls would crowd around in furry hats. A girl with glacier eyes would say, "Hey, now, what's Junior Lewis doing here?"

Dreamer followed this scenario a mile or maybe two, losing interest fast when the Russian girl wouldn't cash a check. Leaned back and slid down easy in his seat. Watched Houston traffic slug along through the hot oppressive night. Watched the bright sulphur-eyed fish in a hydrocarbon sea. Wondered if a nuke would clear the air. Wondered if a girl in Oklahoma knew his name.

. . .

Dreamer watched Junior Lewis drive. Dreamer wished that he was black too. He felt he had a knack for darker skin, in spite of no talent for the dance. Junior had skin black as night. Not your common Hershey bar tone or a high yellow wimpy kind of black, but undiluted Kenya genes. In the stroboscopic light of passing cars, quicksilver washed the hard angles of his face. Dreamer thought it might be a Pharaoh's face, that Junior had likely done Egypt some time. He asked Junior once if Nefertiti rang a bell, if he had a thing for cats. Junior said he didn't know, said he couldn't quite recall.

All this quite coincidental with a Mako Binder sort of off-the-cuff aside the week before, Mako in Dreamer's Austin store to buy a matched pair of Red Devil Cichlids at a fairly hefty price. Mako Binder looking criminally intent in a Panama suit, and somehow spotting Dreamer's wish for greater soul. He said he felt Dreamer would fit right into nigger life. That he might give some thought to basketball. This without malice of any sort at all, simply mobster insight, storing up shit that could turn out useful sometime. Which was how Mako Binder stayed firmly at the top, in a business where retirement meant free fall without a gold watch.

. . .

Junior Lewis took a nip from his pint and passed it on, a pint in a brown paper sack.

"I guess not," Dreamer said, though a drink seemed proper at the time.

"Might just settle you some," Junior said.

"I feel I'm settled just fine."

"I see that you are."

"I got a firm handle on my needs. When I want a drink and when I don't."

"That's good."

"A man know his needs, he going to be a happy man."

Junior briefly took his eyes off the road. "What you ought to do, you ought to stop talking like that."

"Like what?"

"Dropping words and letters, then sticking one in that don't belong."

"You do it," Dreamer said.

"That's different, man. I got an ethnic obligation to talk the way I do."

"Well see, that's it. I wish I did too."

"You lay off those *Jefferson* reruns awhile, you're going to be fine."

"I envy you minorities a lot. I feel incomplete."

"I've got this Mes'can friend works down on the Gulf," Junior said. "He can read English okay, but he's got this dyslectic tic he try to read any Mex. Doctors can't find a thing. They maybe going to write him up."

"This is the funny looking dude with one eye."

"Who you thinking about is Raoul. Raoul the man bet Sid Pink he could drive to LA buck naked without getting stopped. Which he did, except Sid tips the law and Raoul is out twenty-five grand and a couple of weeks in jail."

"Sid doesn't much like to lose."

"That is a fact."

Dreamer looked out the window at the soupy primal mix that passed for air. Traffic up ahead disappeared, lost in a deadly yellow veil.

"I wouldn't live in Houston on a bet," Dreamer said. "What you got right here, you got the asshole end of the world."

"Nobody going to argue that."

"You ought to come to Austin, get out of this place."

"That hippie dog life's not for me," Junior said. "I'm your big spending type. I got the need for finer things."

"Jesus," Dreamer said, "where you been, man? Austin isn't like that now, hasn't been fun for thirty years. All the old hippies wearing suits."

"You don't say."

"Come over there, you could eat at Mama Lucy's every night. Eat ribs and sing darky songs. You play any banjo at all?"

"You tell Mama Lucy Junior Lewis says hello. You tell her that. Mama Lucy is one fine lady. There isn't many like her anymore."

"I don't guess I'll do that," Dreamer said. "Wouldn't want her to know I even saw you over here. She finds out I'm using you on something like this, she'll have my ass in a sling."

Junior laughed at that. "Don't have to *tell* that woman anything. She want to know something, she know."

Junior thought on Mama Lucy, thought about the long night ahead. "You want some more help on this, you got it. I don't have to tell you that."

"You're doing all you need to do, friend."

"Shit, I'm driving, isn't much to that."

"It's enough," Dreamer said, and said it in a way that didn't call for extra talk.

. . .

Traffic wasn't bad for Friday night. Slow, but better than the other way, better going out than coming in. Fun-lovers groped for the city's strangled heart, weekday people seeking weekend dreams, seeking joy and release, seeking major aggravation and assault. Dreamer thought about a drink, about the bottle in Junior Lewis' sack. A drink seemed the right thing to do. Alcohol abuse would put the night on hold, muddy up the colors in his head. In the morning he could tell himself he didn't need the money, didn't need it bad.

The thought seemed to carry some doubt, seemed to lack true conviction and accord. Money didn't matter and it did. The money was good, too good this time. When it got that good, there was always a bad reason why.

And that, Dreamer thought, was reason enough to call the whole thing off and have a drink. Drive back to Austin and call Eileen. If she's speaking to him now, they can go and have a steak and a beer. Tell the client in the morning things didn't work out the way they should. They wouldn't like that. They'd figure he was holding them up for extra bucks. But hey, you can't help what other people think. That's the way they are, that's what they're going to do.

Just at that moment, as a plan began to jell, as decision seemed complete, Dreamer looked past Junior at the traffic going south, at the yellow wash of light, at the phosphorescent blur, looked and saw the bottle-green Jag, saw the car stalled out and saw the girl, saw the skinny-butt jeans, saw the cool Madonna eyes, saw the bright sequin halter that would make a fag bullfighter cry.

All this in a wink but enough to let him know that love had struck him blind. Love, passion, and romance. True love paperback style, and, if the present is a mirror of the past, maybe something greater, maybe something bigger than that...

INTERSTATE DREAMS

"Pull off," Dreamer said, and Junior did.

Junior Lewis had seen the girl too. "We doing Batman and Robin?" he said, and didn't need to ask.

"We just might." Dreamer got out quickly and walked to the back of the van. Junior slid out on Dreamer's side, unwilling to risk awesome injury or death. He read the look in Dreamer's eyes. Found no trace of reason or restraint.

"Man, you don't want to do this," he said, "this is not a cool idea."

"That little girl needs care."

"Not from over here she don't."

"We can't just leave her there, Junior. That amounts to criminal neglect."

"That Batplane'd do it," Junior said.

Dreamer knew Junior was right, but he kept on watching all the same, searching for an answer through the white electric blur, through the whine of passing cars. He saw her in a fast-frame beat, saw her looking at the Jag, saw her staring at the hood. Knew there was nothing under there she cared to see. There was magic in the motor but she didn't have the spell.

The night smelled of chemical abuse, there was poison in the air. Dreamer felt he could love this girl a lot. Take her to his heart, answer all her dreams. And, with cross-traffic love came a sadness of the soul, a little tenor sax, a little moment of regret. He didn't know how this could be. They hadn't known each other long enough to sing the blues.

"Come on," Dreamer said, "let's go. We got to get off this mother and circle back."

Junior shook his head. "We be three whole days just finding an exit, man."

"Well goddamn, we sure have to try."

Dreamer started for the van and then stopped. Cross-lane motion caught his eye. The car snaked out of traffic and nosed up sly behind the Jag, a *barrio* Buick set gnat-turd close to the ground, a paint job slick and beetle-black, a Tijuana fresco of green serpent gods and a vaguely Mayan Jesus on the hood, Mary there somewhere, lost amid airbrush crucifixion and tears, possibly a yucca and a rose, all this a Sistine taco work of art and clearly trouble on the run.

"Uh-oh," Junior said, "those Mes'can Americans going to *help* that lovely girl."

"Christ, let's go," Dreamer said, unpleasant visions in his head.

"Time and space against us all the way," Junior said. "That gal have two little babies by the time we get over there, man."

"I don't care, it's better than just sitting here."

"Sittin' here's fine," Junior said. "You stay and watch. Stay cool, think black."

"Do what?" Dreamer watched in extreme irritation as Junior ran back to the van. Maybe Junior Lewis had automatic weapons in the back. Streetsweepers, Uzis and Stens. He looked across the lane. Fate dropped a snowcone down his back. All the doors of the Buick seemed to spring wide at once, as if the riders might have practiced such a move till they got it down pat.

There were six dark and fragile young men, jack-knife lean, clothing bright as ocean pearls. Some had Apache war paint across their eyes. Some had the look of Inca kings. One wore a Japanese mask. There was ethnic confusion in the night. They walked around the girl, they circled in a quick dance step with pointed toes, with a matador strut, a touch of the palm to slick the hair. Shy winks passed between them now and then. One seemed to parody the next. They paid no attention to the girl, never let her out of sight.

Dreamer spotted the leader of the band right away, and fear and sorrow reached out for him again. The boy was as pretty as the girl. A scar across his cheek only added to his grace. A Michael Jackson face with opal eyes. An angel with a shadow on his soul. He spoke very softly to the girl. He spread his arms wide and looked to God. Dreamer read his smile. With the help of *El Dios*, he would see this girl through trying times. He would take her to his breast, he would keep her from the night. He would show her razor love, but he would never break her heart.

Dreamer wondered if he could make it through the cars. Maybe so and maybe not. Then Junior Lewis came back.

"You take a nap in there or what?"

"Got us some cellular aid," Junior said. "Got some black road knights coming down. They maybe half a mile back."

Dreamer felt relief but not a lot. "They better do it real quick."

"They on the way now."

"I never heard of black knights. I'm pretty sure you had to be white."

"Who said?"

"You can look it up. A black guy couldn't be a knight."

"I don't remember readin' that."

"You probably skipped class. Went down to the fishin' hole."

"Lawdy, we likes to do that."

The boy stood very close. The girl had no place to go. She was feeling the gravity of this, feeling some alarm, feeling the pure and dark convergence of an alien soul. She tried not to let her fears show, but the boy had seen all this before, there was little that the boy didn't know.

The Merc blinked its lights, pulled off the road behind the Buick and the Jag. Two men got out, two Brothers in shades. One had a shiny bald head. One wore a Bogart hat. The man with the hat walked up politely and spoke to the boy. The man had a very winning smile. He looked as if he smiled all the time.

The boy stood his ground. Stayed long enough to hold his pride, long enough to scare the girl again, then he turned and walked away, turned and walked away as if he'd planned this all along.

"She be okay," Junior said.

"What those dudes'll do, they'll keep her for themselves," Dreamer said, "you can bet on that. A white girl's a black man's delight."

"I heard about that," Junior said.

. . .

He couldn't get his mind off the girl. He turned around and watched until the Jag disappeared, until love was out of sight, until Junior found a spot and tacked neatly in the flow. Her image burned a hole in Dreamer's heart. Where did she come from, what did she do? How would he ever find her now? Love wouldn't have a chance if they didn't get to know each other, if they didn't sit and talk.

He thought about her hair, he thought about her jeans, he thought about her lips, and her cheerleader thighs. An emotional stew began to simmer in his head. Purity and lust. Tenderness and pain. Joy and regret. He imagined them together. What she said, what he said after that. He yearned to buy her a burger and a beer. A triple-dip cone. A double feature at the drive-in, 1956, a soda and a kiss.

The colors in his head made sounds he didn't like. He pushed them all aside. He didn't want to mess with tints and tones. He wanted to think about *her*, and nothing else at all. Dreamer made a picture in his head. A double-strength sack from the grocery store. He stuffed all the colors in fast, rolled down the window and tossed it outside. Looked and tried to find the girl again and she was gone.

"I saw this thing on *Nova*," Junior said. "They got this Death Star circles out wide around the sun. Goes way out and comes back 'bout every twenty-six million years. Flat wipes *everything* out. They think it might've done the dinosaurs."

"Is it coming back again?"

"Sure is."

"Fucking figures," Dreamer said.

INTERSTATE DREAMS

It is past eight-thirty and still close to ninety-four degrees. Houston chokes beneath a heavy ocher sky. Air superheated from the day rises up to meet the hydrocarbon farts of Subarus, Chevrolets and Saabs, Broncos and Beetles, Fiats and Fords. Phantoms from above meet and mix, join with the wraiths from down below. Chemical remorse from the Houston ship channel, from the dead and turgid waters, clotted and congealed, mingles with the sweat-ghosts of bankers, bakers, bums and bookmakers, sinks to kiss the vapors of medical waste, bodies dumped in haste, bad breath from winos, bimbos and girls with broken hearts. Do-do from pit bulls and registered cats, Big Mac sighs and former satiated rats.

Through some emissive law, colors seem to seek their own kind. Yellow and brown and bilious green, a deadly shade of red, all coalesce in a mighty septic pie, in a poison club sandwich nearly half a mile high, a multi-layered dome that masks the city down below, an awesome incandescence in the final light of day.

Beneath the scabrous sky, people scutter this way and that to find a bed or a bar, an all-night movie or an unattended car, anywhere to suck in the chill electric air. Only the truly down and out, people sitting down to a catfood supper and a single color set, suffer from the stifling heat of night...

. . .

The way it all works came to Wallace Pailey Marshall in a two-liter dream, a vision born of malnutrition and alcohol abuse. What he saw was a great lake of ice buried far beneath the earth, a lake as big as Texas, white and deadly cold, cold enough to freeze the awesome magma that rolls beneath the world.

In his dream, Marshall saw a million silver straws stretch up from the ice to the undershell of Houston where he lived. Bright straws sprang to the surface like weeds, sprang into condos and cheap motels, into trailer parks and malls, into cafes and bars, into the bedrooms of billionaires and aging porno stars. And, wherever the frosty straws appeared, high-priced lawyers and half-price whores, K-Mart shoppers and debs with canker sores, fought to find a straw, fought to breathe the frigid air, fought and scratched and lied, killed to suck and stay alive.

Like everything else in the world, Marshall knew, there weren't enough straws to go around. You had to stay on top, get as many as you could. Fuck other people out of theirs, or they'd sure as dirt fuck you out of yours. You either did, or did without...

. . .

This is God's truth, and Wallace Pailey Marshall ought to know. It is 8:42 in the torrid p.m., and Marshall sits alone on a bed of white gravel, dog shit and fast food debris. He leans against the walls of Al-Mustadi's Self-Service beneath the great pillars of Interstate Highway 45. From there, he can see the bright lights of the cars flashing by, listen to the shrill ululation of the tires.

Different cars make different sounds. The little cars whine and the big cars sing. The eighteen-wheelers howl like a pride of hungry lions. And, when the sounds come together, they blend into a song. Marshall loves to listen, and loves to hum along.

Wallace is aware of the cars, but he isn't sure exactly where he is. Demons have erased all his tapes, all his concepts of present time and space. The lack of a universal site makes Marshall uneasy in his head. People who don't know where they are tend to simply fade away. He has seen this happen many times before. People that he knew simply don't come around anymore.

I'd better make sure, Marshall thinks, and he carefully presses one hand against the ground. There. There's where I am, I'm right here. Wino navigation does the trick, and Marshall feels content.

. . .

Sometimes, the fog seems to lift, and Marshall is aware that they've fucked him out of every silver straw he ever had. He doesn't know how or why or when, but he's certain that they did. On really bad nights he has the dream.

He dreams about the woman. The woman's name is Amy and she smells fresh and clean, clean as a BMW off the floor. There's a two-story house in the dream, a house in the heart of River Oaks with a pool and a spa and a four-car garage. There are beds and clean sheets. Fifteen cases of single-malt Scotch and a cellar full of wine from overseas. A Maserati and a Porsche. A BMW and a classic MG in authentic British Green.

Sometimes Marshall sees a BMW on the road. It makes him real happy when he does. For a moment, he feels that he's sitting on leather instead of doggie-do. Mostly, he sees cars in bright, visceral colors that hurt his eyes. He feels that he might be losing touch. He feels as if his life might have wandered down a strange erratic course, going somewhere that he doesn't want to go.

. . .

Something on the freeway seems to catch his eye, something so sweet and purely fine it brings him out of dipso reverie close to a conscious state of mind. He sits up straight to watch a miracle, a vision pass him by.

The vision sits atop a van, painted in the rich, purple hues of kings. It catches the light of passing cars, the neon filaments of red and pink and blue and dazzling green. What it is, and Marshall can scarcely believe his eyes, is a bottle fully ten feet long, resting on its side, the neck tilted high. It reaches out and holds him, like the loving grace of God, the most wondrous thing he's ever seen. It throbs with a plum-colored luminescent glow, a glow that frames the sight in a rich magenta aura suspended in the air above the van.

The vision is so clear, so incredibly real, Marshall can follow the chill tears of violet that bead up on the glass. He can see the nice picture of a French chateau, the red metal foil about the neck. He tries to imagine how much the bottle holds, how long it would take him to drink. The thought shorts every pickled circuit in his head. How long is forever? How far is it to a star?

Marshall follows the bottle with his eyes until at last it disappears. Long after it is gone, he holds the holy wonder in his head. He decides he will never tell anyone else what he has seen. Not Wildcatter Jack or Bob or Sil. Fuck 'em. If Jesus wants to send them a vision, then He will...

In the hot dark of night, Dreamer watched Junior Lewis drive. He watched Junior's shoulders bend slightly to the wheel, watched the skin stretch tight across his skull. Dreamer knew exactly why he liked the color black. One, because he did. Two, because he knew that among the pigment-challenged, there were people who fucked up the colors in his head. He couldn't say why, but he knew that's what they did. Blacks came on nice and easy, at least they did to him. He'd get to talking late at Mama Lucy's Vishnu Jesus Barbecue and the indigos and greens and the midnight blues would start hanging in the air like a smoky magic veil. You'd hardly ever see a yellow or a metal-ripping red. Black people kept his mind straight. White people left broken glass inside his head.

Okay, it didn't work out all the time. Take Steel-Eye Brown, a dude Mama Lucy wouldn't let inside the door. There wasn't a color in Brown's ugly head that smelled anything but blood. Steel-Eye Brown would kill Christmas if he could. Steel-Eye would dropkick a nun. He'd run down an angel in his coal-black Olds.

All of which told him what he already knew. There were assholes of every size and color you could name. He could get along better, and his head felt nice, when the people around him had cool night shades.

He, knew, though, the matter went deeper than that. He'd felt this affinity before he got the colors in his head, and wisely kept the matter to himself. In Lubbock and Odessa, there was little discontent with honky genes. Few boys out in West Texas had the urge for blacker hues. He could not recall a friend at Texas Tech who said, "Man, I sure do wish I wasn't white. I wish I was a nigger instead."

Dreamer knew the need was clearly there. Mako Binder had seen it, and Eileen saw it too. Eileen didn't like it, and didn't mind letting him know. Mama Lucy saw it, and didn't much approve. Mama Lucy felt God put color where He wanted it to be. That a man ought to stick with the skin that he got, even a man who was doomed to be fish-belly white. Faded, sallow, pale as flour paste, bleached and washed out.

Maybe, Dreamer thought, he'd picked up some soul along the way. Maybe he'd shot a little pool with Junior Lewis and Tut in a former Dreamer life. Maybe, some rich Swahili sap slipped in the family tree in Tennessee. If it did, why that'd be fine. Just so his dead daddy never heard about that...

. . .

At Conroe, Junior left the freeway and headed due west. The nuclear haze over Houston was forty miles south, an olive-yellow worm against a lint-colored sky.

"It's eight or nine miles," Dreamer said. "You want to stop before we get to the wall. Those people got gadgets in there can hear you farting in the car."

Junior flipped a switch to let the lights in the bottle overhead begin to cool. Dreamer searched around for shoes. They were all-black Nikes, worn to fit his feet, worn to where toe shadows scruffed the canvas top.

"Anywhere here's just fine," he told Junior, "you don't want to get close."

The road was two-lane, new black asphalt with highway-yellow lines. Tall murky pines lined the way on either side. Two cars passed from behind. A pickup came the other way, a boat on the trailer in the back. Junior pulled up and doused the lights.

Dreamer sat and listened to the dark. Crickets and frogs, locusts buzzing in the trees.

"Thanks for the help, pal. I'll catch you tomorrow sometime."

"I can wait, man. You don't have to be getting back yourself."

"No way," Dreamer said. "This ride's about as subtle as the circus in town."

Junior couldn't argue with that. Dreamer used the window to climb to the top of the van. In spite of the distance from the city, the air was hot and still and smelled faintly of chemicals and dust.

There were four metal snaps on the big plastic bottle. Dreamer lowered himself in, careful not to break the lights. He tapped two times, and Junior started up again. In three seconds flat, Dreamer was soaked with sweat, but there was nothing he could do about that.

He listened and waited, then Junior slowed and turned left. Tires snapped on a good gravel road. Junior eased the van to a stop. Dreamer heard the guards' heavy steps, one to the left, another to the right. A hand slapped the side of the van.

"Hey, Junior Lewis, you doin' all right there, boy?"

"Makin' out jus' fine, Mister Bill," Junior said, properly indolent, walking real slow, tossing in a watermelon grin. Dreamer felt him step out of the van, go to the side and slide back the door.

"That all you got," the guard said, "one case?"

"Shit, man," Junior said, "that be your Chateau fucking somethin' or other, nineteen fifty-six. You lookin' at five-hundred ninety-five dollahs a whack."

"Goddamn," the guard said, "you reckon it's any good?"

The other guard laughed. Junior did a suitable shuffle to the door and climbed back in the van. A flash found the bottle, and filled the inside with a milky purple light.

"You got a bulb or something out," the guard said.

"Motha *always* going out," Junior said. The engine came to life, and the van rolled slowly up the drive...

INTERSTATE DREAMS

Dreamer knows a case of good wine at 10:30 Friday night won't make any waves at Enchanted Mesa West. The order is for real, and they see Junior Lewis all the time. Someone likes a little red with the Letterman show, that's fine. The people here order what they like. Vans drive in day and night. Vans bring condoms and Jamaica Blue Mountain Coffee beans. Vans bring Czech Pilsner beer and Hershey bars. Vans bring Cuban cigars and unborn Italian suits. Vans come from Gucci and Pucci and Sears. Vans bring pizzas and fine Sulka ties.

The French-gray van from Pauliano's brings signed prints and paintings, cafeteria style. Picassos and Pollocks and Klees to match the drapes. The chocolate-brown vans from Aunt Sally's Home Bakery Shoppe bring flaky croissants and chilled eclairs. Coral-pink vans from the Friendship Florist bring flowers still kissed by the dew of Sumatra and Belem.

Those in the know--and everyone at Enchanted Mesa is--can ask Aunt Sally for some gingerbread men (good Turkish hash), oatmeal cookies (Colombian coke), or Angelfood cake (Acapulco Gold). Aunt Sally's is fully owned by Mako Binder, who also owns Pauliano's and the Friendship Florist chain. Customers at Enchanted Mesa West state age, sex, and color persuasion of the driver who comes with the Friendship van. A call to Pauliano's brings up-to-date video delights: Sniff, snuff or S&M. Man, woman or Pekinese.

Dreamer knows the A-list refers to these services as Sally High, Port-a-Whore, and Twenty-First-Century Fuck.

But never, *never* do they say it where Mako Binder can hear...

The van slowed, and Junior tapped on the roof. Dreamer waited. Junior tapped again. Dreamer raised the plastic lid, emerging like lobster thermidor into air scarcely cooler outside. Squatting on the roof, he secured one snap on the bottle and jumped into the thick green hedge beside the road.

He lay on his back and watched the tail lights disappear. Looked at the map in his head and knew exactly where he was. Less than twenty yards to the building, and cover all the way. Manicured shrubs in the shadow of tall Texas pines.

Dreamer closed his eyes and let his breath go shallow and still, let the colors go to work. He smelled the scent of cinnamon and Spam. Blue Crayolas and clean athletic socks. Gold electric ants in his hair, and beetles on his skin. He distinctly heard a line from a Bette Davis film.

It took a good minute and a half. Dreamer sat up and looked around. It was all right there, as clear as it could be, thin green wiggles going this way and that, a holographic map spread out before his eyes.

Jesus, Dreamer thought, they got an awful lot of stuff. It was all on Paulo's chart which had cost him a bundle to get. Still, he'd never seen anything like it anywhere. It was sheer electronic assault. Radio Shack and the CIA were holding a sale at Enchanted Mesa West. There were video cameras on the twelve-foot walls, stone and razor wire, and that was just a start. The system worked out from the wall. The strongest defenses were closest to the building itself. It reminded Dreamer of a firebase in Nam, though that was one war that he'd missed.

An infra-red nighteye system backed up the TV snoops. A marble-chip path wandered out from the wall like a lazy little stream; water-worn stones placed artfully about in the Japanese style. Within this area, thin copper wires stretched an inch above the ground. They wouldn't kill a man, but they'd knock him on his ass. There were pressure mines in the grass, ears that could hear a flower grow. Closer to the building, red laser spiders spun their webs, daring anyone to break the spell. There were pinecone mikes in the trees. Sensors in the yucca and the sage. A thousand crystal eyes, blinking blindly in the night.

It was overkill beyond all reason, protection past any conceivable need. Dreamer knew it, and the people who'd installed this million dollar system knew it too. But this was not your ordinary rent-a-cop Tinkertoy two-dollar whoopa-whoopa listen-to-the-sirens-go-off kind of place. This was Enchanted Mesa West, and the folks inside liked all the good shit they could get.

. . .

Dreamer sat on the grass and watched the colors mix and flow. At first, the pale shades and hues were all lumpy and bumpy and slightly out or synch. Ice cold and hot, gritty and slick. Soft as a feather, harder than a brick. Colors that didn't quite match, and some that nearly did. Like flour and eggs, and sugar in a bowl. Nothing looked right until you whipped it all up into something really good.

This is how it worked: The colors and the sounds and the smells came together and baked an electric chocolate cake in Dreamer's head. Dreamer tasted copper, cobalt summer rain. A hum like a pretty girl's hair. A smell like a kitten's olive eyes. He watched the videos sigh and take a nap. Heard the pink lasers curl up on the lawn. Felt the sonics yawn, tasted fresh vanilla on his tongue.

He didn't have the faintest idea how it worked, he simply knew it did. Two-thirty-six a.m. Ninety-two degrees. The chopper screamed down in banana-land burning like the fires of inner Hell, burning like the center of the sun. Everyone shrieked, everyone smelled like bad barbecue. Everyone died, and Dreamer lived on.

He didn't know what happened, but it did. What he knew was the colors in his head told him all he had to know, every sly device, every trick and every trap. When he walked through the shrubs beneath the trees, he winked at every gadget, every ruby laser eye. The electronic tigers knew exactly what he weighed and what he wore. They knew he'd had chili with Junior Lewis the night before. They didn't turn off and they didn't look away. They didn't start to whimper, they didn't start to howl. They simply didn't give a shit that Dreamer was around...

Enchanted Mesa West is twenty-two stories high, built like a horseshoe, built like one of Mickey's ears. The materials are weathered pecan, copper the shade of old moss, Hill Country limestone, and honey-colored glass that filters out the harsh Texas sun.

The style of the building is harder to define. A New York critic called it 'Texas Babylon.' *Time* said it was 'Greco-Mayan Fort Knox.'

The residents liked this description a lot. It was close to what they'd really had in mind. Newton Fielder Forbes, Houston's leading architect, had sternly warned the builders to avoid any "middle-class cozy sort of crap." Those who could afford Enchanted Mesa West, Forbes said, wanted luxury, comfort and security, a place that would keep out the you-know-whats, people from other lands than ours, people who were born with a permanent tan of some sort.

Within the twenty-two stories are a hundred and eighty two spacious homes, each boasting five-thousand-two-hundred-six square feet in the gracious Southern style. Each unit has a view of a virgin forest from the Tuscan veranda on the building's outer curve. From the inner span, residents gaze at a lake-sized pool. Past the building is a 36-hole golf course, riding paths and stables, an artificial trout-stocked hydraulic river and a blue lake for sailboats and shoreside fun. A meadow stocked with semi-conscious quail. A landing strip for jets.

All this splendor, set amid eight-thousand-one-hundred-seven well-guarded acres, formerly a haven for endangered birds and plants. Gracious living starts at three million-five. And every square inch of Enchanted Mesa West, inside and out, is protected by security that surpasses state-of-the-art. Residents steal from one another now and then. There is murder and suicide, rape and assault, but all in-house and all perfectly discreet.

Twenty-seven burglars and eight skilled assassins have tried to breach the grounds. The electronic tigers have eaten them one and all.

All except Dreamer, who has now scaled fourteen lovely Tuscan gardens, and is climbing higher still...

Junior had tested him out on a limestone wall the night before. "Shoot, you better than the Green Hornet," Junior said. "You as good as The Shadow, man."

In fact, the wall was easy enough. There was ample space between the limestone slabs, deep enough for fingers and good athletic shoes. The sky was dark and overcast, and very little light escaped the richly curtained windows that he passed. The balconies, now they were something else. If anyone walked outside and cared to look, they'd see a man climbing up the wall. Dreamer didn't think they'd do that. Texans had good common sense. Texans didn't go outside on a hot and sticky night.

. . .

On fifteen, the curtains were slightly parted. The room was bathed in soft light from Tiffany lamps. Tiny leaded shards of citron, topaz, amber and a brilliant blood-red. Dreamer looked at the lamps a long time. He dearly loved Tiffany lamps. He knew these were real and what they cost.

The walls were blue silk. The furniture was French; seventeenth century, he thought, but he didn't know for sure. The carpet was a real Oushak. Eileen had one that was nearly as fine. There were paintings in heavy gold frames. A small Renoir and a Monet, some he didn't know.

The thing that turned him on was the fire. It was maybe ninety-four and the air was heavy as a sauna outside. And here was this fireplace, flames dancing off the silken walls, like Christmas Eve in Vermont. Now that is fucking class, Dreamer thought. Turn the air down to forty-two and build a fire. He waited for a moment to see who lived in this place, but no one appeared.

The curtains were drawn on sixteen, seventeen and eighteen as well. At nineteen, he pressed himself flat against the outside wall. The drapes were wide open and a painful white light stabbed the dark. He knew he shouldn't stop. The system couldn't catch him, but a guard who looked up would surely spot him, pinned against the light.

Still, the sight held him entranced. The ceiling and the walls and the carpet were white as bleached bone. Furniture was sketched about the room. Harsh squares of black and silver chrome. The table was a glass slab thick as polar ice. Six black cushions planted about the table, commas that appeared to have fallen off a page.

Yet, it was not the room that held him, but the picture on the wall. The only color in the room was this massive, unframed canvas, fully ten by ten. Narrowing ellipses of apricot and coral, shrimp-pink and rose, hues that seemed swollen, plush and overripe, steamy with a rich tropic heat, a growth intense and uncontained, a bright, carnivorous bloom poised to grab a tasty fly.

In spite of the danger of discovery, the picture held him there. It was ready for a treat, ready for a snack. It might slick right through the glass and pull him in. It might just--- --Holy shit, Dreamer thought, for as he watched, as he lingered, as his vision seemed to work some magical displacement of the eye, some trick to bring illusion into place, he saw this was no hungry flower at all, saw color and dimension had played a sly game inside his head. With a blink and a mouth gone dry, he saw a mighty vulvar display, a gnat's eye view of super love, an alpine labial ascent. And, at the crown, at the peak, at the crest of this lubricous array, a bright and shiny pearl the size of an NBA basketball.

"Jesus," Dreamer said aloud. He wished Junior Lewis could see the sight himself. Junior was really into art, and it would go with everything in Junior's house.

. . .

At twenty-two he stopped, the penthouse level of Enchanted Mesa West. He watched for signs of life on the balcony to his right, then slipped over quickly, dropped down behind a pot of ferns and out of sight. Vines clutched the walls, and made a thick arbor overhead. Dreamer peered through a glass door that led inside.

The room was lit by a single pale lamp. He studied the layout in his head. Past the den and down the hall. Take a right up the half-stairs. Library past the second door on the left. Desk in the southeast corner of the room. If the client's information was right, Halloran Horn and his wife were at the Houston ballet that night. No one else was in the house, he'd been assured of that. And, if his client was wrong, someone would wake up and shoot him in the head.

Inside, there was no sound at all, only the hiss of cold air that turned

Dreamer's sweat to ice. He let the small penlight guide him through the room. Up the half stairs, a faint smell of lemons in the air. Left. Second door. English hunt scenes, water-color ducks in flight. Dark paneled walls and pewter lamps. Carpet the color of port. A perfect set for a good whisky ad. Guy in a smoking jacket, salt and pepper hair.

Dreamer found the desk with his light. Whoever set it up had done his job well. He knew about the ducks, knew the color of the carpet on the floor. He had been in this very room himself. Standing where Dreamer was standing now. Not as an intruder, as a guest. Someone Horn would invite into his home.

Dreamer thought about that. It didn't seem right. You shouldn't have a drink with a guy, and figure out how to steal his stuff. It didn't bother Dreamer stealing from Horn. He was only taking back what Horn had stolen himself. Horn was a thief. Not a retriever like Dreamer, but an out-and-out filcher of other people's goods.

The man who bothered Dreamer was the man who'd set Horn up. A guy like that, you could never trust at all.

He found the envelope in the second drawer, right where they told him it would be. Nothing else there but scattered paper clips. He glanced at his watch, stuck the envelope under his belt and turned to go.

At the balcony, he paused to look down. Everything was quiet below. Easing himself over the edge, he made his way past twenty-one and twenty, nineteen and eighteen after that. His foot struck something hard. Easing his grip, he bent down and touched a potted plant.

Dreamer let out a breath. Jesus, he'd let his mind wander and nearly knocked it off. Now wouldn't that be fine? All that work, and the pot wake up every whoopa in the place.

Kneeling in the shadow of the balcony wall, he set the plant carefully aside. Waited for a moment, stood to try again. Heard the sound behind him, felt the hair stand straight up behind his head. Stooped in a crouch, stabbed his tiny light into the dark. His beam struck the child in the face. A girl-child with fine golden hair and great luminous eyes, dressed in a nightgown that kissed the pink tops of her toes.

He waited for the scream that would bring in an outraged grownup, a sitter or a nurse.

"Would you kindly take the light from my eyes?" the girl said. "It is not very pleasing, you know."

"I'm sorry," Dreamer said, and shined the light on the floor. "Look, don't be scared or anything, little girl. Just turn around and go inside and I'm out of here. I'm a real nice man, and I'm not going to hurt you at all."

"I know," she said. "You've a noble mien about you. In spite of your actions, I would never take you for a baseborn lout."

"Good," Dreamer said, "I appreciate that. You mind me asking, who else is here besides you? Is, uh--mommy and daddy in there?"

"Sadly, no one at all," she told him. "I am quite alone, all by myself."

"You are? You're sure of that now."

The little girl sighed. "Did I not *say* so? Do you doubt me, sire? Sit, now. I have never met a burglar, I'd hear what this is all about."

"I don't believe I said I was a burglar, where'd you get that?"

"Please." She gave him a patient, understanding look. "Will you sit *down*?" Touching the hem of her gown, the girl slipped gracefully to the floor. Dreamer hesitated, then sat down himself.

Reason had him over the balcony and back down the wall. Still, his heart held him fast. He could not resist her charms. She was lovely, she was magic, the fairest little girl he'd ever seen. Hair soft as duck fuzz, framing an angel face. Even in the semi-dark, he could follow every fine blue vein beneath the porcelain skin. He fell in love with her eyes. The SWAT team could break in the door. He knew he'd just sit there and look into her eyes.

"Well," the girl said, giving Dreamer a thoughtful glance, "am I to be ravished now or what?"

Dreamer cleared his throat. "I don't ravish a lot. I just take stuff now and then."

"What kind of stuff? Jewels, booty, gold doubloons?"

"Hardly ever doubloons. Listen, how old are you, kid?"

"Seven. How old are you?"

"Thirty-eight. I'll be thirty-nine in September. What's your name?"

"Diane. What's yours?"

"Lamont Cranston," Dreamer said, feeling oddly uncomfortable with the lie.

The girl showed Dreamer sad and lonely eyes. "You've not the face of a felon. A common cutpurse or such. You *have* to steal, I'd say. Your father the duke was falsely imprisoned by the king, and you must find the means to set him free."

Dreamer wondered if the little girl had a beer. "Diane, listen, you don't mind, don't talk like that, okay?"

"Like what, sire?"

"You know like what. Where'd you pick up that stuff?"

"Alas, I am an unwanted babe," Diane sighed. "The chaff of a moment's idle lust. My father's in the pen. A problem, it seems, with the savings and loan. I'm afraid he's a greater thief than yourself. My mother was a wench in Las Vegas, a stately showgirl. Comely, but desperately poor. She is not with us anymore."

"I'm real sorry to hear that."

"Oh, she's not *dead* or anything. She's in Mexico, I think. Getting another divorce. That's what Mother does. Gets divorces, and reads romances by the ton."

Dreamer grinned. "And you read 'em too, right?"

"I fear that's so. It's all we ever had about."

"Well you better ease up. I'd get into Nancy Drew if I were you. You don't want to grow up talking like that. You're going to have enough trouble, seeing as you're pretty as a peach."

Diane gave a little girl shrug. "I don't especially *want* to grow up. Or be pretty either. It didn't do Mother a lot of good."

"Now don't say things like that."

"Especially if it's true."

"Right. Especially if it's true. Besides, things have a way of getting better. They do it all the time. Look, I know you don't live here by yourself, they don't let you do that. Is there an aunt around or what? They just leave you here tonight?"

"Aye, that's what you'd hear, is it not? That there's nary a guardsman about."

"It occurred to me, yes."

"Alas, no." Diane broke into a little girl giggle that somehow seemed out of place. "Lucky for you, right? They'd fair have you in a stew, like as not." She brought her hands together like a prayer. "As you guessed, I do not reside here by myself. I have a crew of nannies, and a very great trust. Funds, I take it, that the Feds can't touch."

She reached down and took Dreamer's hand. Dreamer helped her up and stood himself.

"I *think* you'd best be gone, Lamont. The nannies are out on a spree, but they'll return at first light."

"It's been a pleasure," Dreamer said. "I would climb these heights again, just to see my lady fair."

Wow, you're kidding!" Diane's eyes sparkled with delight. "Up the castle keep to rescue your maiden in distress." She looked down at the floor. "If only it could be. I don't suppose you really would. Free me of my chains. Get me *out* of this dismal place."

"I don't think I'd better," Dreamer said. "I'd get us both in an awful lot of trouble, Diane."

"I suppose. Just a thought..."

"Goodbye," Dreamer said. "I hope things work out better for you soon. I've got an idea they will."

Diane raised her hands and he lifted her into his arms. "One kiss, m'lord," she whispered, "a kiss and then be gone."

Small wet lips touched his cheek. Dreamer squeezed her tight and set her down.

"I suppose you are pledged to another."

"I think I'm kind of pledged to you," Dreamer said.

"I wouldn't be any trouble. Not any at all."

"It's not you. I just can't settle down right now. There's things I got to do. My lands have gone sere, and I really ought to clear my father's name."

"I understand," Diane said. "If honor be not golden to a man, then love is all but lost."

"I couldn't have said it any better, hon..."

INTERSTATE DREAMS

Far down below across the lawn, Rabbit trembles in fear against the twelve-foot wall that surrounds Enchanted Mesa West. He isn't sure at all where he is. He can sense green shoots very near, yet something keeps him still. The earth doesn't smell the way it should. A slight breeze carries the acid taint of metal, and this is not a natural smell. Something is wrong, thinks Rabbit. This is very bad shit. The green shoots can wait for a while.

In that very instant, Ears shout a warning to the Brain: *"Owl! Owl at two o'clock!"*

What Ears really hears is a swift and not an owl, but Ears is on edge like everyone else. Rabbit doesn't stop to ask. He moves in a blur from the shadow of the wall, right into the path of the alien smell. There is a quick, startling blue sizzle of copper light, and a pain Rabbit never dreamed could ever be...

. . .

In the morning, while all the fine gadgets rest a while, a security guard named Earnest Allen Clay makes his rounds at Enchanted Mesa West. First he finds Rabbit. Farther along, he finds Bird and Mouse and Squirrel. Earnest puts the night's catch in a Hefty bag and sells it later in the day to a man named Carl Dancer Ray.

Ray is one of fifty-eight men who pick up similar collections in Harris, Fort Bend, Brazoria, Montgomery and Walker counties. Each collection comes from a home, business or condo property protected by Lektra-Fide Security. The collections find their way to one of thirty-nine locations of St. Sarah Jean House, a semi-non-profit bird nest on the ground that offers low-cost meals to the South Texas poor and out of synch. Men and women who've lost their homes and even their second cars.

Rabbit will find his way into Beef 'n Rice Surprise at St. Sarah Jean Number Nine. Later in the evening, a part of this horror will be served to Wallace Pailey Marshall, who is, unaccountably, sober enough to eat.

Dreamer stole a document from Halloran Horn, who lives in the rooftop villa at Enchanted Mesa West. Horn owns 22% of Lektra-Fide Security, and 13% of the St. Sarah Jean House deal. Horn's wife is named Amy, the former

Mrs. Wallace Pailey Marshall. Once, Horn and Marshall were very close friends, as well as partners in prime oil leases, real estate and a BMW dealership. Horn saw a chance to fuck Wallace Pailey Marshall out of all his silver straws and his beautiful wife, and so he did.

Partial financing for the takeover deal came from mobster Mako Binder, owner and operator of Aunt Sally's Home Bakery Shoppe, Friendship Florist, and Pauliano's Mobile Art. Binder also owns a piece of Lektra-Fide, plus 85% of the St. Sarah Jean House public service mother lode scam.

Horn, then, is responsible for Wallace Pailey Marshall's ruin. Still, as a stockholder in Lektra-Fide, he can also take a little credit for frying Rabbit on the lawn, turning him into the Beef 'n Rice Surprise that will fill Marshall's belly that night. Marshall will sleep behind a Honda dealership and have, as is his custom, a semi-erotic Amy dream. In the morning, he will find half a bottle of Aqua Velva good as new.

And who says God doesn't even up the score, passing out good shit and bad, touching us each and every one now and then, in His own mysterious weird and wacky way...?

INTERSTATE DREAMS

At two in the morning, Dreamer waited by the hedge where Junior had let him off. There were still a few lights at Enchanted Mesa West, constellations of the super well-to-do. At 2:35, he hopped on the back of a Freezy-Ice van, and pulled himself up to the roof. The van passed through the gate and headed south. The guards didn't bother looking up. People broke *into* Enchanted Mesa West, people didn't try to break out.

Riding atop the van through the pines, through the hot oppressive night, Dreamer had the sudden manic urge for a high-priced overseas beer. Beer and a burger and fat onion rings. Onion rings the size of a Kawasaki tire. He would pick up the rental where Junior had stashed it the day before, near the turnoff to Highway 45. Then he'd grab a bite, drive back to Houston and go to bed. Get a little sleep and call the client, get the bucks and get the hell out.

The job had been easy. All the extra gadgets had him slightly uptight for a while, but they didn't mean a thing. How many didn't count. One little crackerbox alarm or all the fancy stuff at Enchanted Mesa West. There wasn't a system made that could hope to keep him out.

The thought brought sweet exhilaration. An *apres*-burglary high. Followed, at once, by a voice that said, next time, baby, it won't work at all, they will surely burn your ass.

. . .

The van slowed and turned, left instead of right, heading for the lake or maybe Huntsville town where they kept careless felons locked tight. A road Dreamer didn't care to take. He dropped off the back and hit the bushes running fast.

The air was thick as syrup, the night hot and still. The pines on either side black as printer's ink. Nothing artsy here, no fine delineation, nothing stark against the sky. The chatter of insects filled the night. Water was close at hand, somewhere past the trees; frogs took up the chorus, low and mournful sounds as if they suffered mortal pain.

He thought about the morning, how he'd get his bucks quick and head for home. He ticked off things he had to do. Scratched off an item, put another in its place. The basic idea was to make his life appear as if it might be something else. This, in case someone looked a little closer than he liked. People who sometimes wondered what he did, where he'd been the night before.

The whole idea of this irritated Dreamer a lot. He remembered when getting out of town meant walking out the door. Now, there were too many doors, too many keys, too many people to think about. Good folks and bad, and they all had pieces of his life.

Now there was Dinh and the fucking tanks of fish, which had seemed like a good idea at the time. An honest, marginal enterprise with a chamber of commerce sticker on the door. A very nice front that worked for the IRS, but failed to fool Detective Sergeant Asher, or Mako Binder himself.

Lawmen and outlaws heard things they shouldn't ought to hear. Most of the time from the very same ears. Mako and Asher knew he made a lot more bread than a half-ass fish store could bring him in the very best of times, even though he seldom spent cash around town.

Still, a man had to try and look straight, and fish did the trick as well as anything else. You couldn't just take out an ad that said, 'semi-honest, reliable guy, desires opportunities in break-in and retrieval. I am not a common cutpurse, a felon or a thief.'

"Sweet Diane," he said aloud, "grow up and be mine. Let's get the hell out of here and fly to foreign climes!"

And that's not fair, he thought, not fair to another with skin pale as medieval art, a lady dark as ebony who smelled of Samarkand. Not fair to Eileen. Not fair at all to the angel in the Jag. They'd had so little time together, he couldn't break her heart. And, as much as he loved Diane, he simply couldn't wait around.

. . .

He was close to the highway now and he could see a patch of neon from the truckstop cafe, hear the songs of the heavy-duty tires, the big rigs growling through the pre-dawn night. He thought about the tanks that needed cleaning in the shop. He ought to tell Dinh to put an eye-catcher out in the window, a Rainbow or a Blue. The fish were too big for the average tank, but they'd pull new people inside...

...As he thought about the fish and arranged the wood and gravel in his head, as the lights grew brighter, as the sound of the cars seemed to reach a higher pitch, seemed to whine up the scale, bring the frogs to a single rowdy

din, Dreamer looked up, heard the clatter of the pistons, heard the rattle of the engine, heard the shudder of the canvas in the wind, smelled the sweet and sour tang of castor oil, smelled the dust of St. Mihel, saw the stark moth shadow overhead, felt the jolt of heated air, saw it disappear back into the night...

It was there and it was gone, leaving Dreamer shaky in a still summer hour before the sultry dawn. He was slightly off-center, he was vaguely discontent. He wondered if what he'd seen was real or in his head. It was one of those times when he really couldn't tell, and he didn't care for that. It pissed him off and it scared him half to death. Worse than that, it made him itch in the middle of his back where he couldn't get to scratch...

He dreamed three times. Dreamed about nasty little wars in jungles and deserts and muddy street towns. Wasted women and stick-leg children and gummy old men. Camou colonels who thought poor people were better off dead.

It was always bad and it was always the same. They took groundfire and the chopper went bright and blossomed like a rose. The rotors turned to shit and Happy McCall yelled 'mothafuggah!' in his ear. Dreamer tried to stop it, to make it do right, but everything turned to macaroni in his hands. A little jerk a little twist, then straight for the turf and the scenery turned red...

Slight intermission. Dreamer sweats for a while. Turns on the tube. Learns what cable is like at a quarter past five. The second dream is an OBF, your standard everyday Out of Body Fuck. Which, he's come to find, is one of the pleasant side effects of having all the colors in his head. The woman says, 'hi, how've you been?' Dreamer says, 'fine, babe and you?'

He always wonders who she is. A dark-haired, hard-eyed lady who never gives her name. There is no foreplay, no horsing around like your ordinary earthbound affair. They crackle and they sizzle, they split a little proton or two. They leave each other dizzy in the head. No cigarettes, no long goodbyes. He always wakes with a jolt, with the feeling that he's screwed a generator, that he's dated Hoover Dam.

The final dream stars the girl in the Jag. She whispers 'forsooth' and 'varlet,' turns into a cherub named Diane. Diane turns into the lovely Eileen, who has spotted the others and is mad as all Hell. This is more than he can handle and he drags himself up and out of bed.

. . .

The rental was a stove. He got the air going, finished off a beer from the 7-Eleven store. Called up the client on the phone. Drove past the Astrodome and daytime bars, bars with windows dark as open graves, drove past lots full of hopeless used cars. Neon signs fought the sun, offered chicken-fried steak and topless fun, offered fine transmissions, offered tires as bald as Andy Gump.

He found 610 and let the traffic draw him north. His early morning call had shaken Cochran good. Cochran yelled at him a while and then Dreamer hung up. He wasn't mad now. Mad was gone now, plain pissed off was the password of the day.

He'd thought about wearing the patched-up jeans and the scruffy boots, with a Willie Nelson T-shirt to match. Instead, he picked a charcoal, summer-light suit, slate-blue shirt and black tie. All this and the big Italian shades. The shades were a gift from Eileen, who said if he was older and a tad better looking he could pass for Clint Eastwood's evil twin. Maybe, on a very cloudy day.

Leaving the car in a space marked 'reserved,' he walked past the concrete fountains and the tall glass incorporated spire, walked like he might have a .44 Magnum in mind. Walked as if he might decide to squint.

Cochran met him in the lobby looking short, bald and apoplectic, looking sallow and intent. He didn't speak at all until the elevator whisked them to the top.

"You got it," Cochran said. "You got it with you now. I saw it when you came in the door. I've got this uncanny knack."

"I've got it," Dreamer said.

"Jesus..." Cochran looked relieved. "Shit, man, you are something else. I bet Max they'd have your ass. Okay. Fine. I gotta to tell you, this is not a good idea. This is not the thing to do, you coming out here. We talked about this you might recall. Max is unhappy, he is very disappointed in you.

"What you gotta know is there's a right and a wrong way, pal. No offense. Our way is right and your way is wrong. You are not on-line, you are out of synch, babe. Your behavior is erratic and possibly extreme."

"I've been reading a lot of Travis McGee."

"Who the fuck's that?"

The elevator door slid open with a sigh, and Cochran led him quickly down the hall. Opened an unmarked door and ushered Dreamer in. Table, and mid-level chairs. They were keeping him out of sight. No secretaries, no executive suite.

Max stood, hands on the table, clearly unhappy, possibly disgruntled and annoyed.

"I am furious with you. This is not a good idea, you coming here. We don't care for this."

"I told him," Cochran said, "I told him that."

Max looked at Cochran. Back to Dreamer again. Studied the black suit, studied the cool Italian shades. Max and Cochran wore light beige suits, a color Dreamer didn't like at all.

"All right. That's done. *Finis*." Max waved the past aside. "Let's take a look, let's get down to the meat."

Dreamer drew the envelope from an inside pocket and dropped it on the table. Cochran tried for casual and couldn't bring it off. He pounced like a dog, and handed it to Max.

Max opened the envelope, taking his time. Dreamer watched them scan a dozen sheets, then reached across the table and took the papers back.

"Hey, now what the hell is this?" Cochran looked surprised. Max didn't.

"He is holding us up," Max said. He smiled at Dreamer, told Dreamer he clearly understood. "I could see this coming, I could see it down the street. You walked in here I could smell contention, possible dispute."

"Bullshit," Cochran said. "He delivers the goods, he gets the rest of the fifty Gs. Not a fucking penny more than that."

"Well spoken, Cochy," Max said. "My very thoughts indeed."

Dreamer slumped down in his chair. "What happens, is, I keep the half I've got. You keep the rest. I kept my end of the deal and you weaseled out."

"You watch yourself!" Cochran said.

"Reading you loud and clear," Max said. "Cochy is right, we do not haggle here. A man's word is gold, a deal is a deal. You don't have that, what the hell you got? Still, I think what you're saying to me, I think you're saying, 'Max, you've got a major enterprise here, a business that is flexible and strong. Let's use that strength, let's *use* that flexibility, let's work this fucker out.'

"What you're saying is you'd like another helping on the plate. You did the job, you took a lot of risks. Growth and enterprise. We are playing on the same course, friend. A little chip shot and we're on the green in par. Lay it on the table. What's it going to take to make you happy here?"

Dreamer was getting real tired of the business world, he was getting tired of Max. He wanted to get on the road, he wanted another beer.

"I read this stuff," he told Max. "I threw the old envelope away and put it in the one I got here."

Cochran started to fade. Max kept his cool. This is why Cochran worked for Max instead of the other way around.

"Now why did you want to do that?" Max said. "It's just a lot of science and technical shit."

"I went to a good state school," Dreamer said. "I can even do numbers in my head. I don't think what you got here's a good idea. I think a chromosome ought to be happy with itself, and not try and be something else. I don't feel I need a ninety pound cat. I don't want a little hippo on a leash. I sure don't feel we ought to have any pigs look kind of like me or anyone else.

"I don't like what you guys are doing, or Horn either one. What you are doing, you are fucking with people, you are fucking with the zoo. I think they're both just fine the way it is."

"Shit," Cochran said, "will you listen to this?"

"Okay," Max said, "how much. I am not fond of talking with you."

"There isn't any how much, Max. You people jacked me around. Right here on page three. It talks about the other labs doing work similar to yours. One of those companies is Nu-Gene, Inc., where I'm standing right now. It wasn't your document, it was his. I stole it, I didn't steal it *back*. I told you up front I retrieve, I don't steal. This stuff belongs to Halloran Horn, it wasn't ever yours."

"Business is business," Max said. "We've got to keep an edge or we go in the dumper. You're not a company man, you don't understand this kind of shit. All you think about is yourself."

"I don't like what's in here," Dreamer said, "but I'm going to mail it back."

"Shit," Cochran said again.

"We've got us an impasse here," Max said, "we got to work something out. I want you leaving here entirely satisfied. Say you get another twenty-five K. I throw in another ten. That sounds more than fair to me."

"No."

"No. No what? Ten's not the number, what is?"

"We can find you, mister," Cochran said. "We can spend a little cash where it counts. Possibly with people into basic mutilation, into injury and death."

"Hey, whoa," Max said, wiping the air with his hands, clearing the slate to get on with something else. "There is no need for things to come to that. I'd like to keep this thing on higher ground. Economic need. A sweet little bank in Liechtenstein. A hedge against inflationary trends."

Dreamer stood. "I've got a long drive. I need to get a beer."

"You've got a fucking attitude problem's what you've got," Cochran said. "We are not finished with you, don't think we are".

"I think we all need to back off," Max said. "You've done us wrong, friend, but I feel to blame for bringing in someone not real commerce-minded into this. So let's just leave it like it is."

"Good thinking," Dreamer said, "that's a sound idea."

"Hey, no goddamn way!" Cochran said.

"Go," Max said, "get the fuck out of here..."

INTERSTATE DREAMS

Halloran Horn and Mako Binder played tennis every Friday afternoon at Enchanted Mesa West. Mako owned 18 1/4% of Horn Life Engineering, Inc. Horn, in turn, had an equal share in the St. Sarah Jean House flim flam delight.

After the match, they drank Margaritas on the terrace high above the pool. The drinks had a thick coat of frost on the glass, the right amount of salt around the rim.

Halloran sat in the shade of a big umbrella. He wore white pants and a long-sleeved shirt. His thinning blond hair was covered with a white tennis hat. He wore dark shades and a thick patch of sunscreen on his nose. A moment's bare exposure would turn his flesh a fiery red.

Horn hated tennis, but he never turned Mako Binder down. Turning down Mako was not a real a good idea. Mako remembered every slight. He kept a mental list. Sometimes he'd tell you how many slights you had. You wanted to ask: How many can I get?

Mako always won, not because people always let him, though usually they did. Mako was a hard-driving player who could slam a ball right down your throat. If he missed, he would smash his racket on the court and curse his opponent in the harsh Sicilian tongue. After that, Mako didn't have to try. A Mako tantrum was enough to wilt a Wimbledon contender on the spot.

Horn never waited for a miss. He let all the hard shots go so he could get the game over and get his white body in the shade. Mako wouldn't play on the indoor courts. Indoor courts were for women and little kids.

Halloran Horn looked at Binder, stretched out on plastic in the sun. Clad in black Speedo trunks, his hard and muscled frame absorbed the searing Texas sky. Mako was tanned a rich St. Tropez brown, a shade that faded slightly in the winter, when he went on gangster business in countries that seldom saw the sun.

Horn hated Mako's body as much as he hated his own. Horn knew he looked like a fish; Mako looked like the bronzed Greek god who'd hauled him in.

Amy, now, Amy took the sun and turned it into gold. Amy was what tan was all about. Fabulous body, legs down to here. And who really cared if she didn't have a brain in her head? You want a wife who can walk and chew gum, marry a PhD. He got enough of that at the plant, women from Prague, Budapest and Minsk. Women without any tits and brains out to here.

He thought he probably loved her. He was almost certain that he did. Still, for a reason he could scarcely define, he seldom touched her anymore. At night, he laid very still and watched her sleep. Watched her breathe, watched the rise and fall of her breasts, watched the flutter of her eyes. Sometimes he lifted up the sheet. Looked at that marvelous body, tried to imagine they were making love again, the way they'd done before. Sometimes he'd touch her. Touch her everywhere. Amy never woke. Amy took a lot of pills. Amy shopped all day, and at night she took her pills.

Sometimes he watched her through the night. Sometimes he'd turn away and desperately bring himself off. Sometimes it worked. But not if he was looking at Amy. It simply wouldn't work, not if he was looking at her. He didn't understand it, he didn't know why...

. . .

"Listen, that's interesting stuff you guys are doing," Mako said. "It got me thinking's what it did."

"Uh, about what?" Horn said, Mako jogging him back to real life.

"Genetics. Shit like that."

"It's a great field. Lots of opportunities for growth. You've got a good investment, Mako."

"Uh-huh."

"You can make things bigger or smaller, right? Change the way they look."

"On a very limited scale. We're just at the beginning right now."

"What about that big fucking rat? Over at your lab, you show me this rat's big as a fucking collie dog."

"That's a start. We're, ah--not primarily interested in making big rats. The most important work's in chromosomal manipulation, for the purpose of eliminating abnormalities, looking for clues that--"

"So what are we talking here? You're sayin' 'limited scale,' and I'm thinking what? A coupla weeks, next month, what?"

Halloran squinted through his shades. "Mako, are we still on the rat?"

"What else? I'm asking, when you going to make stuff bigger or smaller? That abnormality shit, I ain't real excited, okay? I'm seein' this *cloning* everywhere, it's on the TV. A guy's making sheep. I saw the fucking rat. Your guys are making stuff different. This is what I'm talking about, you're talking something else. What I want to do, I want you to talk about what *I'm* talking about, okay?"

Halloran looked alarmed. "Christ, Mako, the media has blown this all out of proportion. Everybody thinks we're making poodle-size elephants you can keep around the house. In theory, now, we could. We have data on that, but that's not what it's all about."

Mako mumbled to himself. He wiped the sweat off his brow and finished off his drink.

Halloran gave himself a mental kick in the ass for ever taking Mako to the lab. Of course, he didn't have a whole lot of choice, since Mako owned a piece of the rock, and it was hard to tell Mako Binder no.

Mako had gotten all excited about the sheep they'd cloned a couple years back, he'd seen the whole thing on TV. Like every other moron in the country, he'd seized upon one little dab of misinformation and wouldn't let it go.

Horn had no idea where Mako was going with this, and he was terrified he might find out.

. . .

Mako didn't like the sound of years. Years meant money sat still and didn't sweat. It sat somewhere while a wimp wearing glasses grew germs in a dish. Mako didn't want a fucking germ, he wanted product on the line, he wanted something you could sell.

Mako waved for a drink. He sat and wiped his face. He loved the fucking sun, the fucking sun was great.

A waiter brought his drink. He took a big slug, smacked his lips and set the glass down. Picking up his Leitz 10 X binoculars, he swept the heights of Enchanted Mesa West, paused at a balcony or two, and settled on the pool down below. Moving past a treasure trove of incandescent flesh, past long and tasty legs and coffee thighs, past foxy gold and cocoa cutie pies, he came to rest on the former Mrs. Wallace Pailey Marshall, the present Mrs Horn. He glanced at her husband, who seemed to dozing for a while. And hey, if he wasn't, who the fuck cared?

The glasses were the best you could buy, strong enough to bring the fine hairs on Amy Horn's arm into stunning detail, into startling array, so close that Mako nearly laughed aloud.

"Goddamn," he said, "if that ain't something to see."

Mako knew fine goods when he saw them, and Amy Horn was first class merchandise. Tight and slick as she could be. A honey of a girl, a looker and a half. He followed the line of a leg to an ankle to the little-flip-curl of her toes. He stayed on the toes for some time. He liked toes a lot. A girl could do a lot of fun things with a toe, and not everybody knew that.

Working back up, he paused at the awesome carnal mound, a secret swell of flesh only scarcely concealed by white bikini net. He swept past the high, polished bone of the hip, a spur caught in the sun, followed pubic trails and found the finest belly button ever seen. Through the magic and precision of the clever German glass, this small indentation gained Olympic proportions to the eye. A sugary lake of baby oil and sweat, a sweet reservoir that flooded tummy plains with each measured Amy breath.

Mako could have spent days at this site, but he traveled up the hollows of her ribs, past Himalayan breasts to another pool gathered at her throat. Beyond, to a stronger chin than Mako liked to see, a chin that liked to have its own way. On to a very likely Oklahoma jaw, the high cheeks of Cherokee or Choctaw somewhere down the line. Swollen lips and a fine straight nose with a huffy little tilt on the end, a go-to-hell tilt that meant trouble on the run, some guy breaking his ass to keep champagne in her tub.

Nice little nostrils sharp and clean, not a bugger in sight. This kid is prime, Mako told himself again. A girl that looks good up the nose, that's a girl who looks fine. And who cared if she was dumb as wheat bread? You want a babe with smarts, find a good hooker who's been around a while.

. . .

"What I'm thinking," Mako said, "you're taking maybe years and maybe not. Maybe you get a little break."

"It's mostly hard work," Horn said. "Science is slow, science isn't fast. You don't want to count on a break. What you're going to do, you're going to miss a lot more often than you hit."

"Yeah, right." Mako turned his dark, Mediterranean eyes on Horn, taking in the sunscreen nose, the homo tennis hat.

"This chromo-whatever, it makes things different in animals and people. If you *were* makin' something, I mean."

"Double helix," Horn said. "Protein chain. Atoms and stuff. Recombinant DNA."

He desperately wanted Mako to stop. Maybe high-tech chants would do the trick.

"You take something like it was," Mako said, "mix it around, stir it up good, you come out with something else. It takes a lot of time, it takes a lot of bucks."

"Absolutely," Horn said, ready to agree on anything to make the man stop. "A great deal of money, a *great* deal of time."

Mako, though, was on his own ground. This part of the action he knew. The seller bitches there's a lot of stuff the buyer doesn't know, additional expense, money to spread around. You talk around the price until your points and the other guy's are close enough.

"What I'm thinking, your crew sorta slicks the package up. Leave out stuff you don't need. Get down to basics, give the consumer what he wants to see. Stuff you don't use, leave it out. You get the package down to where a guy or a lady, they're maybe outta town, they don't want to go nowhere, they don't wanta order in."

"What?" Horn said, "do what?" He had no idea what Mako was talking about, not any clue at all.

Mako Binder didn't hear him, Mako was on a roll.

"What the guy or the woman, what they want's a decent lay, you don't have to dress and go out. They pick up the phone, we send 'em the package in a van.

"There's got to be a handle you can hold while you're using this thing. And a nice case to carry it in. We're talking high-class here. We get Blass or Gucci to work something up. Good looking leather, which is costwise out of sight, but we gotta go Cadillac on this..."

Before he could stop, before he could regain control of himself, Halloran Horn gave a long and raucous laugh. More than a laugh, it was a cackle and a honk, a splitter and a roar.

As soon as he realized exactly what he'd done, he prayed for lightning or cardiac arrest, but it was too late for that. Mako Binder had cut through the harsh realities of science, the complexity of chromosomes and genes, right to the heart of the merchandising core, right to the product that left out the parts you didn't need, right to the Mako Binder handy-dandy travel-size portable fuck.

Mako smiled, which was much worse than Mako getting mad.
"I'm talking bidness here. I don't remember doing a joke. Did I do a joke, you hear me do a joke?"

"Hey now, it wasn't you, I was thinking of something else."

"So you like it, right?"

"It's good, it's terrific. Absolutely tops."

"You talk to the guys in the lab. I'll check back in. See how we're doing, okay? Don't talk to no one doesn't have to know. We're not sharing this mother, we're keeping it all for ourselves."

Mako looked at his drink. The frost was all gone. At the pool, Amy Horn stood and walked toward the shaded *cabana*, walked in a manner that induced hydraulic dreams, that suggested glacial drift. Mako followed her with his eyes. Jesus, the woman was pussy on the hoof. Did a jerk like Horn deserve a honey like that?

Maybe, he thought, after the deal was sewed up, he'd give some thought to Mrs. Horn. Hey, it could happen. Nothing was out of reach if you wanted it bad enough, and the woman had toes that wouldn't quit.

Mako already had a few ideas in mind for Horn. Not anything that hurt, nothing like that. Just something to remind a guy that bidness was serious stuff, not something to fucking laugh about...

INTERSTATE DREAMS

Dreamer left Houston behind, pausing only long enough the drop the stolen envelope to Horn in the mail. At Brenham, he pulled off 290, gassed up and took a stretch. The grocery there had a butcher's counter and take-out barbecue. He bought a cold six-pack, two beefs on white bread to go.

Back on the road, he ate and drank beer and let the uninspiring miles roll by. There was nothing to see but Exxon signs and dead grass. A station in Austin was having Merle Haggard day, and he listened a while to that.

Outside Giddings he spotted a single brown and white. The cop was at a Dairy Queen, standing by his car, dripping ice cream down his shirt. Two high school girls sat on his hood. One wore a cheerleader jacket, the other wore the trooper's Smokey Bear hat pulled down about her eyes. She made a face at her friend and the girl in the jacket laughed.

The trooper followed Dreamer with his big mirror shades. A line cut the trooper's brow above his eyes. The lower half was red, the upper as white as Dreamer's bread.

Dreamer wondered what Halloran Horn would do when he got his stuff back through the mail. Did he know it was gone, that it was missing from his desk? He'd figure it out, and he'd figure half wrong. That someone had stolen the package, made a copy, sent it back. A kind of Texas fuck you gesture, a finger through the mail.

It didn't bother him much to leave half the fee behind. Twenty-five grand was okay, four days in Houston, meals, motel and the car. Three grand to Junior Lewis, another five to Paulo for setting up the job. The thing going sour wasn't Paulo's fault, and Dreamer would send him the whole ten percent. He would also tell Paulo what the clients tried to pull. Paulo would see that their names got on a list. Assholes like Max would be wanting help again sometime.

. . .

He drove straight into the sun, a fireball that sucked all the color from the land and laughed at the factory air. At IH 35 he turned south into town, past sad motels and the Army-Navy stores and the radiator shops, still near the heart of the city, but lost in a backwater now. Austin had moved on north to new shopping malls and homes, and computer office parks that served the proper end of town.

In the sixties, Austin was a laid-back-take-it-easy town, skinny dipping in the Colorado's cool and shady pools, getting high and coming down. It was a college fun town, big white houses on steep and narrow streets, live oaks older than God. On a hot afternoon, lawmakers took off their jackets and walked down Congress from the pink granite capitol for a beer and a look at college girls. It was Lyndon Johnson's town, and Willie's after that. And Charlie Whitman's for a day, when he woke and saw the sun had turned to broken glass.

Dreamer wished it hadn't happened but it had, the town gone Sun Belt crazy with high tech delight, and shiny buildings that strangled the capitol dome. For a while the money came, and the good ol' boys had a spree before the bankers lost their ass, passing loans out for land deals and oil, and the fun times came to a halt. But not before the town sprawled out of sight. Not before the river turned a funny looking green.

And, just as things will do, Austin hit bottom, got its second wind, and swelled up bigger than life again. Now, as the century died and another one began, you wouldn't send your kid to the 7-Eleven store if you wanted to see him again.

Mama Lucy said corruption came wrapped in a pretty pink ribbon, so you couldn't see the bad inside. A lady starts taking little presents when a gentleman comes to call. Pretty soon it's money on the dresser and hey, there you are.

. . .

Dreamer drove past the capitol, turned on Sixth, and saw the lights flashing him to stop. He pulled over easy and rolled the window down. Watched in the mirror while the cop came over and poked his head inside.

"What you say, Dreamer," the cop said with a smile, "you gettin' any I haven't had?"

"You're letting air out, Bennie," Dreamer said, "I don't like to breathe down here."

"Asher wants you should drop by. Said if I saw you tell you that."

"Tell Asher okay. Tell him I've got stuff to do, and I'll come by when I can."

Bennie took off his shades. "I'd go and see him now, I was you."

"Why's that?"

"I just would is all. That's what I'd do."

"Shit, Bennie. I got three kilos of good Colombian in the trunk. I don't get that over to the governor he's going to have my ass."

"There's a new Mes'can band over to Ortega's. You ought to catch 'em while they're here."

"Over at Ortega's."

"This isn't no plastic chili pepper band. These dudes are the real stuff."

"I'll try and do it."

"You go on and see Asher, okay? Don't fuck me up now, I got to call in and say you're here."

Dreamer said he would and rolled the window up and pulled the car south on Congress Avenue. What he wanted was to get back home and get a shower and a drink. See if Dinh had let all the fish die. See if he had a clean shirt and any socks. What he didn't want to do was talk to Detective Sergeant Avery Asher about anything at all. That it might be about the night's event didn't even cross his mind, and yet it did. When a cop wants to talk, you think about everything you've done and a few things you only thought about, and that leaves a lot of doors open you wish you'd thought to shut...

Fate plays poker around the clock.

Go to the john or get a beer, the hand you left behind is going to be there when you get back. When the play comes around to you again, you have to bet. It's not fair at all but neither is the deck. If Dreamer had turned due north instead of south, he would have seen the girl for sure. He would've known at once she was the girl in the bottle-green Jag, the love he'd lost the night before. Maybe it would have turned out different, and again maybe not.

. . .

She stands in the doorway of a bank that went under the year that she was born. Wind blows a fine mist of hair across her cheeks. She wears Reeboks with no socks, white shorts slit at the thigh. The white is a lovely counterpoint to the nut-brown tone of her legs. The gray T-shirt says University of Texas across the front in orange. Heaven seems alive beneath the shirt, a place of pointy dreams and soft delight.

One of the men says something and she laughs. Her eyes are green and bright, her teeth are straight and white. She tells the two she's glad they didn't get the wrong idea about her, being friendly and all. If she'd thought for a minute that they had, why she wouldn't be talking to them now.

She's good at that, she says, learning how to size people up. This is what a Psych major does, see, learn how to study different people from the way they move and talk. When she doesn't have a class like she doesn't right now, she likes to study people on the street, meet and talk to folks like mature businessmen, guys who nearly always wear a suit. This is how you learn, don't you think? Interpersonal stuff is where it's at. She's flattered that they noticed her, and fine, she could go for a drink somewhere and talk. Then she could get back over to the dorm and hit the books for the big Russian Lit test tomorrow afternoon.

The two men are Charles D. LeLong and Walter Orin Kirsch of Fort Worth. They both work for Phil Boa Properties, Inc., a firm of the real estate persuasion that knows how to scoop up land that lies directly in the path of something big. Something like office parks or shopping centers, or places where the highway's going, only no one's supposed to know that.

Kirsch and LeLong can scarcely believe their luck. This girl is no ordinary hooker, you can tell by the sparkle in her eyes. Her body is electric with the glow of health and the energy of youth. The bones in her face show intelligence and grace, breeding somewhere along the line. She looks very clean and brand new. She couldn't be infected with the you-know-what, and hey, safety is for sale at your nearest drug store.

It might be true that she really goes to school, a plucky college girl who likes to have a little fun and pick up some extra cash. The men watch her as she talks. They try to see behind those lovely eyes. Will this girl do what they want her to do? And will she even do *that*? And, if she will, each wonders to himself, will he dare tell the other such a dark and secret dream is in his heart? Will a friend think you're less of a man, or admire you even more if he knew that you liked to do that?

Detective Sergeant Avery D. Asher was thirty-six when his body began to slide. He paid no attention at the time, having muscle to spare from his semi-pro years. He compared himself to men his own age, and came off looking fine. He was twice divorced now, and not even tempted to ever try again.

Asher lived and ate alone. For lunch he liked Juan's Fiesta Special Plate. Two beef tacos, cheese and sour cream enchiladas, refried beans, soft flour tortillas with butter and hot sauce on the side, a dark bottle of Dos Equis beer. Monday through Friday, in the evening after work, he ate at Mama Lucy's Vishnu Jesus Barbecue. Tuesday and Thursday, Karma Ribs. Monday, Wednesday and Friday, the St. Thomas Aquinas Sausage Plate. No one knew where he spent his Saturday nights, and his Sundays till noon. No one except Dreamer, who made it his business to get a little edge on life, when and where he could.

At forty-four, Asher puffed into second base and made it safe. At fifty-two they tagged him out. Asher didn't care. He'd miss the ninth inning, and possibly the seventh and the eighth. And who'd give a shit if he did? A few old hands on the force. The friend he saw Saturday nights. Mama Lucy, and Juan Cordova, who ran Juan's Authentic Mexican & Chinese All-Night Restaurant. These were the people who would mourn for him twenty, thirty minutes after they lowered him in the ground. Fine. As soon as he was dead, he'd forget about them, too.

. . .

Asher didn't stand or look up when Dreamer walked into his glass-walled office late that afternoon.

"So what's going on in Houston," he said, "let's hear about that."

Dreamer sat. Asher never said hello or goodbye. "I don't know, you tell me."

"Hey, come on, I got stuff to do."

"I hit the gay bars. Took in the ballet and the tractor pull. Ate some lemon pie."

Asher looked up. "That's a nice suit. I don't guess I ever saw you wear a suit."

"I don't ever wear it."

"You're wearing it now."

"You want to talk about the suit?"

"Friend of yours is on the road to getting her pretty ass in a sling. She ought to think some on the people she runs around with. She ought to give some thought to maybe doing something else."

"And who is this we're talking about?"

"What she's doing is she's hanging out with folks she shouldn't ought to. Maybe you know this, I don't think you do. These people are new in town and they're clean as Ivory Soap. Except if you look real close, they're connected to some really bad dudes. I'm just saying how it is."

"What friend are we discussing here, is this maybe Eileen?"

"Did I say a name? I didn't say a name."

"Okay, you didn't say a name."

"None of this leaves my office, I didn't tell you anything at all. You remember that. These people I'm referring to are talking to Mako Binder himself. Binder doesn't come here often, and anytime's too much for me."

"Asher, let's not do this," Dreamer said, "it's all the same to you. I sell Binder fish. You want a fish, I'll sell a fish to you. You ought to get a tank. A little ten gallon, we'll work you up from there."

"I don't give a fuck you sell the mother fish. What I give a fuck is other things you and him do."

"I don't do anything with him. You know I don't, if you thought that I did, you wouldn't be telling me this, whatever the hell it is."

"Yeah, I would, too." With a great deal of effort, Asher slid his barbecue-enchilada-egg roll butt a little deeper in his chair.

"Under certain circumstances, I would. If certain conditions prevailed, which they happen to do, I would tell you what I'm telling you now. You might be fucking with Binder somehow, but you wouldn't do something that'd get this friend of yours severely hurt or dead. Whatever is going on here is not healthy for your friend. That's why I know you're not involved in this. That, and I think these dudes who are mixed up with Binder, I think they're way out of your league."

"Everything's out of my league," Dreamer said, "I haven't got a league, I haven't even got a team."

"If you did, though, if you did have a league, I just did you a big favor, you and this friend. You tell your friend these assholes are serious people. Tell this friend to find some other clients somewhere. This friend is good at what she does, she can easy find something else to do."

"When I see her I'll tell her."

"You see her soon. I'm not talking later soon, I'm talking now is the soon I'm talking about. Anybody tell you you look like a fag in those shades?"

"These shades are Italian design. They cost over two hundred bucks."

"Fine. You look like a fag from overseas."

Dreamer knew their talk was over. You could always tell because Asher was suddenly gone, even if his very large body was definitely there.

Dreamer walked out of the building and back into the sun. He hurried to the rental car, shedding coat and tie on the run. The tie had a spot from Brenham, Texas. Dreamer wondered if Asher had noticed that. Asher had an uncanny knack with spicy food, and especially barbecue sauce.

He was sort of like Holmes, who could tell you where an ash came from, what the smoker had on. He could sniff a spot of sauce and say, "Yeah, that's from that place east of Waco, the old boy from Corsicana runs. That one, now, that's commercial stuff, that's your grocery brand, I wouldn't be caught dead eatin' that."

Which, Dreamer thought, with a pang of slight regret, is exactly what Asher would be caught doing just before he got caught, just before he got dead. Eating something he should have quit eating twenty years back...

INTERSTATE DREAMS

When Dreamer got back from the small and deadly conflict south of Mexico, the first thing he did was buy a house set back among pecan trees and oaks, a house that was paint-peeled with age, not far from town, not far from college fun. He could well afford a better home. The backwater war had left him with a bag full of bright green stones. The stones came his way through a man he didn't know. The man had a bullet in his gut and maybe thirteen minutes left to go. He didn't want a stranger to steal his bag of stones. Dreamer was there, so the man said Dreamer was his friend.

Dreamer sold the stones to Paulo in Houston, who sold them to someone else. There was plenty of cash money left. Dreamer put a little down on the house, and arranged for a loan to pay the rest. He didn't need the loan, but you don't ever tell anyone you can buy a whole house.

This was really the second thing he did, the first being consultation with Paulo on the wrong side of Houston in a room above a ship channel bar. And, after all their business was done, Paulo took him on a three-day gastric adventure that left Paulo's digs in styrofoam decay, Indian take-out and Tex Mex debris, and a herd of dead bottles of overseas beer.

Paulo, performing the *paso-doble* now and then, worked Microsoft magic on the keys, turned out a financial fugue and a cavatina scam, a nice little riff designed to confound the Infernal Revenue till 2066. And, on occasion, he'd stop for some Chinese or Thai, drink another beer and show Dreamer his guns, his grapeshot revolver by Le Mat, 1856, his eighteenth century Wooldridge musket, and his Mauser rifle, 1918, designed to stop the British tank. Dreamer didn't give a hoot about guns, but he surely loved the beer.

When Paulo was done, he'd effectively forever changed the fine green stones into overseas Donald Duck accounts, Mormon municipal bonds, and a tax-free bonanza from a mythical uncle in deepest Tennessee. Paulo took delight in the product of his art, took twenty-two percent, took Dreamer out for curry at a place that didn't have any license on the wall.

And Dreamer moved into the paint-peeled house and filled the first floor with tanks of multi-colored fish. He began to meet some women who were semi-balanced and partially out of synch, women who were black, who were brown and bronze and white, women who shared his passion for Mozart and ribs, radio tapes of *The Kate Smith Show*, and old Stan Kenton 78s--women who wanted as much of himself as Dreamer had to give.

The women in Austin are fine. A capitol dome and a big state U draw a wealth of far left and neo-fascist ladies into town. Thinkers and doers, women on the go, a reasonable number consumed by lust to some degree, even in these scary carnal times.

He began to hang out at Mama Lucy's and relax in the cool insulation of darker skin. Mama Lucy liked him, and the people who ate there didn't seem to care if he was melanin-impaired. He tried not to think about the colors in his head. A VA doctor in Dallas said the colors were echoes of post-trauma drift, something like aftershock from LSD, which tends to hang around. The colors, he said, would go away with time.

Only that wasn't how it was at all; they didn't go away, any more than the gnat-sized fragment of steel that had found a new home inside his head, a spot on the X-ray neuro whiz Dr. Jackie Slagg of Fort Worth, said didn't seem to cause any harm.

It didn't hurt and it didn't go away. What it did, Dreamer learned, was fuck with all the wiring in his brain. Purely by chance, installing alarms in his house, he found that the colors could charm electric shit of every sort. He made a few runs, just to test the thing out. No matter how he tried, he couldn't set anything off. He could pass through an airport with an Uzi in his jeans. He could jam all the phones, he could lock all the doors. He could empty Cartier's in a flash. He didn't want to, but he could. He didn't need the bread. He would never have to go to war again. The green stones and Paulo had taken care of that. He couldn't spend a lot in Austin, but a lush vacation every year would be a lark.

Dreamer sold enough fish to keep a step ahead of the welfare crowd, but not enough to call much attention to himself. He learned to put the color thing aside, or at least turn it down, like a radio playing somewhere inside the house. The nightmares were sometimes very bad. He couldn't count the times he woke in stink and sweat, the chopper blazing and dead men screaming all the way to the ground.

He had always loved to fly. Flying was his life. Now, he ducked when an airplane flew overhead. He knew that he'd never fly again, or go up with anyone else. If an airplane appeared on TV, Dreamer switched it off. He wouldn't help a friend catch a flight. "Get yourself a taxi," Dreamer said.

. . .

If he couldn't understand about the colors, the other part was just as big a mystery as well. Seeing things that might or might not be really there. Like the crate from the past, shattering the silence in the hot dead hours of the dawn. Real planes buzzing overhead were bad enough, he didn't need ghosts on top of that.

And, earlier the very same night, undefined vibes about a girl in a bottle-green Jag. The girl was really there, he knew that. Junior Lewis had seen her too. But Junior didn't see what he saw, didn't know she shimmered in a cloud of indigo, in a burst of azure and mad electric blue.

There was love, there, love and sweet intent, denial and desire. And, skirting just outside the edge somewhere, fear and apprehension, pre-coital tears.

Then there was the other sensation, the OBF, the Out of Body Fuck, with a woman he'd never seen before. Nice, and a hedge against AIDS and the problems of romance, but he could do without it fine. Fornication in his own dimension was good enough for him.

It all seemed more than a tiny hunk of metal ought to do.

Better, still, than coming back crispy in a green body bag.

. . .

All things considered, life was okay for a couple of years. A time of adjustment, unhurried enterprise. A time to catch up on minor deviations, barbecue ribs and foreign beer.

Then, on an April Tuesday night, fifteen minutes past nine, he sensed the beginning of an itch. Clear and uncertain, precise and ill-defined. A tankful of Tetras failed to stimulate his mind. The joy and sad transition from the last romance was revealed as a cyclical event. As easy to predict as a linebacker's grade in English Lit.

He knew what he needed, he needed something fun, what he needed was a kick. He had vowed not to ever use the stuff inside his head. Not ever not once no matter what. I am not a crook, Dreamer thought, but there's a way around that. Steal from the stealers, keep it all legit. Hi Ho, Silver, or maybe Robin Hood. Wear green tights or a big white hat.

So he did. It was risky, very stimulating, and seemed to make him better in bed. The only thing is, when you're real good at something, word tends to get around. You can cover your tracks, but they're going to find you out. Clients can't keep their mouths shut. People like Mako and Avery Asher keep an eye on a man who's got the knack. They didn't *know* what he was doing.

They couldn't even say he really did. They surely had no idea how. But things got done, things no one else could do, and sometimes Dreamer was in the neighborhood.

. . .

Now, he wondered how he could have been so fucking dumb. The fact that he might draw attention to himself, doing the impossible, pulling magic rabbits from a hat, simply never crossed his mind. Now he had to watch what he said, and who he said it to. He had to be careful what he spent. There was so much money coming in, Paulo had to squirrel it away in flim-flam deals and Sudanese accounts.

He could quit. He could take up Portuguese stamps. He knew that was what he ought to do. But he couldn't do that. The Green Hornet doesn't quit. Batman doesn't back out. That, and it's a kick to wear a cape sometime...

INTERSTATE DREAMS

Dreamer liked to walk through the long rows of tanks, through the mini-shoals and reefs, through the tunnels lit by eerie water light. He stopped to watch Neons explode into phosphorescent glee, then vanish in the spiny needle grass. The smell here was slightly stale water, the sound of tiny motors out of sight, a meditative hum just right for lace guppies with a yen for the higher planes of life.

Dreamer tapped the glass to get a loach to come out and say hello. The loach gave Dreamer a real or imagined barbel smile.

"Don't tap," someone said, an inch from Dreamer's ear, "don't be tapping on fish."

"Jesus!" Dreamer did a quick little two-step jump.

Dinh stood in fish-light shadow, between a tank of Firemouth Cichlids and Pearl Danios, a breed Dreamer felt was likely gay.

"Don't spook around like that. I told you, I don't like it, I don't care for that."

"I do not spook," Dinh said.

"Yes you do. You all do it. It's some kind of thing you people do. Your VC person, he's got to spook around."

"You lose war, okay? Don't be tapping on glass. Fucking fish don't like it, you tapping onna glass."

"What they don't like, Dinh, they don't like starving to death. They don't like to do without air, they don't like to freeze to death. This is what you want to think about, not tapping on the glass. What did we get while I was gone, anything I want to see?"

"Red Devils. White Clouds. Rosy Barb. Bunch of cats."

"What kind of cats?"

"Bumble Bee. African Polka-Dots."

"I don't need the Polka-Dots, I told you that twice. A guy wants to spend that much, he's going to get him something else, he isn't going to spend it on a cat. You call in the morning. Tell Gates he's got to take 'em back."

"Okay," Dinh said.

"No, not okay, I want you to *do* it. I don't want to come down tomorrow and find those cats, you're standing here playing with yourself, you're saying okay. And I want you to check on the nitrites, Dinh. Now I told you that. You get the nitrite and ammonia screwed up all the fish are going to die. You remember we had this discussion before, how fish have got to pee, and they don't have anywhere to go but in the tank? You remember that? You check the tanks, Dinh."

"Okay," Dinh said.

He wouldn't, and Dreamer knew it. He'd have to do it himself. He'd have to call Gates and he'd have to check the tanks. Dinh would agree with anything you said and he wouldn't do anything at all. He liked to look at fish but he didn't like to work. Dreamer didn't have the heart to let him go. He was useless in the shop, and he'd be just as useless to anyone else. He stood there staring in his combat pajamas, looking wise and fairly dense, looking slightly unhinged, a dark Asian madness in his eyes.

"And get rid of that suit," Dreamer said. "Get yourself some jeans."

"No way," Dinh said, "I gotta ethnic obligation. I no be wearin' jeans."

"Fuck your obligation. In Austin, ethnic is jeans."

"Okay," Dinh said...

INTERSTATE DREAMS

When Dreamer bought the house he took the second-story southeast corner for himself, a large and airy high-ceiling room amply shaded by pecan trees and oaks, a room which had served as a screened-in porch in simpler times, when air-conditioned comfort meant the family took their bedding outside on summer nights to catch whatever breeze might happen by. Now the screens were gone, replaced by thermal glass, and window units the size of Subarus.

There are plenty of rooms like this in Austin, Texas, where people like the Tarzan treehouse effect. They feel these surroundings might insulate them from the world outside--that they might be happy grad students, stretching out the academic years instead of working at a bank, sweating out a mortgage by the lake.

Dreamer soaked in the tub with a scotch on ice in a Mickey Mouse glass, and hummed along with country radio. He reflected on life. He thought, as he always did, that he ought to get out of the burglary trade and into something else. He promised himself he would. He wished there was more hot water. He wished he'd fixed himself an extra drink.

Wrapping a towel around his waist, he stepped out of the tub and walked into the bedroom slicking back his hair. Eileen was sitting in a straight-back chair, drink in hand looking lawyer smart and trim, looking fairly strung out, looking partially content. Cool as shaved ice in a white linen suit that said expensive and correct, yet cut to enhance the slightly rangy and long-legged Eileen effect. Dove-blue shoes. Hose so sheer they required a second glance.

"How'd you get in?" Dreamer said, and mixed himself another drink.

"My, what a nice thing to say." Eileen crossed her legs and set an ankle a-twitch. Possible aggravation on the way.

"Came up the back. You don't ever leave it locked, someone's going to steal your TV. How'd you find Houston, by the way?"

"Who said I did?"

"You got a Houston rental outside."

"I guess you got me cold."

"Fix me another drink?"

Dreamer did. He took it to her and she whipped off his towel and started drying off his chest.

"Turn around. You don't ever get your back."

"I can't see my back."

"Other guys get dry they don't see their own backs. You're always soaking wet."

"You do a lot of backs?"

"I feel I've done a few."

"Guess it's better not to ask."

"That's pretty sound advice."

Eileen stood and patted his shoulders and his back and ran the towel down his arms. It seemed like stimulating fun. Getting toweled off by a fully-dressed, professional person had a pleasantly perverse and clearly visible effect, which Eileen discovered at once.

"Well. Now how about that."

"I can't help it."

"I don't guess you can. You better lie down."

Dreamer took his drink to bed. Eileen started taking off her clothes, undressing in an orderly and systematic way. Unbuttoned the jacket, zipped off the skirt, hung the jacket on a chair and the skirt after that, slipped off her shoes, sat, slid invisible hose down her legs, stood, peeled off the beige-colored minis, laid them on the chair and unhooked a bra to match, a bra that unhooked in the front, the kind Dreamer liked the best.

He watched her take the pins from her dark-dark hair. He liked her hair a lot. He liked the way it sprang free and tumbled down her shoulders, slid down her back, one feathered curl sort of catching on a nipple, sort of hanging on there. All this wonder like a slo-mo ad for shampoo, including the parts they never show on TV.

Eileen found a brush in her purse, stroked one side of her head and then the next, naked and lovely and totally detached, thinking, perhaps, of the Texas penal code, of the wonders of criminal intent.

As ever, Dreamer was stricken by her charms, by the tall ivory woman slick and bare, every sweet hollow revealed, every secret exposed. She stood by the window, against the fading light. Her body seemed sharply defined, possibly a special effect of some kind. A not exactly rawboned look, but plainly angular and lean. The thing about Eileen was that big town look, those opal-black eyes that could turn an opponent into mush. Those eyes and a strictly legal nose were somehow mystically fused with a Fort Worth mouth, a much too wide and clearly carhop mouth designed for backseat love and unwholesome delight.

Dreamer marveled at the sight, at the wonder of creation, at the splendid idea of carnal strife. Then, to make the picture complete, Eileen came to him through the waning afternoon, moving from the waist in a manner women know how to do, a motion that starts along the planes of the thighs, tautens at the tummy and slicks around the ribs, a muscle or a tendon that lifts the breasts impossibly high, a graceful little tilt that made Dreamer want to cry.

. . .

As it sometimes comes to pass, a moment will occur in conjunction with the stars, in absolute cosmic accord. It happened just then, and Dreamer held his breath, afraid the world would vanish, that they'd both disappear. She came into his arms, followed by a sly manipulation of the light, filtered through the dirty window glass and polluted atmosphere, an awesome coronal effect that gave the real and true illusion that Dreamer and his love were inside a great luminescent orange. Dreamer felt her skin next to his, felt her burn into his soul, felt the hard points of heat against his chest.

And, sometime later, stricken by the muse of afternoon delight, Dreamer said, "Christ, Eileen, you know what? You've still got cheerleader tits."

"And you ought to try and grow up," Eileen said.

"Why would I want to do that?"

"You'll never know until you try. Shit, Dreamer, you don't even try. I could go for Chinese right now."

"I didn't think we were on a dinner date, I thought we were doing something else."

"We are. I'm just saying it's something to consider when we finish up this. What was Houston all about?"

"How'd we get back on that?"

"You don't need to take offense. You don't want to say, that's fine."

"I went to see the French ballet. I was taken by debs and forced to stay the night."

"I hope you didn't get something awful. A deb won't keep herself clean."

"The ones I was with, they seemed clean to me."

"Shoot," Eileen said, and reached across him for her drink. "You must've not looked real close. Those girls take a bath twice. Once before the prom, once before the first divorce."

"I guess I caught 'em just right."

"So what did you do down there? Besides that."

"You're going to keep on doing this, aren't you? I don't feel you're going to stop."

"You want me to stop?"

"I don't think it's important, is all. I do business sometimes, I see about a fish. You want to hear about a fish? Fine. That's what I do, you do something else. I don't want to hear about some poor jerk you're suing for half a million bucks."

Eileen sat up. "Don't you do it, don't you start on me."

"I'm not starting on anything at all."

"Good. Don't you smirch my profession, Dreamer, I won't stand for that. I am proud to be an attorney, and I'm goddamn good at what I do. And if I'm *suing* someone, you can bet they fucking deserve it. I represent some of the finest people in the city, some of the finest in the state."

"Some of 'em *guests* of the state, I understand..."

"What?"

"I said--"

"You want another drink?"

"I don't guess I do."

Eileen tossed her glass in Dreamer's face. Single malt was fine, but it tended to smart.

"All right, now what the hell was that?" Dreamer said, the kind of a question you know the answer to, and don't really have to ask...

INTERSTATE DREAMS

Dreamer woke and heard water in the tub. The room was comfortable and dark, the day gone away. Window units fought the heat. He rose to turn them up, stopped to take a peek in the bathroom door.

"You sure look good in the tub," he told her. "I'd like to hop in and be your duck."

"You don't mind," Eileen said, "I'd like to take a bath by myself. That's what I'd like to do."

Dreamer worked his way up her long and lovely self, to the cold judicial eyes.

"You're still mad. I don't know why, I can try and make a guess. I said something bad about the law. I wouldn't tell you where I been. I don't think it was the debs."

"I'm not mad about anything at all."

"It seems to me you are."

"I said I'm just fine."

"We had a little scrap. We also had a lot of fun."

"I am not having fun right now, Dreamer. Leave me alone and close the fucking door."

Dreamer did. He turned up the cool, got back into bed. His watch said a quarter past nine. Eileen emerged at ten, wrapped in a towel from head to toe. She dressed in the dark, keeping her back to Dreamer, hiding parts she hadn't tried to hide from him before.

"I don't guess you want to eat."

"I don't guess I do."

Dreamer sat and pulled on his jeans. You're always at a slight disadvantage, someone's dressed and you're not.

"I would like to get to the bottom of this, whatever this is, all right?"

"I don't want to do that right now." Eileen searched about for shoes. "Explaining things to you can be a chore. You act like you listen but you don't. I feel we're out of synch."

"Out of synch."

"Yes."

"Sometimes we're not."

Eileen looked at him then. "I know that's what you think. Maybe I'd like to think it too. I don't guess I'm real convinced."

She had pulled her hair up for the tub. Now she let it down and combed it out, Dreamer feeling this is where he'd come in, that the film was winding back on the reel, and he'd liked the plot better the first time around.

"Something's wrong, you ought to tell me what it is. I think I'm entitled to that."

"I don't see you are. A person's not entitled if they don't really care. That's the whole thing right there, you don't really care about me."

"That's not true. I care a whole lot."

"No you don't. What you want right now is me to stop. You don't care what I'm stopping *for*."

Eileen stomped about, driving her semi-sensible heels into the floor.

"What I thought," Dreamer said, "I thought we had a relationship here. Maybe I'm wrong, this is what I thought, Eileen."

"We don't have a relationship, pal. What I think we've got here is an itch. What I think we've got is the restless urge to fuck."

"Well I feel deeper than that," Dreamer said.

"Not a lot you don't."

"I do too. I think about you in a caring sense is what. I care what happens to you. I'd have called you up if you hadn't come over when you did."

Eileen looked slightly intent. "What for? What kind of care are we talking about?"

"Word's come to me you're maybe mixed up with some very bad types. People inclined to illegal enterprise. People mixed up with Mako Binder is who I'm talking about."

"Christ, Dreamer." Eileen let out a breath. "I do not believe this. I do not fucking believe this at all."

"I'm saying what I heard."

"Heard where? Where'd you here anything about me?"

"Are you, then? You doing some kind of legal stuff for somebody mixed up with him, somebody maybe new in town?"

"If it's any of your goddamn business, no, I am not. Mako Binder's *your* client, Dreamer, not mine."

"Don't," Dreamer said, "don't get off the track, that's dumb, Eileen. We don't call them clients, they come in for a fish. And let me say I'm greatly relieved you're not mixed up in something, because I really care."

"Don't you ever do this again. I keep out of your affairs, you keep out of mine."

"I can do that."

"Fine. See that you do."

"We'll just make it sometimes, we don't even have to talk. You get horny, you call, I'll do the same for you."

"Oh, man." Eileen let out a breath. She came back and sat on the bed. "Listen to me, hon. You're right about the talking part. We don't have a lot to say to each other standing up. I'll take half the fault for that. Chemistry's a killer, and I let myself yield to your masculine charm. You fuck good, pal. You fucked me good tonight. The only thing is, it was somebody else, it sure as *hell* wasn't me."

"Come on now--"

"Huh-unh, don't even start." She poked him in the chest. "I"ve got feelings, Dreamer, and I'm not talking 'bout the ones down there, I'm talking in my head. I get carried away, and I'm not excusing that. I've also got some self respect, friend. I'm engaging in a porno flick, I expect the star to be *me*. I can read you like a book, and you get this clear. I am not a carnal vessel for your dreams. I will not offer up my lovely self while you're mind fucking a waitress or a rodeo queen."

"You are really nuts, you know that? How could I think about anyone else, I got you in the bed?"

"I don't know. I thought maybe you'd tell me." Eileen got up, straightened out her skirt. "And don't plan anything for Friday night. Rent a good tux. Go downtown where the frat boys go. Do something with your hair. This party's out of town."

"I don't go to parties, unless it's just for two."

"You're going to this one, pal. I've got to go and I've got to bring you. My very best client wants to talk. God knows why, but he wants to talk to you."

"Who does, who is this guy?"

Eileen hesitated, just long enough to let Dreamer know she didn't want to say.

"Augustus Brauweiller. I've told you about him before. In case you don't know, he's--"

"I know who he is. He's the dude who's stolen half the state."

"Maybe a third. I don't think it's any more than that."

"I guess I'll pass. Brauweiller's not anyone I really want to know. You said out of town, out of town where?"

"Houston. Enchanted Mesa West."

"Jesus," Dreamer said...

He wished Eileen hadn't caught him in the act, but she did. Lawyers seemed to have this keen insight, and he hadn't thought of that. He didn't know they watched you in the sack. And, the truth was, he didn't mean to do it but he did. The girl in the Jag just popped in his head and he didn't even try to toss her out. He kissed her on the rosy flush of Eileen's breasts, kissed her in Eileen's magic loving place, kissed her on Eileen's lips. And Eileen sensed, and even told him so, that she'd picked up an Oscar when the winner didn't show, and she didn't much care for doing that. Dreamer was glad he didn't know the girl's name. You call out a name, it's hard to try and lie your way out. Calling out a name, that nails you down flat.

Still, there was something else that troubled him, something even more than getting caught. That seemed almost a misdemeanor now; there might be a major felony here, and he wondered how he'd come to that. They'd had little fights now and then, that's simply what they did. He'd offend her, and then she'd hurt him, then *zap*! they were back in bed again.

This time, though, sitting in the dark in the near dead silence, with only the rattle of the trees against the house, it didn't feel the same at all. He was sorry that they'd fought, but he always felt that. This time, a shadow of doubt, a sad and lonely chill, came with the usual regret. Her image was clouded and he couldn't see her face. And, to make sure he got it right, a livid slash of red, a raw assault of color that razored through his head.

He stood, shaken, and held onto the wall. "Christ," he said aloud, "now what was *that* all about?"

He wished she was there. Wished that she hadn't thrown a drink in his face and bolted out the door. If she hadn't run off they could talk things out, they could have another drink and then go to bed again. Now she was gone and the bed was empty, and he was empty too, empty and sad and hollow without her, and there wasn't any Scotch at all...

She was flat out of Scotch, not a drop in the house. There was bourbon, tequila, half a quart of gin. Well shit, where did *that* come from, she couldn't stand gin, never could.

She poured a shot of *Cuervo,* felt the heat all the way down. One weekend they'd gone to San Antone, tried to hit every bar in town. She damn near made it. Threw up on tourists, passed out inside the Alamo. Dreamer got her in a cab, she threw up in his lap. Jesus, what a weekend, in and out of bed, the room full of bottles and tacky souvenirs--

It hit her hard then, wrenched her apart, plaster lizards and gaudy-colored pigs, lurking in her head somewhere, waiting to set her off. Everything blurred, everything hurt, and the tears welled up and stung her eyes.

She let it go, didn't try to stop, let it wrack her till it all ran out. When it was over, she bent over double, clutched at her belly to keep the pain back.

"Just stop it," she said aloud, "goddamn it, I won't put up with that..."

. . .

This was the part that she hated in herself, the big-girl little-girl crybaby part. The hormones and genes or whatever the hell made females do what they did. It was also the part she liked the best. Being a woman was an awesome, wondrous thing to be. She loved the way she looked, loved the way she felt. Loved her hair, loved her mouth, loved all her private parts. Loved everything about her that drove her to a frenzy, drove a lover nuts.

The good and the bad came together sometimes, and that time was the best. A drop-dead female dressed fit to kill, wiping the other guys' noses on the courtroom floor. They wanted to fuck her, and she was fucking them.

"Hey," some moron would tell her, "you were mean today, babe, you on the rag or what?" It happened all the time. They were the guys and she was the babe, and they wanted her to understand that. It helped make up for the fact she was also a partner in the city's biggest firm, a bad-ass lawyer who billed eight figures every year.

--Which didn't help much when Dreamer came out of the john and her

knees went weak and her tummy did a flip. She knew what was under that towel, how it felt and where it fit...

She cursed herself for that. Blessed herself as well. It happened every goddamn time. She might be thoroughly pissed, ready to slap him silly, ready to slug him with a baseball bat. Then her crotch would kick into second, and that was the end of that.

She hated doing that. Giving in and putting out. Maybe every woman felt the same. Maybe they also liked it as much as she did. It was part of the female bit--the sadness and the joy, the weakness and the strength.

And what did men have? The very same thing, except they were big and behaved like bears. They were sensitive and brutal, and sometimes incredibly dumb.

"We don't have a relationship," she'd told him, "What we've got is the restless urge to fuck." That hurt his feelings, and he said he really cared.

Maybe he does, she told herself. But I don't know if *I* do.

And that was the thing. Right there. She didn't know if she wanted any more. She didn't and she did. *Work* had gotten her where she was, *love* surely hadn't done shit.

Still, sometimes, in the tumble and the heat of sweaty bliss, she wanted to cry out, *I wish I loved you...I wish you loved me!* And, every time it happened, she was smart enough to grab him, hold on tight, and keep her mouth shut.

And there was something else as well. Dreamer wasn't the only lover in her life. It was only a sometime thing, but it was there. It was there and she wouldn't let it go, didn't know if she even wanted to. Certainly didn't know if she could. If Dreamer knew, he'd have a fit. It might be different today, but the double standard was the same. A guy who slept around was a stud, a woman was a whore. A man would tell you he stood up for women's rights: But that was only if she wasn't lying down.

And, you son of a bitch, she thought, *you aren't any different than the rest. That wasn't me this afternoon, that was somebody else!*

"Fuck you, pal," she said aloud, took another slug of tequila and didn't even bother with the glass. Realized, at once, those weren't exactly the words to get Dreamer out of her head...

INTERSTATE DREAMS

"I got guys working night and day on this," Mako said. "I got this mother moving frontways, sideways, up the kazoo. I got people don't do nothin' but package stuff, right? You don't got a package, you don't got shit. I got fag designers doing double overtime.

"I got ad dudes in New York, I got 'em in Chicago, and Butte. Jesus, what a bunch of dickheads *those* guys are. The jerks was going to dump us in the dirty magazines. I said, 'who the fuck you think you're talking to, we're going class on this.' I'm talking *Elle* and *Vanity Fair.* I'm talking fucking *G.Q.* Good-looking guys and skinny babes. We might be sayin' stuff in French. *Moi-Guy, Moi-Gal.* What d'ya think, the dudes come up with that. Hey, where are you, friend, you fuckin' out to lunch, you fuckin' *listening* to me?

"Uh, sure, right here, Mako," said Halloran Horn. "Good-looking babes, skinny guys, saying stuff in French. That's good. That's the sophisticated touch, that's the way to go."

"Yeah, right..."

Mako gave him a frosty gangster eye, a look that told Horn he wasn't off the hook at all.

"All this stuff, the stuff *I'm* doin', it don't mean shit, you're not holding up your end, Horn. I don't like to be complaining, but you're dragging ass, pal. Science is dropping the fucking ball, you're letting down the team."

"We are making progress," Horn said, choosing his words with care, "we have made--definite inroads into the problem. I see growth. I see good indications, positive gains. I see breakthrough here."

"I see a lot of fuckin' talk. I don't see product, pal."

"I've got some charts--"

"Will you listen to this, you hear what you're saying to me? A guy's saying *progress,* he's sayin' he hasn't got shit."

"Now that is not true--"

"Fuck it's not." Mako got up, tossed Horn another killer look, just past injury, close to homicide.

"You want a drink? I got bourbon, I got beer and 7-Up, I got anything you want."

"No thanks," Horn said, "I'm fine."

"You want somethin' to eat?"

"No, I'm just fine."

"Hukka-Hump," Mako mumbled to himself. He walked past Horn, through the living room, through the kitchen door.

Horn let out a breath. Mako rattled glasses, worked the ice machine. Put a skillet on, tossed some bacon in. It's eight in the morning, Horn thought, greasy dishes on the table, whiskey in a glass, and he's having breakfast again.

. . .

Horn wondered what the hell to do. He'd stalled all he could. He was running out of high school science magic tricks.

He knew, if he ever told Mako there was no such thing as a portable fuck, Mako would likely kill him on the spot. He wouldn't remember it was his, Mako's idea, it would all be *his* fault.

It wasn't like he needed any hassle right now. Amy'd just heard about Europe, and wouldn't shut up until he took her over there. Someone broke in and took stuff out of his desk, which he hadn't told anyone about. The son of a bitch got onto the grounds, into Enchanted Mesa West, and that was supposed to be impossible to do.

Competition was fierce, and he'd done a little thievery himself. But stealing stuff--and sending it *back?* What kind of crazy shit was that?

If it wasn't for Mako, and Amy on a tear, everything would be fine. Business was good. Business, in fact, was fucking great. In the eighties, while the rest of Texas moaned and licked its wounds over bad oil prices, a real estate bust and scandals in the banks, Horn got richer by the day. He'd seen the storm coming and shifted his wealth to condom stock. Argentine bonds. Thai insurance and Idaho trout. Enchanted Mesa West. Lektra-Fide Security. St. Sarah Jean House and straight laundromats. Crack snacks for pets. Drive-in brothels in Maine and Tennessee.

He was heavy into fat clinic futures and day-care centers for Czechs. High interest loans for the poor. Organ banks for the rich. Mako had him down for 19% of this Lease-a-Tot thing which was almost perfectly legit. The kids came from Waifland, Inc., thirty-nine branches of the St. Sarah Jean House scam. Waifland took in disadvantaged kids, and found them lovely homes at a very hefty price.

Lease-a-Tot did better than that. Lease-a-Tot rented out moppets and tykes to people who didn't want kids full-time. People who needed little cuties for family reunions, company picnics, Easter time at church. Horn liked the deal a lot. It was good for the grownups and good for the kids. He liked it most of all, because the sucker could go into franchise and bring in money by the pot...

. . .

He didn't mean to pry, but the papers on the corner of the table caught his eye. Mako was still in the kitchen, frying something up. Horn lifted a single page and peeked. What he saw sent a flutter through his belly, sent a tingle up his shorts.

The pictures were in terrible color. The women were innocent and nasty, pure and unsullied, totally corrupt. Lechery and Lust came to mind. Animals in heat.

He had seen it all before in movies and dirty magazines. He'd seen the same breed in a dozen topless bars. And, before his wife came along, when Amy was still Mrs. Wallace Pailey Marshall instead of Amy Horn, Halloran had tasted immoral flesh himself.

What it is, he thought, is seeing this stuff so early in the day. Sin seems a little out of place before ten. Which is why he'd reacted so strongly to an ordinary sight. That, and the fact that *The Sound of Music* had nasty overtones if you watched it at Mako Binder's place--

"Hey, caught ya!" said Mako, and Horn dropped the pictures quick.

"I was just--"

"Right, I know what you was doing, pal." Mako stood in the doorway and grinned. He was eating a fried egg sandwich, the yellow dripping down his chin.

"It's okay to look," Mako said, "you got a cut, you're in."

"I've got a cut of what?"

"SLUTTO. You got thirteen percent. We ain't talked about this? I'm pretty sure we did."

"I think I'd remember," Horn said.

"It's LOTTO with chicks. Your number comes up, you turn in your ticket, you get one of them."

Halloran was taken aback. "That isn't legal, is it, can we do that?"

Mako laughed again, a gangster guffaw this time, that sprayed a little egg on Halloran's shirt. "Shit, whatcha think? We don't sell tickets at the 7-Eleven store. You gotta know where to go, you gotta *know* somebody, okay?"

"Uh, so where do you--"

Mako's phone rang. Mako picked it up, put it on hold.

"I gotta take this. Get back to me, there's somethin' we haven't talked about. Get to the lab guys, tell 'em we're gonna need ethnic coloration on this. I don't give a fuck, but there's bozos out there every shade there is. This is something *you* got to do, this is science stuff."

"Do what?" Horn said, but Mako was off on a criminal adventure somewhere...

The walls of Mama Lucy's Vishnu Jesus Barbecue were covered with photographs and drawings of famous religious figures from the present and the past: Moses. St. Teresa. Ray Charles. Charles DeGaulle. Buddha. Billy Graham. Billy Sunday. Jesus. Shirley Temple. Shirley MacLaine. Abraham. Abraham Lincoln. Murray Abraham. Brigham Young. Gene Autry. Gandhi. Zeus. St. Thomas Aquinas. C.S. Lewis. Joe Louis. Louis Armstrong. Jung. Osiris. Luther Burbank. Martin Luther King. Vishnu. Adam and Eve. Eve Arden. John the Baptist. John F. Kennedy. Pope John Paul. St. Paul. Paul Simon. Paul Newman. Rama. Shiva. F.D.R. Isis, Mohammed, Jesse Jackson and many more.

A lot of these pictures were signed, personally inscribed to Mama Lucy herself. Dreamer felt some of the signatures--people like Zeus and Billy Graham--were questionable at best.

Once, when he first came to town, before he knew Mama Lucy well, he asked her how she could handle so many different and varied beliefs.

They ain't different at all," Mama Lucy explained, "they all just the faces of God. You go and see John Wayne in a movie picture show. You know he ain't a cowboy, he ain't a Green Beret. The man be playin' out a role, dressing up like somebody else. You get your act straightened out, boy, you start seeing God in everyone you meet..."

Dreamer thought of some of the folks he knew, and figured he had a ways to go. Still, Mama Lucy said there was good in everyone if they'd bother to let it out, and Mama Lucy knew. That was the thing. You might have doubts about the pictures on the wall, but Mama Lucy *knew.* Mama Lucy had the power. She knew when a Blue Gourami had to die. She knew the price of oil. She knew about the colors in Dreamer's head and *no*body else knew that. She knew things Dreamer wished she didn't know, like when a lady stayed at his big white house overnight.

"Fornicators got a special place in hell," Mama Lucy liked to say, serving up Dreamer's Elijah Chopped Beef. "They private parts goin' to sizzle and snap for all eternity. I reckon that's a long time to howl..."

Dreamer figured it likely was, too.

. . .

"What I've got," Dreamer said, "is a real bad feeling about this Houston deal. I don't want to go and Eileen wants me to. I'd a whole lot rather stay home. I could clean up the shop is one thing. Dinh's let it get real bad. They're having a Blondie and Dagwood film fest over at the Dobie, and I'd like to see that. I ought to go, I guess, it means a lot to Eileen. We haven't been getting along too good and maybe this'd help."

"I don't want to be hearin' nothing dirty," Mama Lucy said. "I am not inclined to nasty talk."

"All I said is we aren't exactly getting along, Mama Lucy, there's nothing nasty in that."

"Seems to me there is. Seems to me getting along's got overtones of lust in your head."

It did, of course, but he didn't want to get into that.

"Changing words don't change what's on your mind," Mama Lucy said. "You eat your lunch, I got other folks to tend."

Dreamer watched her disappear in the kitchen. She walked straight and tall for a woman her age, whatever that might be. She looked like Cicely Tyson, made up to be a hundred and ten, which might be coming pretty close.

As he ate his sandwich, he heard her yell at Horace E. Temple, a man with the patience of God who made the best ribs in the world, a man who'd done time for assault, a man prone to seizures now and then, related to Junior Lewis somehow, on his ex-uncle's side. Dreamer had tried to get more out of Junior, and Junior simply said there were things about Horace E. Temple that he didn't want to know, and to let it go at that.

The fans stirred the muggy summer Austin afternoon. Mama Lucy didn't care for refrigerated air. Blue flies clung to the outside screens, yearning for the countertops and floors, for the tables and the doors all coated with grease and tasty sauce. The flies stayed out and looked in. No one had ever seen a fly inside. Mama Lucy had ways to keep them out, Junior said, ways that had little to do with mortal insecticide.

It was late for lunch, and there were five other people in the place. A black doctor Dreamer had met once or twice, a man named Billy Shank. Another black man, a banker named Morris LeBlanc having lunch there with his wife. A white man who drove the Coors truck. Betty the Crush, a black velvet beauty of the night who ate ribs at Mama's every day. Dreamer knew the lady had a limited trade, that Betty had a pelvic grip that could do a man bodily harm.

Mama Lucy knew Betty and knew what she did. Mama Lucy saw beyond that. What she saw was the light around your head. Black skin or white was okay, preachers and whores were just fine. But aural segregation could put your ass out on the street in no time.

. . .

"I don't mean to be hard on you, Dreamer," Mama Lucy said, serving him up some apple pie. "I don't but I do. Sin gets me riled, I can't much help doing that."

"I know I've got some faults," Dreamer said, "I won't deny that."

"You got more'n some, but Jesus loves you all the same. That don't mean you ought to let yourself slide. You do, you be headin' for a fall."

Dreamer finished off his iced tea. "Mama Lucy, I feel as if I'm falling right now. What I feel is, somebody's giving me a push."

"That's because you're doing things you shouldn't ought to do. That's the one thing. The other is you're scared of getting caught. And don't be taking Junior Lewis out again, you think I don't know about that?"

He didn't want to look at Mama Lucy but he did. "I don't want to keep doing what I do. What I want to do is quit. I don't like what I got up in my head, I don't want to use it anymore."

"What you got in your head's a special gift. God give it to you, Dreamer. You let it go fallow, you denying His will."

"God's going to get me in jail, is what He's going to do."

Mama Lucy made a sign above his head. "Don't you talk like that. I'll slap you silly if you do. You say you're sorry right now."

"I'm sorry," Dreamer said.

"Tell Jesus you're sorry, not me. You listen real good. There is trouble coming at you, rollin' right out of that big ethereal flux. You're right in what you're thinking. Someone's giving you a push--a whole bunch of someones, it isn't just one. Watch out who you know, be careful where you go."

"Are we talking here about Houston or what? Me going there with Eileen?"

Mama Lucy gave him a frosty look. "I work for Jesus. You want your fortune told, go on down the street."

"I don't think I'd care for that."

"You do something, Dreamer." Mama Lucy poked a sharp finger in his chest. "You bring that woman here. You bring her here to me."

"Do what?"

"You bring her here. You just do it, boy."

"When, you mean now or what? Is that all you've got to say?"

Mama Lucy didn't answer. She took Dreamer's plate and his empty tea glass and walked away. Dreamer listened to the fans and watched the flies. Betty the Crush asked Dr. Billy Shank for advice, or possibly the other way around.

When Dreamer left, he took the memory of sorrow in Mama Lucy's eyes. Sorrow not arrived, possibly in transit somewhere. Sorrow in a holding pattern, circling about in the great ethereal flux. Everything was cloudy in his head. There was something big and scary out there, but nothing he could really make out...

INTERSTATE DREAMS

Enchanted Mesa West. Dreamer couldn't think of any place he'd rather not be. He looked for hints of dread, omens of regret. One bad sign was a tux that didn't fit. He'd forgotten to get a rent. Borrowed a suit from a waiter at a semi-French taco restaurant. There were sure signs of salsa down the front. Not a whole lot, but enough to earn Eileen's fury and contempt.

"Eat the little canapes," she said. "Put the toothpicks *down*, Dreamer, don't put the fucking toothpicks in your coat."

"A person might need one later on," Dreamer said.

"Honest to God..."

"This was your idea, babe."

"Don't you remind me of that, and don't you call me *babe.* Don't say anything to me. Don't feel compelled to talk, don't feel you have to--

--Augustus, how nice. Augustus Brauweiller, this is Dreamer. How's Lee Ann, I haven't seen her in a year my God has it been as long as that?"

"Lee Ann's in the sack," Brauweiller said. "I guess she's got the curse. That woman cramps like a nun. Seems to find great benefit in pain. Dreamer what? What kind of name is that?"

"Just Dreamer, that's it."

"You and me got to talk. I got a job for you, what's it going to cost to make a deal?"

"You boys have fun," Eileen said, and disappeared in a shoal of tuxedos and lavish evening gowns.

"Nothing's going to cost you," Dreamer said. "I'm not looking for work and we haven't got a deal."

Brauweiller grinned, his ball-bearing eyes disappearing in little chubby cheeks. Dreamer had seen him on the TV news, and knew the man was fat, but fat didn't cut it when the man was right there, five-foot-two and maybe three-six-six, it was like you were talking to a fucking manatee.

"I like a man don't cave in right away," Brauweiller said. "We'll get along fine. Money's no big thing. Mutual respect is where it's at. We can work something out, I promise you that. Hey, you humping Eileen?"

"That's no concern of yours."

"Damn right it's not." He punched Dreamer lightly in the chest. "We'll talk later on. You ever hear of a woman does a period 'bout every three days? I never heard of that."

"She might need medical advice."

"Say, I bet you're right. I'll look into that."

Brauweiller grabbed a drink off a tray. It looked like eggnog in a cup. The hacienda rooftop villa was done up in Christmas array. Decorated trees. Festive mistletoe. Mexican pinatas, a hundred thousand lights from overseas. Outside the broad windows, automatic plastic snow drifted through the summer night.

"What do you think?" Brauweiller caught Dreamer's interest in the holiday decor. "My idea. Something everybody likes. Even your Jews and your Ay-rab types. Christmas don't piss off anyone at all."

"It's terrific," Dreamer said. "I bet there's nothing like it anywhere."

"Goddamn right," Brauweiller said.

What the yuletide motif did, Dreamer thought, was partially hide the unsightly mess from bazaars around the world, an awesome collection of overpriced junk, crammed into every nook and hollow, every corner of the room. Phoney furniture from Austria and France. Mayan pottery from mainland China, Soviet lamps. Plastic gods from Africa, Picassos from Iraq. Everything there cost an arm and a leg, and everything was crap.

Dreamer wondered if Augustus Brauweiller was responsible for this, or the lady of perpetual cramps. When it came to bad taste, money didn't count. You could fuck up a mobile home or Enchanted Mesa West. Junior Lewis had better taste than this. A little Day-Glo wouldn't hurt the place a bit.

Brauweiller left. Talked to a man and came back. The man wore white Saudi robes and eyes full of evil intent.

"That mother's richer than me," Brauweiller said. "It's a fact. He's got near everything there is. He says he'd like to buy Fort Worth."

"What for?"

"That's what I said."

"They've got some real nice museums."

"I doubt he'd go for art. Your Mideast greaser don't have a lot of taste. What he's into is pussy and oil. Don't guess you can fault a man for that."

Brauweiller mumbled something else about perverse pleasures of the East, anal acts in Egypt and Sudan. Dreamer didn't hear a thing. He was wholly entranced by the woman coming toward him, taken by the chic dark glasses that covered up her eyes, by the bare and lovely shoulders, by the honey-colored hair, by her legs, by her nose, by her sweet undulation, by her quiver, by her shake, by the motion of her thighs. He hungered for her breasts, for her red-red mouth, for the body meant for lazy summer days, meant for cozy winter nights.

Brauweiller spotted her at once and hauled her in.

"Dreamer, this here's Amy, and that fella's Halloran Horn. This ol' boy's Dreamer. Dreamer hasn't got another name, that's it. What you think of that?"

"Pleasure," Dreamer said, and tried to hide a little jolt. *Jesus*, he thought, *I'm me and you're him. Guess what, I robbed your house, man!*

He shook a limp and soppy hand. Fish-belly skin. Dirt-colored hair and tap-water eyes. A plain generic brand. Still, in spite of Horn's pallor, a man with all the vigor of lint, the colors went *Zhit!* in Dreamer's head. He tasted something bad. Clothes in the attic gone to mold, mice that had died up in the walls.

It wasn't just the stealer, face to face with the recent stealee. It was something he couldn't put his finger on, something that he didn't like at all.

Brauweiller winked, slapped Horn soundly on the back.

"This sum'bitch is a caution. Wants to fuck my commerce and trade. Wants to eat me up and spit me out again. Shoot, Horn, I'll have your ass for Sunday lunch."

"No, now you won't do that, Augustus. I can't let you do that."

Horn showed them all a weary smile. His voice was flat as paint. No ups, no downs, not any life at all.

"I get through with you," Brauweiller grinned, "you won't have a pair of pants. You won't have a fucking hat."

"I don't think so," Horn said gently, "I feel I can bring you to ruin, Gus, I surely think I can."

"Is this guy something, or what? Goddamn, ain't doing bidness fun? Halloran, you want some eggnog? This stuff'd paralyze a buffalo."

For an instant, the pair of tycoons were caught up in the party's tidal flow, lost amid affluent Japanese come to see the plastic snow. In that small moment, Dreamer found himself alone with Amy Horn. He yearned to kiss her neck, to taste her collarbone. To peek down her dress, see if her bra hooked in back or in the front.

"We could live in Mexico," Dreamer said. "Maybe get a goat. I'd do anything you want."

"I don't know," Amy said. "I don't know if I could go right now."

"You think you might, though? It wouldn't have to be Mexico. Waco's fine with me. I won't go to Dallas, anywhere else'd be fine."

"You'll do anything I want?"

"You bet."

"I can't think of anything at all..."

Dreamer felt a little lurch in his tummy, a queasy little flop, as she took her glasses off. He'd been kidding, just jerking around, but the woman didn't know that. Her eyes were blue and empty, there was nothing there at all. The windows were up, but no one was there to get the phone.

"You got any coke, any hash, harmful pills of any kind? A joint'll do, anything'll be fine."

"I'm, uh-- no, I guess not," Dreamer said, patting the pockets of his jacket and his pants. "This is a rental, I don't have a thing."

"That's okay," Amy said, with a smile that gave Dreamer a minor heart attack, "I'll give some thought to Mexico."

He watched her weave a path through the crowd. The snow outside seemed real. On the twenty-two speaker subatomic stereo, Cher sang *Oh, Holy Night* in faultless Lebanese.

He ate a canape that tasted like eel. Washed it down with nog. The mix had a startling effect. He felt desperation coming on, searched through the mass for Eileen. Maybe they could go, get a burger and some fries.

Brauweiller said, "Hey, you sum'bitch," let Horn go, and waddled off after a man in a solid red tux.

"Nice party," Dreamer said.

"Oh, yes," Horn said.

"Your wife is lovely. I hope you don't mind me saying that."

"She'd like to go to France."

"Oh, yeah?"

"You came with Eileen."

"You two know each other then."

"I don't know her at all," Horn said.

"Jesus, Dreamer," Mako said, "how do people swallow this stuff, you wanta tell me that? Who the fuck drinks whiskey and eggs?"

Mako Binder burst upon the scene, grinned at Dreamer and Horn. Sicilian shades. Raw Italian silk. Expensive gangster cologne.

"It's Christmas," Dreamer said, "that's what people drink."

"Not me I don't. I feel I gotta puke. Christ, where'd you get that tux? You'd think a place like this, they got a fucking john."

"Excuse me," Horn said, "I need to find my wife."

Mako grabbed him in a fullback hug and hauled him back.

"Halloran and me's in genetics. What you got, you got a protein chain, you got your DNA, you can mess around with that. You oughta see this fuckin' rat. I'm coming over Tuesday, Wednesday next. I want to get a fish. What I want is a cat that's got some spots."

"African Polka-dot. I can fix you up."

Horn ducked away from Mako and escaped this time.

"You don't want to mess with Amy Horn."

"Why not?"

"I'll be over a couple days. We'll have lunch. I'm talkin' somewhere nice, I'm not talkin' nigger barbecue. You don't like that kinda talk, right?"

"No I don't."

"Who gives a fuck, pal? You ever see so many slopes? Fucking Japs own half the country now, Gus, he'll sell 'em the half they haven't got."

"Doesn't seem right."

"I say we kick ass. Nuke the little fuckers again. You forget all about Amy Horn."

Mako took off. Amy Horn appeared.

"Hello," she said, "I don't guess we've met."

"Dreamer. Can I get you a drink?"

"That'd be nice," Amy said, and floated off again.

Dreamer took a deep breath. Lunged through the crowd. Escaped through linen and gold lame, through silk and cigars, through millionaires and debs. Fought asphyxiation, fought the colors in his head.

"Goddamnit, Eileen," he said aloud, "you got me into this, you better get me out..."

He thought he saw her once, saw her swallowed up in a herd of Nepalese. Spotted Brauweiller, tacked off to port, but Brauweiller ran him down.

"Say, you and me need to talk, let's get a little air."

"I'll call you," Dreamer said, "Thursday afternoon."

"Fuck you will." Brauweiller gave him a macho wink, grabbed his arm and led him through the crowd. Down a hall to an elevator door. Dreamer wished he was back in Austin, back home in bed. With Eileen or Amy Horn, someone he didn't even know.

The elevator opened on an underground garage. Acres of Dusenbergs and Cords. Bentleys and Rolls. Caddies and Lincolns belonging to the help. Brauweiller led him to a '38 Chevy painted blue.

"These mothers are real hard to find. You can't get parts. Get in the other side."

Brauweiller snaked through concrete tunnels and up into the dark. Out past tennis courts and putting greens and spas, out past race tracks and artificial ponds. Dreamer wondered where they were. Decided it was better out here than where they'd been.

Down through valleys and past tall trees, on to a cluster of dark shadow buildings, great beasts settled for the night. Brauweiller pulled up to a halt. Jumped out and waited for Dreamer, grabbed him and led him through the night. Fiddled with a lock, slid back a very tall door, flooded the dark with a bright and searing light.

Dreamer's heart skipped a dozen beats. His knees began to melt. The sight came at him like a loose refrigerator on a spree. His night on the road rolled back in a rush of summer bugs and rowdy frogs. The rattle of the engine, the flutter of the canvas in the wind...

Then, just as quickly, he was back in the chopper, in the white ball of death, in the bone-searing fire. He knew he ought to run but he didn't know where...

"What the hell you doing," Brauweiller said, staring at him under the harsh hanger lights. "You all right, boy? I thought you was having a fit."

"I'm okay," Dreamer said, "I think I ate some eel."

"I'd say sit, but you might get grease on your tux. Say, what do you think of this? Aren't they honeys? Don't tell me you ever seen anything like 'em before."

Dreamer couldn't say he had, he was certain of that. The stubby little planes sat side by side in a military slant, five pesky bulldogs, angry and ready for a fight. Turtle-green wings, moss-green wheels and a mustard-colored nose, stern black crosses on the body and the tail.

"They're--something else," Dreamer said, and knew this wouldn't do. "They look good as new."

Brauweiller made a face at that. "Damned right they're *somethin' else.* And that's not phony-baloney reproduction shit you're looking at, boy, that's the real thing, that's *it.*"

Brauweiller walked over and caressed a canvas tail. "You're going to get some history, you like it or you don't. These here are Fokker D VIIIs. The very last Fokkers in Dubya-Dubya One. There were eighty-five of 'em at the front. Nineteen eighteen, November One. Ten days after that, the war's done. What you got here is a combat monoplane, Dreamer, I doubt you know the import of that.

"I'm borin' you, forget it, you're gonna hear it anyway. The old Red Baron himself was shot down in 1918, April Twenty-one. Manfred left his Flyin' Circus to Willy Reinhardt, a pilot twenty-seven, the oldest in the bunch. Reinhardt gets himself killed right off. Another hot-shot named Hermann Goering takes over as honcho of *Jagdgdeschwader* Freiherr von Richtofen Number One."

Brauweiller paused. "Now I'm skipping on ahead. The huns are getting their asses whipped. On November Ten, the Kaiser tosses in the towel. The order comes down to give up, keep all planes on the ground. Goering calls his boys together and tells 'em, 'Fuck this, we aren't giving up the fight.'

"He gets all his pilots in the air. Something goes wrong and his plan turns to shit. He knows he has to burn his planes or the Allies'll get 'em intact.

"That's the true history part, but it isn't all there is. He doesn't burn the planes at all. What he does is fly six D VIIIs off east, where his mechanic's old daddy has a farm. He takes the planes apart, rolls up the canvas and knocks the frames down. Puts every nut and every bolt in bottles of grease. Has it all labeled and stacked. Your average Kraut, he's going to do everything proper and precise."

Dreamer waited for the rest. It seemed as if there had to be something more to this.

"What for," he said finally, "why'd he do that?"

"Who the hell knows? Man didn't want to quit. Hermann never saw those planes again. Got real busy after that. Tied up with this new Nazi bunch."

"I heard about that."

"What happens, this mechanic whose daddy owns the farm, he runs up a gambling debt. Sells off the planes to a textile merchant in France. The Frenchie sells out to a Hong Kong collector in nineteen-twenty-six. He sells the goods to a Capetown diamond tycoon. These babies have been around. I tracked them down in '86. They were still packed up, no one had ever took 'em out or built them back."

Brauweiller grinned at Dreamer. "I've got five out of the six. One of 'em's missing. I want that mother back. That's what I'm hiring you to do."

Dreamer was too appalled to laugh but he did.

"Christ, mister, we're talking what? That war's been over eighty years."

"I guess I know that, boy, I can add some."

"Fine. Well you've got the wrong man. I wouldn't know where to start. Sometimes I try and get things back. I see Eileen's told you that. But I can't do it, if I don't know where it is."

"Shoot, what kind of business is that? If I knew where it was I'd do it myself. How much we talking here? I'm willing to go a mill-six. Don't try and jack me up. Don't horse around with Gus Brauweiller, son."

The figure nearly overwhelmed all his omens and his doubts, but the colors in his head were screaming violet and pink, howling lavender and red.

"I can't help you, pal. I wouldn't be any use at all."

"Say, that's fine, I like a man who keeps an open mind. You sleep on this. Bunk in with me. Take one of these babies up at dawn. Feel the wind in your hair. We can work this out, I can tell we'll get along."

Dreamer felt distress, felt ice around his heart.

"You mean fly. Go up in one of those?"

Brauweiller grinned. "Don't try and tell me you can't, I know better than that. You've been in a couple of flyin' wars before."

Dreamer wondered how he knew that. Maybe Eileen, but it didn't have to be. Gus Brauweiller was rich enough to dig up anything he wanted to know.

"That's why I don't do it now," Dreamer said. "I've had about all the air time I care to get."

"You think on it, like I said. I'll get back to you Monday afternoon."

"I already thought about it, the answer's still no."

"I might go a mill-eight. Don't push me any further than that. I got money up the ass but I'm nobody's fool."

"I hate to lose out, but I guess that's what I'll have to do."

"Good. You sleep on it. Give it a little thought. Shoot, let's get some more of that nog."

Dreamer looked for Eileen. Saw Mako Binder and Halloran Horn. Saw a bunch of Taiwan microchip kings hitting on an Oklahoma deb. Then he looked far across the room and felt his knees give way, felt his heart slip into overdrive.

Lord God, it was the girl of his dreams, it couldn't be anyone else. The girl on the interstate, the girl in the bottle-green Jag. The same skinny butt and the gold Montana hair. The same tight jeans and the skin like country cream.

Dreamer went for her at once. She was talking to the blackhearted sheik from overseas. He tried to peel her naked with his Middle Eastern smile. Dreamer grabbed her up, took her off and sat her down by a pink Christmas tree.

"I love you a lot," Dreamer told her. "You're the only girl for me."

She seemed to understand. "I guess I am , hon. We've never even met and I've loved you all my life. I knew if I just kept waiting, you'd show up in a while."

"I'm here and I'm yours, you'll never have to wait for me again."

"That's good enough for me," the girl said.

"You got a car?"

"I got an XK, I got a ninety-seven Jag."

"Why, hell," Dreamer said, "I guess you do at that..."

Mako sat at his table in the dark. He liked to watch the sun rise, liked to see the stars disappear and the light bring the world alive again. It was awesome the way night turned into day. Black melted slowly into gray, then pale shades of purple, ragged veils of yellow, orange and blue and red. Then, almost without warning, there was another day. You could watch it a thousand times, it always happened again.

"This is terrific," Mako told himself. "It's a fuckin' miracle's what it is."

It wasn't a sentiment he shared with anyone else. You tell somebody the morning looks nice, first thing you know, everybody figures you're a fag. There was stuff that you thought about, and stuff you said aloud.

The bozos had come in and fixed the place up, vacuumed the rug, picked up empty bottles, got the dishes clean. Mako could still smell grease and fried eggs. The smell made him hungry. He thought he might fix himself a burger, open up a beer. The food at Brauweiller's had given his stomach fits. Eggnog, for Christ's sake. And somebody said the little sandwiches were eel. "Are you fuckin' serious?" He'd grabbed a terrified waiter who said he didn't know.

Still, the night hadn't been a total disaster. Mako had learned a lot, and that's what bidness was all about. Picking up bits of this and that. Anything, no matter what. People didn't know it, everything was a piece of something else. All you had to do was figure how they fit.

He saw Dreamer leave with a good-looking chick. He didn't know her name, but he meant to find out.

He knew Dreamer went off with Gus, and he didn't care for that. Somebody goes off with somebody else, they're doing something you don't know about. That's how you lose out, that's how you get fucked.

He'd known Amy Horn was a flake. Now he knew she was also into very heavy stuff. He wondered why he hadn't known that. Mako gave the Horn's maid a little something every month--plus the chauffer and the butler and the cook. He paid off everyone who worked at the place. Janitors, doormen and guards. Guys who went through the garbage, guys who trimmed the trees.

And that was just Enchanted Mesa West. Mako had stoolies everywhere. All the big companies, the restaurants and bars. Stoolies at the TV stations, stoolies who were hookers, stoolies who were cops. He dropped a bundle in state and local politics. His budget for bribes was into seven figures, enough to choke a horse. And it was all worthwhile. You gathered all the pieces, and you jiggled them around until they fit:

Mako knew from Horn's butler someone had stolen a bundle of papers from his desk. He knew from the maid that someone had sent the papers back.

A jerk named Cochran who worked for a company called Nu-Gene, Inc., bitched at his caddy that an asshole from Austin had really ripped him off. The caddy told someone, who told somebody else.

Mako paid a hacker to pull videos from the big car rental lots. Mako kept tabs on several thousand people at a time. People went on the list and off. The hacker had their pictures on hand. When a picture matched the video, Mako got the word at once. Which was how Mako knew that Dreamer was in town the night Horn's paper disappeared.

There was one other item that didn't make any sense at all, or didn't at the time. Then, *Bingo!* the little fucker fit just right. A little kid lived in Enchanted Mesa West while her daddy did time in the pen. Mako knew who she was, knew how much was in the trust.

The nanny there was on the payroll, because the kid's daddy was a crook. Sometimes the daddy wrote the little girl, and Mako got a copy of that.

This time, though, was something else. The kid had babbled to the nanny that a "knight had climbed up the wall to see his lady fair." So what? Mako thought, little kids are nuts. Then he saw the little girl lived on Level Eighteen. And Halloran Horn was just three floors up on Twenty-One.

Mako laughed when he saw it. Son of bitch, it had to be Dreamer. Who else could pull a stunt like that? And, Mako wanted to know, exactly *how?* He didn't believe anyone could get past security at Enchanted Mesa West. Still, he was sure that Dreamer had, that he'd pulled this kind of shit before. Mako *had* to know just how he did that.

And he would. The same way he found out everything else that he wanted to know. At just the right time, Dreamer would be glad to tell Mako Binder exactly how he climbed up walls without setting off alarms. There was always a way. You gave somebody something they wanted. That, or you took something dear to them away.

There were lots of names on Mako's list. Little fish and big ones. Senators and whores. Dopers, preachers, and CEOs. Super-rich dudes like Gus Brauweiller and Halloran Horn.

Horn, now--Horn was easy, Mako didn't even have to try. He fully owned Halloran Horn, it was only a question of time. Horn was primed and ready, Horn would fucking hang himself.

. . .

And, as the sun began to rise, and the world bathed in dazzling summer light, Mako was grateful that he lived in a state that was nearly always hot, where a man could look at pussy at the pool anytime and sweat a lot. There were places like Boston or Newark where a lot of Family guys hung out, places you could freeze your ass off.

"I love it in Texas, it's fucking great here," Mako said, and got up to fix a morning burger and a beer...

INTERSTATE DREAMS

Junior Lewis feels partially confused. In the back of the *Vins de Jacques* van he's got a case of Wild Turkey and forty-two quarts of chocolate milk. Twenty-five boxes of Oreos, 32 six-packs of beer. Assorted Fig Newtons, Pepsis and gin.

The order doesn't match. The mix seems somehow out of sorts. It doesn't seem right, and neither does a midnight stop in a part of town he's never been before, a place called Davy Crockett Real Estate, Inc.

Junior knocks on the door. There's no light at all, everything is dark. A bald man in shades opens up just a crack and says, "Take it out back."

"I gotta go way 'round, I do that," Junior says. "I got to go in the alley and maybe scratch the truck."

"Out *back*," the man says, and shuts the door.

"Sheeit," Junior says.

He drives around back. Another bald man in shades lets him stack all his goods in the hall. Junior hears music somewhere. He figures maybe cable TV. Two bald-headed dudes doing real estate shit in the middle of the night. You know they watching porn on the cable TV.

Junior walks back to his van. A wino is down on his knees, got his knees in the dog-do and Big Mac debris. Junior sees what he's doing, but he doesn't know why. He's praying to the big bright bottle on the top of Junior's van. He's praying to the bottle, and Junior is glad he can't hear.

"Go on now," Junior says, "get your ass away from that thing."

The wino looks at Junior Lewis. "Jesus loves me a lot."

"Yeah, I can see that. You stay where you are, I'm going to flat run you down."

"Have a nice day."

"You aren't helping much with that."

Junior starts the van, starts to take a little nip, starts to think about painting up his house, starts to think about blue and maybe green. Wonders if he's got any beer in the fridge. Wonders if Mama Lucy knows he's having real heavy dreams about Mary Dee Lamm. Wonders, as he drives down the dark night streets, how chocolate milk and whiskey would be, and decides it's not for him...

PART TWO

BOTTOM FEEDERS, TRIGGERFISH, and CARP

INTERSTATE DREAMS

Dreamer sits back and watches his angel drive...

Watches the wind against her face, watches it whip her flaxen hair. He's loved her from the moment that he found her, adrift on the freeway, lost in a blur of passing cars. Loved her in the sense that he's loved a hundred others, taken by her beauty, stricken by her charms.

Now, though, he's seen her from half a breath away, watched the heart beating in the hollow of her throat, looked deep into her soul. He knows, now, his love for her is more than just passion, more than temporary bliss. He knows, because in spite of her clearly mortal charms, she has to be divine. She looks real enough, and she laughs and she smiles like the girl on *Seventeen*, like the girl who leads the cheers for Happy High.

But that can't be, Dreamer knows, for there's never been a real live girl, born in Texas or even Idaho, who has silver-chrome eyes.

He's seen those eyes and he *knows*. He's driving in an import car with a celestial cutie at his side. She's not simply heavenly, man, this creature's heaven-*sent*.

"What's it like to be an angel," Dreamer wants to know, "I'll bet it's lots of fun."

"I'm not supposed to tell," the girl says, "and you're not supposed to ask."

"Hey, that's fine, I can understand that."

"You're Dreamer," she tells him with a heart-stopping smile. "You live in Austin and you sell pretty fish. But that's not what you do at all."

Dreamer is taken aback. "Now how'd you know that? Is this some kind of power, did Jesus tell you that?"

"No, dopey. I saw you at the party. I knew we'd fall in love at first sight. I thought I ought to get to know your name. I'm Cindy, by the way, you forgot to ask mine."

"I didn't forget, I simply didn't care. I didn't care then and I don't care now. Just so you're here. Just so you never go away."

"What a silly thing to say. Why would I ever do that?"

. . .

Dreamer watches his angel drive...

She drives down Highway 45 into Houston, onto 610 North and 290 after that, taking the road straight to Austin, turning west to Dreamer's without even bothering to ask. She knows where they're going, where fate has decided they should be.

. . .

Dreamer watches his angel drive...

She reminds him a lot of Junior Lewis at the wheel. She drives with firm conviction, with purpose and intent. She is clearly in command, the car obeys her every whim. Dreamer never takes her from his sight. He doesn't see the scenery or the cars that pass them by. If the Jag finds bumps on the rocky road to love, Dreamer doesn't notice, Dreamer doesn't care. He is totally enchanted, stunned and overwhelmed by the vision at the wheel of the bottle-green Jag.

And if he'd had a doubt that she sprang from paradise, the road back to Austin sets him right. You cannot drive one-hundred-thirty-five in Texas, even in the middle of the night. You cannot whine through the sleepy dreams of Brenham, Elgin and McDade, without a Smokey on your tail.

You can't, unless you're a silver-eyed sprite, unless a higher power is guiding you safely toward the early morning light.

. . .

The green Jag slowed for a landing in the semi-cool dawning of the day. Left 290 for 35 South, did a hard right on thirty-second street. Dreamer was glad to find she needed directions--she might get help from on high, but she didn't know how to find the house.

He led her up the outside stairs, up the back way past the high night branches, past the smell of new pecans, past the clean scent of sprinklers down below. A squirrel opened one agate eye, grinned and said, "Hey, Dreamer's sure got a honey this time..."

. . .

The room was dark except for the lemon-white moon, except for the silver in her eyes. In the dark, in the night, she turned and came to him, kicked off her shoes and stretched high on her toes, flowed into the pattern of his arms, parted her lips to meet his own. They held each other in a slow and lazy circle, danced to the music in their heads, danced with their eyes closed, got a little dizzy, never lost the kiss, and never lost the beat.

They undressed each other in the dark, both of them shaky, both electrified by the slightest, lightest touch.

"Are we truly in love, do you think?" she whispered in his ear. "Am I yours and are you mine?"

"There's a magic here," he told her. "There's a spell of some kind." He slid his hands around her, laid her gently on the bed.

"I can feel it," she said, "there's really no question in my mind."

"Who are you?" he asked her, as they lay close together, her head on his chest and her leg across his thigh. "Where do you come from, what did you do? Before you got in the angel biz, I mean."

Her breath was warm against his throat. "I was into banking for a year. I did a little stint in a Swedish submarine. Neurosurgery gave me a fit, and I finally had to quit. I helped out at the Louvre for a while."

"And how old are you, hon?"

"Nineteen," she said, and showed him a lazy grin. "Mostly, Dreamer, I haven't done anything at all. Which is just as well, I guess, since I don't have time now for anything but you."

"I'm thirty-eight," he told her. "I can do this in my head, and it looks like I'm twice as old as you. You don't think that's too--"

--"Hush," Cindy said, and pressed a finger to his lips. "Love me, Dreamer. Love is why I'm with you, love is what I'm for..."

. . .

Dreamer kissed each fine and secret shadow, kissed the corners of her mouth, kissed her ears and kissed her eyes. Breathed the sweet intoxication of her breasts, feasted on the dark and dusky tips. She trembled and she quivered, laughed aloud and cried, twisted like a snake as he tasted the treasure in the hollow of her thighs. Her body was a culinary dream--Fritos, Oreos, hot strawberries on the vine. Pepper and cinnamon, Zinfandel wine.

And, Dreamer thought, as he kissed her and breathed her and watched her body caught in a moonlight web, watched the stars blaze in the silver of her eyes, if this is heaven this is fine...if this is angelfood, let me go ahead and die...

. . .

The phone was a harsh intrusion that thrust him out of deep and downy sleep. Eileen beat him to the draw, didn't even let him say hello.

"You son of a bitch, I will not be humiliated, Dreamer, I will not be treated like this."

"Westside Tropical Fish," Dreamer told her, "we open up at ten."

"Don't you pull that shit on me."

"I don't blame you for being upset," Dreamer said, and suddenly recalled what this was all about, suddenly remembered that he'd left her at Enchanted Mesa West. "I'd like to apologize for that. I was really out of line and I respect you a lot."

"Upset? You think I'm *upset*? You leave with that infant in front of all my friends, you think I'm upset?"

"She's not an infant, Cindy's nineteen."

"Ask her if the word *Tampax* rings a bell. I bet she doesn't blink."

"She's a very nice person," Dreamer said, looking down to check, noting, at once, there wasn't anybody there.

"I know what you're thinking, it's not what you think. Okay, it isn't but it is, I want you to understand that. She's been through a very rough time. Her parents were killed by an Afghani tribe. She's really been scarred, Eileen. She's under professional care."

"Are you through yet?"

"I guess I am."

"Good. So am I. Don't call me, Dreamer. Don't ever come by. I'll have you arrested if you do."

"Listen, that dippy client of yours wants me to find a Hun airplane. I told him no. I'd appreciate it if you'd tell him too."

"I'd tell him yes, if I were you. Gus Brauweiller doesn't like to hear no. No gets him out of sorts. How high did he tell you he'd go?"

"I think a million eight."

"Sweet Jesus," Eileen said and slammed the phone in Dreamer's ear.

. . .

Dreamer found Cindy down in the shop with Dinh. At least Dreamer thought it was Dinh. Short little guy of the Asian persuasion, combat jammies and rubber shower shoes, everything right except the smile. Dinh never smiled, only Dinh was smiling now. Not your sly, Oriental smile, not inscrutable at all. Just your everyday shit-eating grin, and Dreamer saw the reason why. Cindy had made a fashion statement, cut her jeans off just shy of her baby duck nest, cut off her T-shirt high enough to start a Papal riot.

Dinh spotted Dreamer and the grin disappeared.

"Tank full of Harlequin all go belly up. Everybody die."

"Goddamn it," Dreamer said, "that's twice this month. And you know why they die? They die because you're too lazy to check the pH. They don't like it at eight like the other fish do, they like it at five."

"pH fine."

"No. pH is not fine, it's high, you always do it too high."

"I quit," said Dinh.

"No you don't," Dreamer said, "you're fucking fired."

Dinh stalked off, muttering curses Dreamer was grateful he didn't understand.

"He doesn't like you much," Cindy said.

"He doesn't like anyone, he's a vicious little shit. He's afraid to kill me, so he takes it out on the fish. He never kills anything that costs too much, he's far too cunning for that."

"I think he's kinda cute."

"You do, huh? Dinh is a VC colonel. The war is over, but Dinh didn't quit. He says he's on leave till they start it up again. He knows about eighty-four ways to kill you before you can blink. You think that's cute? That's not cute. Let's find some breakfast, I got to have something to eat."

"We slept pretty late. It's a little after one."

"Fine," Dreamer said, "let's go and find some lunch."

. . .

He watched her as they drove down Guadalupe, then past 35, on to Mama Lucy's on the east side of town. He was still enraptured, spellbound and captured by the fever of her touch, by the fragrance of her tummy and her neck. He remembered every moment, every breathless interlude of the magic summer night. He did this and then she did that. Covered him with kisses and trailed soft fingers down his spine.

He recalled every instant, every whisper, every laugh. He rewound the picture and slo-moed it back. Back to the start, to the middle and the end, right before the thunder, right before the lightning sizzled through the air, and what the hell happened after that?

Dreamer lost the thread and broke the spell. The projector went haywire, film piled up on the floor. He remembered everything. Everything but that. Everything but the part where the music gets loud and you moan and thrash about.

Dreamer looked at Cindy. Looked at her long and incredible legs, slick and golden in the sun. Looked at the natty pair of shades, perched on her straight and perfect nose.

We did *it, didn't we? I know we did everything else, we must have done that. Well of course we did that...!*

He felt a little chill, felt a tiny little doubt. He was certain he had never, ever forgotten that agonizing, wonderful detonation, not ever in his life.

He tossed out the chill, quickly set aside the doubt. What happened, and it made a lot of sense, when you really thought it out, what happened, it was just so terrific, such a blast, he'd gone into sensory overload, flat whited out.

And hey, why not? A roll in the hay, an all out whing-ding physical union with an angel, who could handle that? Who could die and come back with his head on straight?

I can always ask Cindy, he thought. Say, that's an idea. She'd think he was nuts, and she'd be absolutely right...

"Chile, you need to take care of yourself, get your life straight, put yourself in Jesus' hands."

"I've been meaning to," Cindy said. "I promise, I'll get on it right away."

Mama Lucy gave Cindy a look, a look that went right through the back of Cindy's head.

"What I'm seein' here," Mama Lucy said, poking a bony black finger in a lily-white palm, "what I see, is a karmic ulceration in your second house. You got a plumbin' problem with Pluto, girl, you got the past backin' up."

"Is that bad?"

"It isn't real good. 'Course, it isn't *real* bad," she said quickly, catching Cindy's eye, the flutter in the hollow of her throat. "What it is, what we call it in the seerin' trade, it's a *indication,* is all. The planets and the stars got signs for us to see. It's up to us if we keep on drivin' down the road they're pointing at."

"Well that's good to know," Cindy said. "I'd like to think we can all, you know, do better, like you said?"

"We all can, girl." Mama Lucy gave her a smile and squeezed her hand. "God's grace is working for us all the time."

"Someone is," Cindy said with a visible sigh. "I've been saved from dire harm any number of times. Can I have another Nehi orange?"

"You can have anything you want, long as you get up and get it for yourself."

"Oh, thanks, you are so sweet, you know that?" Cindy bounced up, planted a kiss on Mama Lucy's leathery cheek, pranced like a puppy across the wooden floor, flushed with sheer pleasure at the chance to run free in an ethnic atmosphere, a room filled with people of every shade and hue.

"You and me got to *talk*," Mama Lucy said, still startled by the kiss, "I don't guess you surprised to hear that."

Dreamer saw Mama Lucy had run out of smiles.

"It's not what you think," he told her. "Okay, it sort of is, but it's not."

"It's not what *you* think either, boy."

"Now what's that supposed to mean?"

"Don't be pushing a prophet, you might get a answer you don't want to hear. Lord help us, Dreamer, that chile ain't big enough to be drinkin' Nehi orange. I'm surprised you're not under arrest."

"She's not a child, she's nineteen."

"She's a child at heart, and she isn't fully clothed. I can see all her privae parts. I don't allow naked girls in here, this ain't a bawdy house."

"She's not entirely naked. She is scantily clad."

"Naked is as naked does."

Dreamer knew better than to chase after that. Mama Lucy was right. Sometimes it's better to remain mystified, to stay completely in the dark.

Laughter came from the kitchen, and Dreamer realized it wasn't just Cindy, but Horace E. Temple as well, Horace, who was meaner than Dinh and about as much fun. Still, like Dinh, he was under Cindy's spell.

"Listen," Dreamer said, "I got this thing in my head, I can't seem to sort it out. You don't think she could be some kinda-- Some kind of *angel*, do you? Some sort of celestial person, am I being silly or what?"

Mama Lucy drew in a breath. For an instant, she nearly showed a hint of surprise, nearly showed a little of herself, which a person of the prophet persuasion never likes to do at all.

"Don't you even be thinking 'bout heavenly persons," she said, "that's God's business, not yours."

"She's got these silvery eyes," Dreamer said.

"I know what kinda eyes she's got. You don't have to tell me that."

"You told me to bring her here. Before I went to the party over there. I thought it was Eileen you were talking about. It wasn't, though, it was Cindy, you didn't tell me that."

"Don't be double guessin' me. You asking questions, givin' back answers to yourself."

"It isn't her or it is?"

"Why don't you tell me?"

"Okay," Dreamer said, knowing when to quit. "You knew I'd meet her there, right, you knew that?"

"I knew *that*, Dreamer, the night you an' Junior Lewis saw her the *first* time, the night you was out where you shouldn't oughta be."

"Junior told you that?"

"Nobody told me anything, boy."

Mama Lucy leaned across the table and took Dreamer's hands.

"You got doubts about what this girl is to you, don't tell me you don't. You'd best listen to your head. *Trouble finds her, trouble binds her.* And you're right squat in the middle of that. Something else, too. You got lots of women trouble coming. Coming from them you know, comin' from one you didn't know you did."

"You want to run over that again?"

"You want to pay your bill? That *angel* of yours has drunk every Nehi in the house..."

Dreamer sat in his shorts, drinking foreign beer before the big AC. He worked on the books, which was always a chore. Doubly hard because Dinh kept a record of everything he sold, every fish and what kind, only Dinh couldn't write in English any more than Dreamer could read Vietnamese.

Cindy left after lunch, telling him she had to freshen up and change clothes. Dreamer was pleased to hear that. It meant she was coming back again. He hadn't even thought about her having a place, a dog or a cat, and possibly a phone. He pictured her adrift, driving through the night in the bottle-green Jag.

He gave up on the books at four. At four-fifteen, he saw the black Lincoln with the blacked-out windows pull up at the shop downstairs. The driver was beef in a cheap black suit. He got out of the car, and his clone rolled out the other side. The clone stepped back and opened the Lincoln's rear door.

Mako Binder stepped out in a black raw silk Italian suit, no shirt and no tie. No socks and black Italian shoes. He told the beefy guys to wait there. Told them to stay out of the car and not to use the air.

"I'm in the car, you use the air. I'm not paying you to breathe my fucking air."

. . .

"Some party, huh? Brauweiller's a greedy bastard, but you got to give him that. You took that little cookie home, right? That is prime pussy, friend, that is nice-looking stuff."

"I've got that Polka-dot cat," Dreamer said. "You want to buy it or not?"

"I'll take it. I'll take maybe two. Hey, you take offense, I'm talkin' like that? You don't like it, what the fuck do I care?"

"You want something else, we're closing at five. You got a minute and a half."

Mako lit up a skinny cigar. "Something you oughta know about Gus. You do bidness with him, what he says he's gonna do, he's doing something else. Like, you get twenty percent, it says right there in black and white. It comes time to pay, *his* contract don't say twenty, what it says is maybe ten. You say, what the fuck is this, yours don't say the same as mine, there's something screwy here.

"What you got then, you got thirty-seven lawyers on your ass--Brauweiller's suing *you*, you're not suing *him*. You want to watch the guy, friend. He'll wring you out and hang you out to dry."

"I'll remember," Dreamer said. "I ever do business with the man, I'll keep it in mind."

"Hey, pal." Mako showed him a razorblade smile. "You got bidness with the man, you don't gotta fuck with me, that's no concern of mine."

"That's what I was thinking too."

"What you oughta get is a franchise deal. One lousy store, you can't even find it, you got a fuckin' map. You got a psycho Chink scares everybody off. You're going in the hole maybe what? Couple grand a month? That ain't bidness, that's playing with yourself."

"I'm doing fine. Things are looking up."

Mako made a face at that. Dreamer wondered where all this was going, and, as ever, why Mako had driven up from Houston for a fish. There was always a reason, something that never had anything to do with Angels or Piranhas or Polka-dot cats. Today, it was maybe Brauweiller, or maybe something else. With Mako, it was always hard to say.

"What I'll do," Mako said, "I'll send a guy, middle of the week. He'll look the place over, check out the books. Won't cost you nothing, I'm taking care of that. What I'm thinking is, we open up, what--six, eight locations right off. Prime spots in Houston. Galleria, River Oaks, keep 'em on the right side of town. Niggers and spics, your trailer-trash whites, fuckers aren't gonna buy a fish. They're gonna piss inna tank, they're not about to buy a fish.

"What else I'm thinking, and this just come to me, it hits me in the head, I'm thinking, we *deliver,* okay? We get a buncha vans, hit the top neighborhoods, like Enchanted Mesa West. The vans are this aqua-fuckin' blue, okay? There's your multi-colored fish, they're painted on the van. There's some bubbles and some plants. We stick in a mermaid, she's got some nice tits. The sign says--what? I don't care what, it says Tropical Treasures, all right? Hey, I already got it, we don't need a ad guy, we're savin' lots of bucks.

"You get twenty-six points, I get forty-eight. That leaves twenty-six for suckers, I got a guy in mind. He puts up the money, we don't spend a cent. What I'm doing, and keep this to yourself, me and Horn, we're working right now on something else. It's in the entertainment field, I can't say no more than that.

"What I'm thinking, this could be a megabuck double-up deal. In bidness talk, that means your feeb, he's backing *two* products, he thinks he's backing one. The one he don't know about, he don't get nothing on that. You work it so you--"

"Huh-unh, I don't think so," Dreamer said. "I don't care for that."

"What, you don't care for what?" Mako looked annoyed. Mako didn't like to be interrupted, didn't like to stop.

"Twenty-six ain't enough? You don't have to raise a finger, you don't have to do shit."

"That isn't what I'm saying," Dreamer said, in the nicest tone he could manage for a man that he couldn't stand at all.

"What I'm saying is, I'm not cut out for the corporate life. I'm a small-time guy, and I'd just as soon keep it like that."

Mako looked at Dreamer, held him with his ball-bearing eyes, held him in an aura of criminal intent, a look between injury and freaking homicide. He dropped his cigar in the tank of a lovely blue Acara, who bellied up and died.

"Fuck you," Mako said, "I'm being polite, okay? You got no manners, you don't fuckin' care. I know what you're into, I know what you do. I know more than you fuckin' think, pal. Do I give a shit? You make a buck, what do I care.

"This bidness with Gus Brauweiller, this is something might be of interest to me, what you're into with him..."

"Hold it," Dreamer said. "Don't go telling me what I do, you don't know dick about me."

"What's Gus want you to do?"

"You killed a nice fish. It's going on your bill."

"Fuck it is. That sucker's dead." Mako laughed. "You little shit, Gus Brauweiller's the eighth biggest crook in the world, I don't even come close. You'd work for him, you won't do bidness with me? You insult me to my face. A guy does this, I get a indication he is maybe not a friend.

"Somethin' else, I'm throwing this in. That bimbo spent the night here? At the party, she's tellin' me, hey, I'm a Russian movie star. Also, she's got a little time, she's a civil engineer. She's buildin' a bridge somewhere. You know what she is? She's a fuckin' hooker, Dreamer. Your little sweetheart's a pro, she's sellin' it on the street..".

"God*damn* you, Binder!"

Dreamer felt the rush of anger, felt the fury and the rage, felt the colors scream crimson in his head. He squeezed his fists to make it stop, knew if he didn't stop now he'd go after Mako, and Mako's goons would rush in and shoot him dead. "Get--*out* of here," he said, as calmly as he could, "get the fuck out of here, now. Don't ever come near the place again."

Mako grinned. He knew what had happened, saw the whole thing in Dreamer's face.

"You know what you need in here? You need a little heat, pal, what you need's a fucking fire."

And to get Dreamer off to a start, he lit a smoke, watched the match burn, tossed it on the floor. Stood and watched a second, ground the flame out, turned and walked out through the door.

Dreamer wasn't dense, he understood the message, got the point at once. He listened for a minute, until the car was gone. Listened to the silence, listened to the bubbles in the tank. Wondered what Mako wanted. Wondered if he wanted anything at all. Didn't have the slightest idea, couldn't even make a guess...

Dreamer started looking for Dinh. Quitting and firing was a weekly event. Dinh would take a very long lunch, kill a few fish, get back to work again. This time he didn't. Dreamer had to feed the fish himself.

A little after six, he checked Dinh's room behind the store. Everything was gone. The VC battle flag, the Russian bayonet. The souvenir pillow of Mao. In the dust on the dresser, Dinh had written PHUC QU. It was possible he wasn't coming back.

. . .

The shower felt good and he shampooed twice. He tried not to think about Mako Binder and the unveiled threat to burn him down. It was possible that Mako's visit had nothing to do with Brauweiller at all. Mako didn't care about airplanes from World War I. Did he know such a war had taken place, was it on the gangster web?

The fish store business was bullshit as well. Or maybe he was saying, I could make you or break you, make you rich or burn you down. Mako had a reason for everything he did, but that didn't mean he had to tell.

Dreamer didn't bother with the stuff about Cindy, didn't give it any thought at all. Mako was baiting him, messing with his head.

And Dreamer had swallowed it, swallowed it whole and nearly lost control. Mako, the son of a bitch, had gotten a kick out of that.

Rinsing the shampoo out, the one a lady senator had given him that smelled like apricots and limes, he scrubbed in conditioner that smelled like pears. Squinted through the water, watched suds course down his belly, off his private parts. There were times when life seemed complete. Biting into ribs, tasting the juice and the peppery skin. Coming with a woman, hitting it right on the beat. Standing in the shower with the hot water drumming on your back. Coming was better, but the shower lasted longer than that. Check in a good hotel, you can do it till your head shrivels up.

As he padded into his room, wiping the water from his eyes, Eileen said, "You can just cover that up, this is not a social call."

Dreamer stopped, dripping water on the floor. "This is my room, I don't have to cover up anything at all."

"Do it. That's the only part I'm attracted to. All I want to do is talk."

"I thought you weren't speaking to me."

"I'm not. That doesn't mean we can't have a meaningful dialogue."

"Right, I forgot. You're in the lawyer trade."

Eileen gave him a squinty-eyed glare. "Don't you piss me off, I will not put up with that."

"So talk. I'm all ears."

"Cover that up. Get something on. Get a jacket and a tie. I'm taking you to dinner, somewhere nice."

"Like where?" Dreamer started toweling off his crotch.

"Oh, God." Eileen looked the other way. "I *hate* this. I'm going to sew myself up."

"You don't want to do that."

"Well that's the fucking point, isn't it? You dressed yet?"

She turned around to face him, looked down and then up.

"You think this is great, don't you? You enjoy this."

"You are acting real dumb, you know what? I am just as susceptible to you. I see you naked, I react the same way. I'm a slave to your flesh, Eileen."

"Huh. You're a slave to a woman's precious gift. Not mine, just any one you see. Where *is* your little friend? I don't smell baby powder anywhere."

"Let's not do this, let's do something else."

Eileen didn't answer. She went to the fridge and dropped ice cubes in a glass. Looked at the glass and tossed the ice in the sink. Went to the kitchen, looked for the Scotch, settled on a bourbon instead. She seemed a little shaky on her feet. Dreamer felt she'd stopped for a couple on the way.

The look was different too. The lady lawyer suit was gone, she was dressed in a killer outfit, black velvet body-huggers, mocha-cream blouse made of spiderweb silk that didn't leave anything to doubt. Dark hair limp across her shoulders, sapphire earrings and bracelet to match, drop-dead midnight high heel shoes.

"I'm guessing this means socks and a shirt," Dreamer said. "Where we're going comes to mind. *Why* comes right after that."

Eileen faced him with a semi-sober look. "There are things you and I need to talk about. This is a business dinner, this is not a date."

"I can see that."

"Don't be fooled by the outfit, pal, I'm not looking edible for you. I am sick of defining myself, my physical beauty and my carnal appetites, through my goddamn addiction to your crotch. That is *all* over now, okay? I've got to do it my way, I've got to be me. I know I can find satisfaction with someone other than you."

"I think you can," Dreamer said. "I think in those shoes, you'll get satisfied before you cross the street."

"You...miserable...shit--"

Eileen began to tremble, tears began to fill her eyes, and he knew he should have worded that in some other way, that it might have struck her wrong.

"I'm sorry," he said, "We're off to a real bad start. We better back off and try again."

Eileen blinked, the wet still in her eyes. It was clear she hadn't heard a thing he'd said.

"You know what I hate even worse than wanting you? I hate you for not feeling anything for me, and what's so awful, so awful and sad is I don't feel anything for you. I want you to fuck me and it ends right there. Is that the shits or what? I'll be out in the car. Put on a clean shirt. Don't you wear that Donald Duck tie. Black socks and no fucking basketball shoes. Don't you ever speak to me again..."

With mascara making little rivers on her cheeks, she ran out the door and down the back stairs.

Dreamer walked to the door, waited to see if she made it to the car. Depraved college boys often lurked among the trees.

"I don't want to make anyone unhappy," he said to himself. "I don't want to cause distress."

It occurred to him, though, it was hard not to do this, that anything you said, even if you didn't say anything at all, someone was sure to think you did, someone would fill in the blanks, write in your dialogue, quote you on a late night show, and, very possibly, sue you for everything you had.

It wasn't getting better, he was sure about that. Once, before you had a PC and a fax, before you had a cellular phone, you could get away with something for a week. Those days were gone and they'd never come back. The world was racing toward tomorrow, leaving Tom Sawyer and even The Simpsons behind. It was very clear to Dreamer that a whisper on the ether, a stutter online, was the new voice of truth in the land. That virtual reality was even more real than reality had ever been itself, and he knew that he didn't care for that.

"And that has nothing to do with making Eileen cry," he told himself, "and I wish I hadn't done that..."

INTERSTATE DREAMS

It had a real name, but no one called it that. What you said was, "See you at the Club." The person you said it to didn't have to ask.

A lot of Austin's clubs were downtown, close to the Capitol, near the hotels, on the top floors of buildings with a view. Somewhere you could see the Hill Country and the good sunsets. The lazy Colorado ran through the city, but the locals called it Town Lake.

The Club, the one that didn't need a name, was in a two-story, white-columned house, with valet parking off the street. This was the classy, quieter part of town, a community of ancient live oaks, well-kept homes from yesteryear, upscale shops and pricey restaurants.

Dreamer had been there before, always with Eileen. Members had to live and work in Austin, and each had to be voted in. You could also be from Houston, Dallas or anywhere else if you had the proper clout. There were bankers, senators and computer moguls here. Oil dudes and land tycoons--prominent people, many who'd been in the Federal pen. Some coming out, some going in.

There were no African Americans, Asians or persons who came from south of the Rio Grande, though many such persons were waiters and kitchen help. Like many of our other fine states, Texas was ready for democracy in action, as long as there were places where decent folks could get a drink.

. . .

"I want you to work with Gus Brauweiller," Eileen said, wasting no time, looking at Dreamer across candlelight and a white tablecloth.

"You don't want to do it for yourself, I'm asking you to do it for me. Brauweiller's business is important to my firm, it's important to me, it's my goddamn future, okay? I'm a real good attorney, Dreamer. I snagged this mother four years ago--I have worked my ass off to get him this far, I do *not* intend to let him go.

" This is asking too much, you make yourself a pile, and make me wealthy for life? What the hell is wrong with that?"

"Wealthy for life."

"Yes, fucking wealthy for--" Eileen looked over her shoulder. "Keep your voice down, I know everyone here."

"You picked this place, not me. Look, I don't have the foggiest idea how to find this guy's plane. I wouldn't know how to start."

"You've found things before. Lots of things, pal."

"How do you know, you don't know that."

"Yeah I do."

Eileen hid behind her wine and a lock of raven hair, a look in her eyes that said she knew all about his dark and secret ways, and even if she didn't, he might believe she did. There were too many people like that in his life. People who knew a piece of this, maybe guessed a piece of that. It made him real goosey that he had to keep looking behind him all the time.

"I've recovered lost items now and then," Dreamer said, "and I'd be grateful if you wouldn't discuss my business with your clients or your friends. Which you obviously have, or Brauweiller wouldn't be on my back now."

The waiter came with fat pink shrimp on beds of shaved ice. He looked down Eileen's front and pondered the mysteries of life.

His name was Hernando Cortez, and his brother, Tomas, was the driver of the *barrio* Buick that had pulled up behind Cindy's Jag and tried to win her heart.

"Listen, I didn't tell Gus a thing," Eileen said, "he already knew. There is not a lot a guy with fifty zillion bucks doesn't know, or can't pretty easy find out."

Dreamer wanted to believe her. Mostly, he didn't want to fight.

"Like I said, I've found things people have lost or misplaced. I have never found an airplane or anything else that's been lost for eighty years."

"I don't see why it'd be so hard." Eileen studied the back side of a shrimp. "I mean, it isn't like he's asking you to find a Toyota, they got about a billion of those. That old plane, you'd know it if you saw it, there can't be a lot of 'em round."

"That doesn't make a bit of sense to you, so don't try and sell it to me. If this is why you're buying me a dinner I feel like I'm wasting your time. And for Christ's sake, please don't tell me your future's in peril and it's all my fault. I am not buying that."

"You want the lamb or the duck? I know you like the duck."

"Duck's fine with me. Listen to what I'm saying. I'd do anything to help but I wouldn't do that. And you don't need me, you just think you do. That old fart's asking something that's impossible to do. He knows that, he's just messing with your head. Guys with lots of money like to squeeze you when they can. He wants you because you're good. He wants to make damn sure he's got you, he wants to nail you down. Get you scared to death that money could vanish any time. Don't fall for that, you don't have to."

"Yeah, I do, too. I need it bad, hon..."

Aw shit, Dreamer thought, and he saw it in her eyes, and he knew right off the bastard had her in a vise. He liked it when she turned off Attila the Attorney and let him in a while, but not like this. Not when the hunger and the anger and the fear showed through. Not when she was naked clear down to the soul.

He glanced around the room, saw the overweight moguls and the ruddy tycoons, heard them merge and heard them steal, heard them slice another deal. Sharks could smell a single drop of blood a mile away, and if anyone was sniffing, they could surely smell Eileen.

"You've got to work this out," he told her, "you've got to be strong. You gotta hang onto your self esteem, babe, assert your inner self. Damn it, caving in to this jerk isn't like you at all."

Eileen tried a laugh but it didn't come off. The waiter brought the lamb and the duck. This time he brought along a friend to share the wondrous sights he'd seen.

"I've got *all* the self esteem I can handle, okay?" Eileen closed a fist around her fork and speared him with her opal eyes. "What I *need* is to keep a tight rein on Gus Brauweiller, to keep the man happy all the time. Which is why I am--why I am slightly on edge and why I am very disappointed I cannot count on someone I thought I was very close to, a person who'd at least make an effort, who would fucking *pretend* to be looking for a fucking airplane and even if he didn't have any idea where it was he could fake it for a while.

"But no, instead, my *friend* is too busy poking his--his goddamn tool into Hannah Highschool, who, by the way, I just thought I'd mention, has neglected to inform big *Daddy* she is also screwing an insecticide king from Abilene, a Waco judge who is under indictment for fraud, as well as business acquaintances of mine who are, at this moment--my, is that a coincidence or what, sitting over there by that awful picture of bluebonnets and cows? So you don't have to say this is bullshit, Eileen, you can hop right over and see for yourself.

"Am I being small and petty, do you think? Oh, God, I *do* hope so, I can't think of anyone deserves it more than you, you unthinking bastard, you rude, unappreciative asshole that I have given my lovely self to, time and time again, without reservation or restraint, allowing you to pump your manhood into my ivory loins on a strictly recreational basis, without asking more than common courtesy, a little respect, like never *ever* leaving me at some fucking party somewhere and going off with a preschool cunt who very likely listens to nigger rap and never even *heard* of Stan Getz..!"

Dreamer heard some of this, but not a whole lot, almost nothing past the Abilene king and the Waco judge. He sent his chair reeling, clattering across the tile floor, launched the very tasty tea-smoked duck into minor orbit and into a local deb's lap.

Rich guys in hippo, emu and alligator boots, illegal waiters without IDs of any sort, all looked up as Dreamer passed, delighted and appalled at such behavior in a ritzy place like this.

Dreamer didn't pause, didn't look from side to side. The men at the table saw him coming. Two looked surprised. The third didn't move, didn't blink, didn't do a thing at all. Cindy merely looked up and smiled, a sweet and smoky angel kind of smile that turned Dreamer's head screaming pink and bloody red.

"Hi, hon, how are you?" Cindy said, juice from a ripe strawberry a fresh drop of moisture on her lips.

"Get up," Dreamer said, not looking at Cindy, looking at Mako in his coffee-colored suit, a cocoa tie that matched his rattlesnake eyes.

"Get up, Cindy, we're leaving right now."

Cindy looked confused. "You mad at me, babe? Honest, you look mad to me."

"I'm not mad. Just get up, Cindy, do it now."

"You're' embarrassing yourself," Mako said, "people are lookin' at you, pal. Sit down, I'll buy you a coffee, I'll buy you a ice cream--"

"You shut up," Dreamer said, and he spoke so softly hardly anyone could hear. "Don't even breathe, you fuck, don't talk to me. You open your mouth, I swear to God you will never watch *Masterpiece Theatre* again. I will come across this table and gut you with a butter knife and spread you on a roll. You want to talk, you try me and see."

Mako murdered Dreamer with his eyes. Shot him through the ears, stuck an icepick up his nose. Tossed him in a vat of roiling fries. He did all this in his head, but he did what Dreamer said. He swallowed his enormous gangster pride, he didn't say a word at all. This was not the time, and it was surely not the place. Mako decided then and there exactly where and when that place would be. The fun part would be exactly how.

. . .

Dreamer took her by the hand and walked her through the Club, past the waiters and the diners, and out through the heavy oak door. And everyone there watched them go, and everyone there told everyone in town what had happened, and exactly what they saw. And no one but the waiter, Hernando Cortez, who didn't know eight words of English, got half the story right...

Amy Horn, wife Halloran Horn, of Horn Life Engineering, Inc., leaves Enchanted Mesa West around noon in her chauffeur-driven Rolls. Amy listens to a Karen Carpenter CD. The chauffeur's name is Maurice, from Paris, France. His real name is Bob, and he's wanted for crimes against badgers in Boise, Idaho.

Maurice-Bob drives Amy all around the seamy side of Houston, searching for a poor person costume to wear to the Annual Waifland Home Charity Ball. Amy buys the clothes off Wallace Pailey Marshall's back for three dollars eighty five cents. Maurice-Bob puts the clothes in a Hefty Bag to be sterilized at Enchanted Mesa West.

Wallace Pailey Marshall doesn't recognize Amy, and Amy doesn't recognize him. There is no sign at all that the two shared wedded bliss.

Wallace Pailey Marshall, unaware that going naked in a Texas liquor store is a minor offense, is picked up spending his bonanza and tossed in the Harris County Jail. On the way to Enchanted Mesa West, Amy listens to Tom T. Hall sing *Who's Going to Feed Them Hogs,* pops a few pills, and for a time seems quite content...

Mako Binder has a piece of the Phil Boa Properties deal, which is presently underway north of Austin's Highland Lakes. The two men present at the Club face-off between Dreamer and Mako were Boa reps Charles D. LeLong and Walter Kirsch. LeLong and Kirsch are still reeling over meeting such a cutie on the street.

Neither Kirsch nor LeLong is aware of the fact that their company's a front for the mob. They think they're simply real estate crooks, and they're satisfied with that.

Augustus Brauweiller and Halloran Horn, always bitter rivals, but eager to make a buck, are in on the Phil Boa action as well. Both, however, are only aware of the project's Level One: The purchase of land adjacent to the pricey new estates called Heavenly Heights.

Mako Binder, who knows the man in Miami who tells Phil Boa what to do, is aware of Levels Two, Three and Four. After the land is purchased, streets and utility lines will be laid in a maze of colored string. A color brochure will picture two-mil homes to be built in the Fer de Lance Estates.

Soon, a great many ill-dressed Blacks, Rednecks, Latinos, and people of the Asian hue will appear in ancient cars. They will show a lot of interest in Fer de Lance Estates. Word of this will get around fast. People in Heavenly Heights will get in touch with their real estate agents at once. Signs will appear on the well-kept lawns. Buyers, working for Boa and Mako Binder, will make insulting offers for their homes. At first, the owners will balk and turn them down. Soon, people with chickens and goats will begin to appear at Fer de Lance. The people in Heavenly Heights will set reason aside, and take whatever they can get.

Investors like Brauweiller and Horn, Japanese czars and the mad-eyed Arab at Brauweiller's Midsummer Christmas affair, will feel they've made a profit on the deal. In truth, most of the money they should have received will finance Levels Two through Four. After the trial run in Austin, the scheme will go nationwide, in cities from coast to coast.

Some of the profits will be used to bribe Legislators to vote for open gambling on the Texas Gulf Coast. Ten mil-five will go into a fund called "HGG," Honkeys Gotta Go, a project designed to ship white people back to

England and France. Another ten five will go to "Liberty for All," a group dedicated to laws requiring "Niggers, Spics, Jews and persons with names like Wang," to wear funny hats at all times.

Mako Binder will handle these funds for a very hefty price. Mako believes neither race, creed nor color should interfere with free enterprise. But you have to pay in cash, he won't take Visa or American Express.

. . .

Everything's going as well as it possibly could. Mid-year figures show Friendship Florist (Port-A-Whore), Aunt Sally's Home Bakery Shoppe (Sally High), and Pauliano's serve-yourself art, (Twenty-First Century Fuck) at new profit highs. St. Sarah Jean House was down six points, and he knew the reason why. Highway safety had made roadkill near impossible to find, cutting out the basic ingredient of Beef 'n Rice Surprise, which fed the South Texas homeless every night.

On the other hand, Waifland Homes was up ten. There were always parents who wanted a kid, didn't ask questions, and were willing to pay a hefty price. And, when Lease-A-Tot got off the ground, Mako was certain he could milk the other end--people who wanted a kid for the company picnic, but didn't want it messing up the house.

There were several loose ends to tie up. Bidness demanded a guy's full attention, you couldn't take a fucking day off:

Horn was okay, Horn was a wrap.

Gus Brauweiller. Mako had some ideas about that.

Dreamer was something else. Dreamer was small potatoes, but Dreamer had stepped across the line. Twice, now, he'd spit in Mako's face. He had a few surprises for Dreamer, then *whack*!--kiss your ass goodbye. The start of the surprise was the setup at the Club. Christ, the look on Dreamer's face when he'd seen the babe there! It was almost worth the insult, standing there taking Dreamer's crap. Almost, but not quite.

He thought about an egg and ketchup sandwich, a peanut butter on rye. Mako liked the crunchy, he didn't like the plain. You finish up a sandwich, there's little bits of peanut in your teeth. Next day you find one, tongue it around, hey, you got a little snack right there...

"You're mad at me, aren't you," Cindy said, "I can tell. You do that thing with your lips? Like you're chewing on something but you're not? See, that's how you tell. The ordinary person, they'll give themselves away all the time and they don't even know it, okay? If you're into body language you can catch these signs right away. That's how I know and I wish you wouldn't *do* that, hon, 'cause I love you so much I could die."

Dreamer didn't care to get into body language at the time. Cindy was perched on his bed wearing very short shorts, legs drawn up, chin resting on her knees, hair in curlers, painting tiny toes. Cindy as Lolita, Dreamer as the guy, partially convinced this girl was maybe twelve or thirteen.

"I am not exactly mad," Dreamer said, which wasn't true at all, "it doesn't make sense to get mad, that never solves a thing. What I am is surprised you'd--that you'd engage in such a thing. It doesn't seem to me you'd do that, Cindy, it doesn't seem at all like you."

"You mean doing it for money. That's the part you don't like."

"Not entirely, but that part especially, yes."

"You never did that. You never paid a girl, right?"

"I know where you're going with this and it's not the same thing."

"Well did you or not?"

"Once. A couple of times. And that was a long time ago."

"You paid a girl to fuck."

Dreamer blushed at the word for the first time in his life.

"That sort of cheapens the act, I think, to refer to it as crudely as that. I--don't feel bad about the experience at all. I have very good memories in fact. She was a real sweet girl."

"Which one was that?"

"What?"

"You said a couple times. Which one was the very sweet girl?"

Dreamer knew he was digging a hole, had known it for a while, couldn't see his way out.

"A couple of times, now that's just a figure of speech, it does not imply a specific number at all."

Cindy inspected her toes. "I'm a very sweet girl too."

"Cindy---"

"Well I am. I'm just as sweet as whoever it was and if I'd been her, you'd have a nice memory of me. But you don't like me now I can tell, you're doing that thing with your mouth."

"No I'm not, I am not doing something with my mouth."

"I'm tired, Dreamer, and you've hurt my feelings real bad. I'm going to sleep. I'd be grateful if you'd turn off the light."

She bounced off the bed, peeled off her T-shirt, slipped off her shorts. Caught Dreamer watching, shot him a frosty stare.

"You don't mind, just look at something else, there isn't any point to that." She was back in bed in an instant, the sheet pulled over her head.

"Ignoring the problem won't help," Dreamer said. "I think we ought to talk about this."

"Talk to yourself," Cindy said.

Dreamer looked at the shapely lump beneath the sheet then turned off the light. He closed the door and got a blanket from the closet in the hall. Downstairs, he thought about taking Dinh's bed, but only for a second and a half. The vibes in there would hurt his head. The people Dinh dreamed about were dead.

There was a couch at the entry to the shop. It wasn't meant for sleeping, but he curled up on that. He liked the low hum of the motors that fed the fish air. He liked the sound of bubbles in the tanks. Eileen said it sounded like farting in the tub, and Dreamer didn't care for that.

He tried not to think about Eileen. He knew she didn't mean it, that he'd brought it on himself. He couldn't help falling for Cindy. He didn't ask it to happen, but it did. Anyway, what he and Eileen had was different. What it was, it was sort of like--a little like--he couldn't think what. Every time he thought about who and what they were, another dozen questions came to mind.

Maybe she'd call, say she was sorry. If she did, he'd tell her he forgave her, and she'd hang up in his face.

. . .

It was nearly three. Dreamer lay on his couch and stared, feeling the day's accumulation of stress, gravity, ocular grit, harmful rays from Oklahoma and emotional lint. Still, he wasn't so dense that he couldn't see sophomore ethics was not the way to get in Cindy's head. With scarcely any effort, she had lobbed that one back across the net.

And, to be perfectly fair, which he didn't intend to be at all, selling sex and buying it were two sides of the very same coin. One party was as guilty--or innocent--as the next. Which was fine if you were watching *20\20,* but not if the hooker in question was the all-time honey of your dreams.

Even the word made his stomach do a flip. Okay, he could tolerate 'hooker.' Julia Roberts had sanitized that. But he couldn't put those other words to Cindy, she wasn't one of those at all. Goddamn it, even if she was, someone had gotten her into it, she couldn't have done it to herself.

A sudden image of Mako, sharp red needles in his head, and the aftertaste of duck. Did Mako have something on her, was she into hard drugs of some kind? He tried to remember ugly punctures on her arms, on her thighs, between her toes. Not a blemish, not a mark. These visions only kindled new desire.

Christ, the thought of that slimeball touching her...and what about the two suits with him, had they had their way with her too? What was she doing at Brauweiller's place, who'd brought her there? Mako, or somebody else? That Arab with the dead black eyes?

He swept the awful images aside. Thought about the first time he'd seen her, stalled on the highway in the bottle-green Jag. He hadn't ever told her, she didn't even know about that. Mama Lucy did, though, and Dreamer remembered this with dread: *"Trouble finds her, trouble binds her."* Mama Lucy goofed sometimes, but not much. She was sure as hell right about that.

. . .

He finally dropped off to the hum of the motors and the bubbles in the tanks, and the sadness and the sorrow followed him down into dark and troubled deep.

He drifted off with heavenly confetti in his head. Did Buddha like chocolate ice cream? Was Jesus into sports? And, didn't it seem unlikely that God would let his angels go and sell it on the street...?

Eileen gave the valet a five or ten. She couldn't remember, couldn't recall even getting in her car. Knew that she'd driven somewhere, nearly hit a dog, nearly hit a truck. Knew that she'd thrown up on somebody's lawn.

God, how could she *do* such a thing? There had to be somebody else in her head, had to be an evil twin. Even if the son of a bitch *deserved* it, which he did, there was no way she'd put him through that.

Yeah, there was, too.

She remembered the anger, the gut-wrenching fury that welled up and choked her, tore out her heart, left her with murder in her eyes.

Gus Brauweiller, just a casual call, how's it coming, how's the weather over there, and by the way, hon, that cutie ol' Dreamer picked up? He's got him a firecracker there, she's humpin' ever'body in town.

Which, it turned out, after Gus named a few, included Charles D. LeLong and Walter Orin Kirsch, of Phil Boa Enterprises, Inc. Eileen had met with them twice, because Gus had his finger in three dozen pies, including a real estate deal out at Heavenly Heights.

She was mad at everyone. Furious at Gus for telling her this, for being the asshole that he was. Furious at Kirsch and DeLong, because she'd had breakfast with them an hour before Gus's call, and they seemed like pretty nice guys.

Never mind crotch-ripping furious at Dreamer himself.

"They ain't ashamed of her, either," Gus added, before he hung up, "they're taking her to lunch at the Club, before God and everyone. 'Course, you got to remember those boys come from Fort Worth..."

. . .

He had set her up good, and she'd stepped right in it. Gotten Dreamer there and set *him* up, as neat as Brauweiller had done it to her. She hated him for that. He *knew* she'd have to do it, and she hated him all the more because he did.

And *why,* she wanted to know, now that she'd screwed Dreamer good, and it was too late to ask? Because Dreamer wouldn't knuckle under, wouldn't look for Gus's stupid plane? Or was it her instead? Like Dreamer said, just before it hit the fan, Gus liked to keep people under his thumb, and had to let them know it now and then.

. . .

It worked out fine.

The guys came in with the girl and sat across the room. Eileen waited till just the right time. Lowered the boom, zapped Dreamer good. Only--it wasn't supposed to happen like that. Dreamer was supposed to be embarrassed, yell at the girl and stomp out.

So what was that goddamn gangster doing there? Eileen hadn't seen him when the others came in. Didn't even see him till Dreamer and Mako squared off, nearly went at it right there.

Eileen didn't like it at all. She felt like something was crawling up her neck and she had to get it off. Sitting in the car, tossing down Certs with the A/C on, she picked up the phone and dialed Gus, put it down again.

She knew what he'd tell her. That he didn't have any idea why Mako was there. That if Mako Binder had business with the Phil Boa guys, that was none of his business, and none of hers as well.

What she wanted to do was find Dreamer, tell him she was sorry, tell him she didn't want to speak to him again, they could maybe have lunch. No fancy clubs, no nigger barbecue--

Wups, sorry 'bout that, I know you're kinda touchy there...

"Jesus, how does anybody do it," she said, talking to the car, "how does *any*body ever get close to anybody else?" So many secrets, things you can't share. Your bodies can show each other everything they know, but your head will never tell. Dreamer wouldn't open up, wouldn't tell her who he was and what he did. On pain of death, wouldn't tell her how he felt.

And I'm worse than that. Worse than Dreamer is, worse than anybody else... I don't know if I feel any fucking thing at all...

In the morning, Dreamer's house was empty. Cindy wasn't there. Dreamer wasn't too surprised. But that didn't help fill the lonely in his heart, the place where he kept her lovely image, and an old Teddy Bear named Bill.

The long uneasy night had polished and concealed every blemish, every flaw, every slight imperfection that might have marred the picture in his mind. All his doubts had vanished, she was shiny, she was pure, transfigured and renewed. And, if she'd been truly been a floozy or a strumpet, or a harlot or a tart, that was surely not her fault. Somehow, his love had been duped and cruelly used, maybe hypnotized. Nothing really mattered anymore, nothing but the fact that she was gone.

. . .

His second irritation of the day came when Brauweiller called.

"Listen," he said, "how's it coming, you find that Fokker for me yet?"

"I haven't found it," Dreamer told him, "because I haven't looked. I haven't looked, because I didn't take the job. I've told you this several times before."

"Good, terrific," Brauweiller said, "keep at it, son."

The moment Brauweiller hung up, Dreamer called Paulo in Houston. Paulo, sometime drinking buddy, fence, purveyor of secrets, master of illicit and semi-legal enterprise, collector of guns, middleman and offshore banker to the Great Southwest, and, the only person in the world, besides Mama Lucy herself, who even had a hint of what was really going on in Dreamer's head, that rare and quirky talent that soothed every lock, every bolt, every latch and alarm, every bright electric tiger and sent them off to bed.

"What do you know about Augustus Brauweiller?" Dreamer said, when at last he got Paulo on the line. "This bozo's a real fruitcake, and I want him off my back."

Dreamer told Paulo all about the party at Enchanted Mesa West. Told him about Hermann Goering and the Fokker D-VIIIs. Told him about Mako's visit to the shop. How Mako was hot to know what Brauweiller was talking to Dreamer about.

"Which, like I said, isn't anything at all. I'm not looking for his goofy airplane. I hate airplanes. I don't care if they're old or brand new, it's all the same to me."

"One mil eight?" Paulo remembered everything anybody said, but he remembered big numbers best of all.

"Forget about it," Dreamer said, "I'm not interested, I told the guy that. I don't care about the Fokker, what I want to know is why Mako cares about Brauweiller's business with me. I don't like mobsters breathing down my neck."

"Amigo, I got no idea," Paulo said. "Brauweiller is the biggest frog in the pond at the moment, which is something you already know. I could download you fifty pounds of shit about his business empire, which, by the way, would scare the mothers on Wall Street half to death. But that's not what you're looking for."

"And you don't have a thing on Mako and the guy? You're telling me there's no connection there."

"Hey, I didn't say that. Everything's connected, pal. That is the nature of the fucking universe, yes? If it wasn't, I'd be selling used cars somewhere."

Dreamer frowned to himself. "You don't know anything, or you won't tell me? What are you saying here?"

"I'm saying that kinda hurts, Dreamer. I take exception to that."

"Right. I apologize."

"And well you should. Shit, *compadre*, this brings great sorrow to my heart and my heart doesn't need more trouble than it's got."

"I'm sorry. Okay?"

"Fine. I graciously accept. And I am not charging you a thing for this consultation. I didn't tell you anything."

"Thanks anyway."

"Por nada, my friend."

Dreamer set down the phone. He knew exactly what had happened here. Paulo gave nothing away, not in his manner or his voice, not in any way at all. Still, Dreamer knew him well. He could sense a very small hesitation, smell a word that ended up instead of down. Paulo walked a tightrope all the time, a tightrope lined with razorblades, but everyone knew he played fair. Playing fair was how Paulo stayed alive. So Dreamer knew Paulo would never betray him; he also knew he would not betray anyone else.

. . .

Brauweiller was subtle as a Cape Buffalo. Before the day was over, a snoop from the IRS dropped by and said he'd like to have a look at Dreamer's taxes back to 1968. Dreamer told him he was nine at the time. The man said, tough, that the cutoff was six.

Dreamer hung around the house, ate a jelly sandwich and went to bed at ten. He could smell Cindy's hair and the sweet scent of her skin. He finally got to sleep, three minutes into *The Jolson Story,* Larry Parks, (1946).

At seven in the morning, a building inspector showed up at his door. He said Dreamer's wiring looked fine if this was 1952. The fire marshal showed up at noon. The men from immigration came at five.

Dreamer kept his cool. He found Brauweiller's number, his very private line. A voice said she'd gladly take his name, that Mr. Brauweiller wasn't available at the time.

"Listen," Dreamer shouted into the phone, "you tell that fucker I am *not* looking for his Fokker, and he'd better call off his dogs and leave me the hell alone!"

The woman said thank you for calling. She'd see that Mr. Brauweiller got the message, whenever he returned.

Brauweiller's tactics didn't scare him, but they did. Building inspectors couldn't hurt him. Still, there were aspects of his life that he didn't want brought up to the light. Anyone who had the means to dig deep enough could find out a hell of a lot. Mako had begun to sniff him out. He knew about Houston and a couple other deals, but he didn't know what. Sergeant Avery Asher knew a little too. So what, he asked himself, can I do about that?

. . .

He thought about Mama Lucy's, decided on tomato soup instead. Mako might decide to fire the house. Cindy might come back while he was gone.

On the six o'clock news, he saw a half-familiar face. It belonged to the mean-eyed Arab from the party at Enchanted Mesa West. The Arab was Prince Abd-el-Yusuff. He was clearly in a rage. The anchor guy explained: Abd-el-Yusuf believed he had purchased Corpus Christi, and he had a bill of sale. The price was fifty grand, and the seller was Samuel Houston, President of the Republic of Texas himself.

Yusuf announced he would declare a *Jihad*, a holy war, on Texas, if the entire matter was not resolved in his favor by noon the next day.

The news brought a moment of cheer to Dreamer's otherwise disappointing day. Cindy had left sometime before Wednesday morning. It was now Thursday night. Logically, he told himself, there was no reason to think she had come to any harm; no more harm than a hooker angel could expect to bring down upon herself.

Still, he felt a certain sense of dread--more than just a feeling, an everyday concern--this was apprehension of a higher degree, this was a fear that loosed colors in his head.

A beer didn't help and neither did a bath. He thought about calling up Paulo again. Something told him not to do that. Sergeant Avery Asher would do what he could, but he'd want to know more than Dreamer cared to give.

He could go to Mama Lucy--she'd told him Cindy was trouble on the hoof, and she'd tell him so again. Besides, things were bad enough on this sorry plane--he didn't want to mix it up with Moses or Martin Luther King.

When the phone rang, he nearly trashed a tankful of tetras getting across the room.

"Hello?" Dreamer said, apprehension clear enough for anyone to hear.

"Do I call you Dreamer, Mr. Dreamer, what? I don't have any idea."

Not Cindy for sure, a woman's voice he'd never heard before.

"Who is this?"

"I'm Lee Ann Brauweiller, Gus Brauweiller's wife."

That stopped him for a second and a half.

"Okay, fine. What can I do for you, Lee Ann?"

"I have to see you. Now. It's important that we talk."

"Is this about airplanes? Listen, if it is--"

"The Inn and Out Motel. That's I-N-N. On South Congress. You know where it is?"

"Yeah, I do. I'm real surprised you do, though."

"It's ten-thirty-seven. I'll be there at eleven-ten."

The line went dead. It sounded like a cellular phone. Anyone who cared to listen in would know exactly where he'd be.

Of course, it didn't have to be Brauweiller's wife, it could be anyone else. Someone calling for Mako Binder or Gus.

Either way, ugly looking guys might be there to greet him, guys named Bubba, Nick or Chuck, Vinnie, Al or Buck. And what's in a name, if the fucker shoots you dead?

He knew about the Inn and Out Motel. Everyone did, though no one said they'd ever been. Part of South Congress boasted Mexican restaurants and antique stores, auto parts and motels--some okay, some even worse than then the scabby Inn and Out.

The cops tried their best to keep the hookers off the street. They even used lady cops as bait. The lady cops were good looking, and the Johns caught onto that. The real tarts vanished for a night, then popped right up again.

Lee Ann Brauweiller was sitting in her car with the A/C on. The car was a Lexus, shiny beetle-black, showroom new, and worth much more than the motel itself.

It had to be her, who else? Dreamer parked and got out, standing clear of the bright headlights.

A window whirred down. Someone said, "Come on, get in."

"You didn't get a room? I drove clear across town."

"Cute," Lee Ann said. "Buckle up, stay on your side."

Dreamer did as he was told. Lee Ann Brauweiller tossed a lot of gravel and smoked the big car back on the road.

"Where are we going?" Dreamer wanted to know.

"Nowhere. Enjoy the ride."

"Love your car."

"You don't smell like a smoker. That's good, I simply won't tolerate that."

She drove on south, under the Ben White Freeway, left toward 35. The car smelled of leather and fifty dollar bills. The woman smelled fine. Not perfume, though, more like good Italian soap.

He didn't want to stare but he did, out of the corner of his eye. Lee Ann was a good looking woman. Slim, long-legged, fine bones and angles in her face, a model's features and neat, close-cropped raven hair. She was dressed like everyone else in Austin, rich and poor alike. T-shirt, blue jeans and boots. Some wore the optional athletic shoe. Dreamer couldn't tell in the dark, but he imagined the labels said *Jordache, Tony Lama, GUESS.*

Gus Brauweiller was somewhere in his sixties and bigger than a tub. His wife was a honey, and still very short of thirty-five. No big surprise.

Billionaires didn't have to shop, they could send out for brides. This was the one, Dreamer guessed, who seemed to have a permanent cramp, though he didn't feel he ought to ask.

"I met your husband at the party," Dreamer said, more to break the silence than anything else. "You've got a nice place. I'm sorry I didn't get to see you there."

"Why's that?"

"Uh, well if you'd been there, see, we would've met then, we'd have met before now, not here. Not that here isn't fine with me."

Lee Ann didn't look up from the road. "You wait for me to go to a party, you're going to be waiting for a while. I can't stand parties and I can't stand Gus. If you're thinking of hitting on me, don't. I'm not into men. I know somebody knows you, and don't ask who. Says you're okay, but I'll be the judge of that."

"You mind me asking who?"

"What did I say? Did I say don't ask who? And you're wrong about us, by the way, you and me. We've met lots of times, I'm sorry to say."

"I don't think so, I'd remember that."

"That's because you're not awake, pal. Look real close next time, you'll see for sure it's me."

It took him a second then it hit him. He felt a little jolt, a little thrill. "My God, you're kidding, that's *you?"*

"I'm afraid it is."

"Well I'll be. I'm riding in a luxury car with my Out of Body Fuck."

"You don't mind, can we call it something else?"

"You don't look like you. You look different somehow."

"The me you know is an aberration of the unconscious Id. God knows I wouldn't do something that sick. I've tried every sleeping pill there is. I've been in therapy for years."

"I'm sorry," Dreamer said. "I didn't used to do it myself."

"Something happened to your head."

"How'd you know that?"

"Don't panic, there are things I can see when we're together. Not a whole lot, just some funny colors when we--you know what. You got hurt bad. I don't know exactly how. You're different, now. I'm not sure what the difference is."

Dreamer didn't answer. For a moment, as passing headlights flickered on her face, he felt he could see that other self, the one who seemed to like him quite a lot.

A sign said Onion Creek. Lee Ann turned off 35 onto the exit road, drove for a minute, pulled over and stopped.

"I didn't bring you here to talk about our nauseating sex life," she said, turning to face him in the dark. "I never go to Gus's parties but I peek sometimes. The minute I saw you, I knew who you were. Believe me, it was just as big a shock to me.

"Gus and I have a wonderful relationship. He hates me and I despise him. He knows I sleep with women. I make damn sure he finds out. Sometimes it gives him little cardiac attacks. You never know when that'll lead to something big. I keep my eyes open. Most of the time, I know what he's up to, I know what's on his sneaky mind. This is *not* because I find him fascinating, let's be clear about that. If I didn't know what I do, I'd be feeding the fish right now."

Lee Ann took a breath. "This is where you come in. My maiden name is Burkette. My sister's name is Cindy. She doesn't use her last name, but that's who she is."

A blow to the gut, a flash of crimson in his head. He knew in that instant, she didn't have to tell.

"Where is she, Jesus, what's happened to her?"

Lee Ann waved him off.

"I don't think she's hurt, I think she's all right. Look, I'm sorry to drop it on you like this. I know what she does, and I can't help that. We didn't have a great home life. The kind of love we got is the kind you don't talk about. I got out the year Cindy was born. I was thirteen. She compensates with men. My bad habit was coke. She's still got her habit, I got rid of mine. You know about the Arab, the one with the name I can't pronounce?"

"I caught it on the news."

"He's the one. That's the son of a bitch who's got her."

"What?" Dreamer stared. "He was talking to her. At your husband's party. I got her out of there."

"Saved her from him, right? You're a prince. This whatsisname was pissed about the Corpus Christi mess. He backed out of a zillion dollar oil deal with Gus. Said he wouldn't do business with Americans anymore. Gus gave him Cindy. As a gesture of our nation's goodwill."

Dreamer closed his eyes. Cobalt razors danced inside his head. "Where is she, you know where he's got her? Goddamn, I don't believe this. You can't do that, you can't give people away!"

"You can if you're Gus Brauweiller. And no, I don't know where she is, I don't have the vaguest idea. I don't know if the Arab's still in the country.

He's got a bunch of jets, he could be anywhere."

Lee Ann looked at him. He could feel her anger and her fear, and somewhere back in a cold and feral corner of her mind, the dark coils of strength, retribution and revenge that she'd caged back there, held until she could let them loose again, snap their chains and set them free.

"I know what you're thinking, Dreamer. I don't know if Gus himself could get her back, even if he wanted to. I know you think you could make him try. Believe me, you can't. Not even with those crazy colors in your head. You can't get near the man. Nobody can."

"I won't accept that. I won't sit around and do nothing while that raghead drags Cindy off to his tent."

"If money'll help, I've skimmed about thirty mil from Gus. Don't they have those mercenary persons for hire?"

"I can't see another Mid East war. I don't feel that'd do Cindy any good. Listen, I don't think we ought to sit here. Some cop comes by, he'll think we're making out."

"My God," Lee Ann said, "what a sickening thought. I think I might have to throw up."

"I'm not that bad. If you'd take a little nap, we'd get along fine."

"You even look at me funny, I'll kick you in the balls."

"I've been getting a lot of that lately," Dreamer said. "I think my chart's out of whack. I don't feel Neptune's lined up like it should. I don't feel the moon's exactly right."

"I feel I'm taking you back to your car," Lee Ann said. "I'll try and keep in touch, anything I find out. Do me a favor, all right? If you gotta go to sleep, for Christ's sake, think about somebody else..."

There's a point where anger, fury and despair, heats the body's juices to one-hundred-twenty-two degrees. This is what your science person calls the Critical Mess, and two things can happen after that. One, you can slip into homicidal bliss. Two, you can strip all your gears, go into overload. That's maybe best. You're too fucking goofy to care after that.

Dreamer, driving home in the saddest hour of the night, back from his meeting with Brauweiller's wife, with his Out of Body Fuck, is somewhere between one and two. He would like to hang Gus Brauweiller by his balls, turn the Arab into Spam, anything to get Cindy back.

He can barely keep the car on the road, he can scarcely see through the bloody rage that's shrieking through his head. This is why he nearly runs over Sergeant Asher, who is standing in the middle of the road, waving his arms in the glare of Dreamer's lights.

. . .

He slammed on the brakes, turned the car sideways as Asher waddled for his life. Dreamer opened the door and got out.

"You okay, you all right?"

"Goddamn, you could kill someone like that. You ever go to high school? I bet you didn't take Driver's Ed."

"You were in the middle of the street."

"I'm an officer of the law. I can be anywhere I like. Come on, we can't stand around here, let's go."

"Go where?"

"Your house. It's four blocks west of here."

"I know where it is, I live there. I've got an idea. Why don't we drive?"

"Huh-unh. Can't do that."

Asher found something with his tongue and spat it out, started off into the dark. Dreamer could follow, or watch him disappear.

"How come you always take Duval? I told Bennie, you wait, he'll come down Duval. There's an easy way to get to his house, but he'll go the other way. What we got, we got us a situation here. I had Bennie Kern watching your place. Figured somethin'd happen after they snatched the girl. You're not reacting, so I guess you know that.

"Shit, get that look off your face. Brauweiller owns half the state. You think I don't know all his plates? I bet you one thing, I bet you didn't get any pussy from Mrs. B."

"Goddammit, Asher--"

"You're going to ask me 'bout the sister. I'm telling you now I don't know. We've got information that Ay-rab took her. It's likely he got her on a plane at that private airport in Enchanted Mesa West."

"Christ," Dreamer said, and his stomach took a dip. He'd figured on the plane, but he'd hoped he wasn't right.

"Everyone's going light on this. That dude's a diplomat of sorts, nobody wants to step on his toes."

"Your information's right," Dreamer said. "Brauweiller's the one who gave Cindy to the prince. His wife told me that."

"Well I'll be." Asher raised a brow. "Now we didn't know that. I'll talk to the people at the Governor's place. Don't know what he can do, you don't go slapping a zillionaire around. Even if we could find the sum'bitch. I doubt if the Rangers or the F.B.I. would have the stuff to dig him out..."

Asher gave Dreamer a curious grin. "'Course I expect *you* could get to him, if you knew where he was. I believe you've demonstrated skills in that direction from time to time."

"That's *Captain Marvel* you're thinking about. I'm into tropical fish."

"Uh-huh. Speaking of which, this situation I was referring to. There's three of 'em. Two skulking about, one driving the car. The driver's local, I think the others are talent from out of town. They got to your place five minutes after you took outa here. If their timing had been a little better..."

Dreamer blinked. "You mean they're still there? Jesus, Asher, what are you waiting for?"

"No big hurry, they're not going anywhere. Wanted you to be there, see your local law enforcement in action."

"Don't ever feel you have to wait on me. How many men have you got?"

"Just me. And Bennie Kern."

"But you don't need him."

"I don't like to be foolhardy where the criminal element's concerned."

. . .

Asher stopped in deep shadow. Dreamer's house was on the corner, at the end of the block. "You got a lot of trees. Don't get closer than the big live oak that's bucklin' up the street. The last thing I need's a civilian come to harm. We haven't discussed who wants your ass dead. You curious at all about that?"

"There's the kid I sold a guppy to. It died before he got it back home."

"I'll look into that."

Dreamer watched him slide a weapon from under his oversized coat. A dark Sig-Saur 928. He didn't keep weapons in the house, but he'd spent a few hangover days with Paulo's gun magazines.

"I feel I ought to help," he said. "It doesn't seem right, hiding out behind a tree. You could deputize me. I could take a vow too."

"Yeah, right."

Asher disappeared in the dark. Dreamer felt a twinge of guilt, and a great sense of relief. Relief, because the colors in his head were no good against lead. Guilt, because Avery was too old and fat to be farting around with hoods among the trees.

As his eyes got used to the night, he could make out details of his house, the front door a ghostly square past the thick-boled pecans. The trees were one reason he'd bought the house. You could hardly see the place from the street. He wondered, now, how he hadn't noticed the trees offered very fine cover for intruders, as well as protection for himself.

Something moved in the corner of his eye, a shadow blurred against the clapboard siding of the house, there for an instant, just as quickly gone, lost in the shrubs he'd meant to cut back for several years.

One by the door, then, another likely in the back, near the outside stairs up to his room. So what about the driver? Behind the house, he guessed, in the narrow, overgrown alley past the semi-rotten fence--

Something went *"phiiiit!"* Something went *"phiiit! phiiit!"* again. Dreamer stood very still.

A dead branch snapped on the ground. Avery stepped out of the trees by the house.

"Come on over here," he said very quietly, "I want you to take a look at this."

Dreamer walked toward him. Avery unscrewed something from the end of his pistol, something long and slim and black. Just before Dreamer got to him, he slipped it in the pocket of his coat.

"Right there." Avery shined a small flash on the ground. A man lay on his back, one leg over the other, his hands on his chest, like he might be taking a nap. The little blue hole just beneath his right eye said this was more serious than that.

"You know him, you ever see him before?"

"No. Not that I recall," Dreamer said.

"You sure about that?"

"If I knew him I'd tell you. I don't know who he is."

Asher looked at him, then led the way around to the back. The second man was on his side. He was staring out at nothing and his mouth was open wide. He was stunned and appalled at this tragic event. Death had come as a total surprise.

"How about this one?"

"Nope." Dreamer shook his head.

"Neither one of 'em, then."

"Not that I recall."

"You don't recall a whole lot. That's something *I* recall."

Avery muttered to himself, and walked toward the back of the lot. Just as Dreamer thought, the car was in the alley, a dark green Pontiac, 1982. Billy Kern was leaning against the hood, arms across his chest.

"How's it hanging, Dreamer? You ever get over to Ortega's like I said?"

"I never did."

"Shit. That band's gone now. You should've went."

"I could kick myself," Dreamer said.

Sitting in the Pontiac was a guy in a short-sleeved shirt with marble-blue eyes, thinning hair swept back across his head. He was forty, forty-five, and he looked at Avery with a very nervous grin.

"This here's Tommy Waco," Asher said. "Tommy's in a awful lot of trouble, he's up to his neck is what he is."

Asher shook his head. "I guess you know that, Tommy. I don't guess I got to tell you that."

"I guess," Tommy said.

Avery slapped him hard across the face, hard enough to jerk his head aside. Tears flowed down the man's cheeks but he didn't look at Avery, he looked straight ahead.

"You want to tell me who those ol' boys were, Tommy? I got to tell you they were both killed resisting arrest, so you're not going to come to any harm."

Tommy stared. Little balls of sweat popped out on his brow.

"They're gone, Tommy, you know I wouldn't lie about that."

"I don't know 'em, Mr. Asher, honest, they didn't give me no names."

"You're sure now."

"I ain't lying, I swear."

"I hope that's so, because I know God's listening to this. And there's something else me and God knows, and I expect you don't. Those fellows was bent on murder tonight. They wouldn't have left you to talk about it, son. I don't guess you figured on that."

Tommy didn't answer, but his sudden lack of color said this had not occurred to him at all.

Asher pulled out his wallet, drew out a dirty white card and squinted at it in the dark.

"Here's what we're going to do, Tommy. I know you were hired help here, and I don't feel you meant any harm."

"I didn't, no sir."

"I can't just look the other way on this, you understand that."

"You got to do something. I flat broke the law."

"You feel you could put this incident aside, forget you were ever here tonight?"

"Lord God, Mr Asher, I surely can..."

"You got loved ones in town?"

"I got family over to Kingsbury. Wife and two girls."

"You all real close?"

"Yes sir, we are."

"Here's the thing, Tommy. You don't live there no more. You live up in Buffalo, New York. They got loved ones up there, I'm sure you'll get along fine. I know that's harsh after living down here, but justice has got to be served, you know that."

Tears filled Tommy's eyes. "Yes, sir, I do."

"Fine, boy. This card's got Sergeant Spencerio's name on it up in Buffalo. He'll see you get settled, get you work of some kind. I'm letting you off easy, I hope you appreciate that."

"If it's all right, sir, I'd like a little time with the wife and my kids."

"I'm certain you would, but that won't happen, son. Bernie, get this asshole down to Greyhound soon as you clean up here."

Asher led Dreamer back into the darkness of the yard.

"Go upstairs to your room and go to bed. Nothing happened here. You haven't seen me or Bennie, you haven't seen shit."

"I don't have to go to New York?"

Asher found a crushed pack of Camels in his pocket and poked one in his mouth.

"I regret this habit. I also regret being fat but what the hell, it's kinda late for that. You ever talk to Eileen about what I said? Messing around with those new friends of hers?"

"I did. She doesn't take advice real good."

"I hear that." He took a puff on the Camel, looked at it in disgust and tossed it to the ground.

"Those two fellas having supper with Mako, the day you and him had words at the Club. Which everyone in Travis County's heard about. Those are the boys I was warning you about in connection with Eileen."

"I didn't know that."

"What happened tonight--I mean if anything had--it could have come from Mako himself. Just as likely from Gus Brauweiller, anticipating you'd be pissed about the girl."

"He'd be right," Dreamer said.

"And you're going to do what, in regard to that? I don't know why I'm asking. Just because I saved your sorry ass I don't expect eternal gratitude."

"Thanks."

"Well you're not welcome. You keep any weapons in the house? You want to borrow one of mine?"

"Do I get a Dick Tracy silencer too?"

"Fuck you," Asher said. "Get in your house, I got stuff to do."

The first thing he got was a drink. The second thing he got was another, bigger than the first. He sat down in the dark. He thought about Cindy, what he could do to get her back. No big deal. She was either in Switzerland, Kansas, or Iraq. Pakistan, Thailand or Buffalo, New York.

In his spare time, he'd save Eileen. Eileen had no idea the shit she was into with Brauweiller and his pals. Eileen was smart, so smart she scared him sometimes. But Eileen had a blind spot. Eileen was certain money and position would smooth out all the kinks, all the worries in her life.

He set down his drink, wondered if Asher knew more than he was telling about their adventure in the night. Asher was a cop. Dreamer hadn't known one yet you who'd tell you a tenth of what he knew. Which was why Dreamer hadn't told *him* that he recognized both of the hoods Asher whacked. The last time he'd seen them, they had stood outside while Mako came in and bought a Polka-dot Cat.

So that told him what? Did Mako send them himself, because Dreamer pissed him off? Or did Mako loan them to Gus? And did anyone care, besides Dreamer himself?

He went to the sink and splashed water in his face. It had been a long night and he'd forgotten to eat, and the whisky was fuzzing up his head.

Outside, someone slammed a trunk. An engine started and a car drove off. Billy Kern had finished cleaning up. Avery's police work was unorthodox, but it saved paperwork.

Another thought: If the two hoods never checked in, someone would want to know why. Someone would check, and then maybe try again.

Well fuck it, pal, you can't sit around and wait for that...

He ran downstairs, checked the tanks, checked the windows and the doors. Ran back up, dug through his closet for everything black. Black shoes, black shirt, black pants. Surgical gloves and pocket flash. Dentyne gum. Nine hundred dollars in fifty dollar bills. Seiko watch, black dial, black band.

What else? He wished he'd turned in the rental car, traded it for another at a different rental place. His pickup was in the garage but he never liked to use it on a job. The safest thing to do was get a rental, leave it somewhere, borrow a car off the street and bring it back. Leave a fifty on the seat. Prove to himself he wasn't an ordinary thief.

It made no sense to go after Brauweiller. Not a chance in hell he could run the man down. He might be at Enchanted Mesa West. He might be in Dallas or Nepal. And, even if he found him, Lee Ann was likely right--he probably didn't know where the Arab had fled.

The wind was whining through the trees as he made his way back downstairs. Made a sandwich and ate it standing up. Chugged a glass of juice. Rinsed out the glass and heard the sound. Someone walking on last year's leaves. Someone bigger than a squirrel or a cat. The bell chimed once. He peeked through the curtains by the couch. Two men, one he recognized. Slid back the deadbolt and opened the door.

"We've met at Mama Lucy's," the taller man said. "I'm Dr. Billy Shank. This is Jay Turner, a lawyer and a friend."

"I'd offer drinks, guys, but I'm in a kind of rush."

"We're not here to stay, take you up another time." Billy Shank looked at his friend.

"I'll make it short," Turner said. "My wife's got a sister works in security at Enchanted Mesa West. This lady's got a friend who's a maid. The maid works for a little kid. Kid's daddy's in the pen."

Oh, shit...

Turner nodded. He hadn't missed the look on Dreamer's face. "This woman's close to the little girl lives there, Diane? Child's full of fairy tales. Told this lady a knight come to see her a couple day's back. Knight didn't use his right *name*, but the little girl saw it in her head--"

"What's happened," Dreamer said, "what's happened to Diane?"

"She's gone. She didn't run away, the lady's sure of that. Someone took her. Someone came and carried her off."

The chill that started at the back of his neck swept all the way through him like a storm, filling his head with broken glass, with a fear that he'd seldom felt before.

Sweet Jesus, not both of them...not Cindy and Diane, both of them gone...!

If you know *anything,* Mama Lucy, if you could--try and see anything at all? I wouldn't be in this mess if I was black, Mama Lucy. I know I've got soul, but I grew up in Lubbock and never got a chance to let it out. You've gotta help me, I don't know where to start!"

Mama Lucy gave him a look, somewhere between sorrow and disgust, somewhere between love and patience running out.

"You are smart in a lot of ways, boy, but in others you are dumb as a stump. 'Spite of all the time you spend with black folks, you haven't got no idea what being colored means."

"I think you're wrong about that. I feel I've got a good idea."

"Shoot. You skipped right from field nigra to the *Bill Cosby Show,* without all the sadness in between. Which isn't over yet, 'case you hadn't noticed that. You want to do like I told you 'bout a hundred times before. Which is get yourself used to being white, which the good Lord intended you to be. I expect it's a burden, all right, but this time around that's what you got to be..."

"Mama, no offense, we could talk about this some time--"

"That girl you're worried about, they got her all right. Don't know where, but that ain't American they're talking to her now."

"You can see that?"

"I believe I said I could."

"You can't see anything else?"

"I tol' you before, I am not a Gypsy fortune teller, I am a *seer.* That comes from the African root word *sees-clear-over-the-hill*, which means you be looking and keeping your inner eye open all the time and your mind on purity and grace instead of low and nasty thoughts."

"Yes, ma'am. I try to do that. I don't guess it works every time. Okay. Fine That'd be--that'd be Cindy we're talking about, I brought her in here. There's another one, a very small child, a little girl..."

"I know who she is."

"You do?" Dreamer drew a breath. "Listen, that's fine, if you could, if you could maybe help--"

Mama Lucy's eyes went cold. She stood, suddenly, stared down at him, stared right through his head. Dreamer could feel the awful chill, feel something dreadful, something old and dark and damp.

"Listen, if I said something wrong..."

"Leave me be, boy. *Leave me be!"*

Her eyes were a fright. Her voice nearly finished him off. It wasn't Mama Lucy anymore, it was somebody else. Whoever was in there, he didn't want to know.

Dreamer sat there, too stunned to move, watched her walk off, watched her disappear in a jerky half-step behind the kitchen door. Looked in the booth where Shank and Turner sat. They'd seen her too. For a moment, they were both white as Dreamer himself.

Dreamer walked over and sat. "I don't know, I never saw her like that. I love that lady, and she scared the crap out of me."

"Me too," Billy Shank said. "I hope I don't see it again."

Dreamer looked at his watch. "I can't sit here, I'm going to go nuts. I got to get on the road."

"And do what?" Turner asked.

"How do I know? Goddamn it, I don't know *what* to do. Listen, you couldn't know this. There's another one out there, someone's got *her* too."

Jay Turner frowned. "Another what? You talking 'bout another little girl?"

"This one's bigger. I mean older. Not real old, nineteen. An Arab's got her. I don't even know where. She might be out of the country somewhere."

Jay Turner looked at Billy Shank. Looked back at Dreamer again. "I can see why you're looking for help. Anything we can do."

"Thanks. I don't know what."

"You going to start looking. You don't know where."

"That's about it."

"No problem, then," Billy said. "We'll be just as good at this as you."

Dreamer looked at the kitchen door. Wondered what Mama Lucy was doing back there. Wondered what he ought to do. He watched flies clinging to the black screen door, watched them tremble in bliss, watched them shiver as they sucked in the subatomic mist from Mama Lucy's Vishnu Jesus Barbecue. Now and then a fly would simply spread its dirty wings and let go, caught in a culinary seizure as its tiny heart went into overload.

Betty the Crush came in, a woman both beautiful and scary, soft as a baby duck, hard as river stone. Skin somewhere close to caramel, Chinese honey and Polynesian tan.

And, as he watched this wonder cross the room, watched her bend, watched her sit, an action entailing some fifty-two muscular events, the god-awful sound began...

...A shriek and a croak and a horrible moan, an unearthly scream and a terrible groan....it came from the kitchen, swept icy breath against the grease-encrusted walls...a sad and awful sound full of misery, sorrow anger and regret...

But no one there heard what Dreamer did, every shriek and every groan, every fright, every dark thing flapping through the night, turned into hellish tones inside his head, turned into colors that no one used anymore, turned into colors that were dead...

Dreamer stood, ran for the kitchen, shaking the nightmares from his head. Billy Shank, Turner and Betty on his heels He'd never been so scared since he was ten. Double feature, *Snow White* and *Gungha Din*.

"Huh-unh, hold it right there!"

Horace E. Temple crashed through the double doors, spread his long arms, blocked the way with his six-foot four.

"Can't let you in there, man. No way, not you or anyone. That ol' lady in a *state* of some kind, sittin' there staring at the wall. Got those candles and shit, stuff you don't want to get anywhere near..."

Horace E. Temple looked disturbed. Not just disturbed like he always did, like a former nutso flipping lunatic, a man who only chopped barbecue now and seemed content with that. This was 'disturbed' like worried, anxious, severely overwrought. Semi-normal behavior, troubled and concerned about a friend.

"She's got candles back there?" Dreamer said.

"Candles and incense too."

"That's not good," said Billy Shank, "I don't like the sound of that."

"Horace," Dreamer said, "I would never disturb Mama Lucy but I really need her help. How long you think this'll last?"

Horace shook his head. "No way of telling. I've seen her go deep three times before. Twice I figured she was dead."

Horace hesitated, looked Dreamer straight in the eye.

"And you *not* going to bother that lady, you're right about that."

"I respect Mama Lucy, I think you know that."

"Cool, then. That's fine."

Horace didn't move. The chromosomal fires that often raged in Horace Temple's eyes appeared to fade. Still, it was hard to trust a man with a cleaver in his hand, even a man Mama Lucy had purified, cleansed, purged of every sin.

"We are fucked," Dreamer said, backing off with Jay and Billy Shank. "Long as Mama Lucy's out to lunch, she isn't going to help us with Cindy and Diane."

I admire that woman a lot," said Dr. Shank. "Seems to me, though, she could've picked a better time than this."

"That's a fact," Dreamer said.

"You're wrong about that," Betty said, stepping up and shaking her head. "I got a seer on my mama's side. Something turns bad, Miss Pru start doing exactly like this. Shit starts to fly on the other side, your seer going to know it, going to have a petrified fit."

"Blowing a fuse," Turner said.

"Having a seizure what's she's doing," said Dr. Billy Shank.

First Cindy and now Diane. No wonder she's stuck in a spell. This thing's taking everything she's got...

The screen door sighed and slammed shut. Dreamer turned and saw Junior Lewis there. Saw the set of his mouth, saw the Pharaoh eyes, knew there was nothing he could tell Junior Lewis Junior didn't know.

"I nearly wrecked my truck," Junior said, "nearly hit a semi head on. Dreamer, Mama Lucy put some real bad pictures in my head. I never saw anything like it, don't want to see it again."

"Thought transmission through time and inner space," Turner said, "Not a bit surprised. This kind of thing is strong in times of great strife."

Junior looked at Dreamer. "I saw that gal in the Jag. Plain as she's standing right here. There's another one, too. This one's a little girl child. I believe it's someone you're acquainted with."

Dreamer took a breath. "I believe it is. Anything she showed you, Junior. Anything that might tell us where..."

"Huh-unh, nothing like that. Just a real bright picture, like the TV's 'bout to go out. They both all right, but that's not gonna last. They need help, man, need it real fast."

"What we got, we got young ladies in real dire straits," Dreamer said. "We're sitting on our butts, Mama Lucy's talking to Thor."

"Satchmo," Horace said from the door. "Louis Armstrong. Know she talks to him sometimes. Him and Luther Burbank too."

"What your seer's going to do," Betty said, "they're going to be having a mystic interlude. Pru, she'd do it all the time. Roll up her eyes, say somethin' like 'Baka-baka do.' Something like that."

"Baka-baka do."

"Words to that effect. Doesn't mean a thing to anyone. That's what a seer'll do."

"This isn't much help," Junior said.

"Avery Asher's got cop friends in Houston," Dreamer said. "I could find out what they know over there."

"I don't think so," Turner said. "This woman works for the child? I didn't tell you this before? She didn't *call* the police. Didn't call anyone at all."

"Huh?" Dreamer looked up. "Why the hell not?"

"Says the security folks told her not to. Said that might endanger the child. That doesn't sound right to me. Sound right to you?"

"Jesus," Dreamer said, and no, security wouldn't do that at all, but somebody would. *Diane, Diane, where are you, what are they doing to you, hon...!*

"Junior, you've got connections in Houston. Get on the horn, use the one here. See if you can find out anything at all about the child. I'll call from the 7-Eleven store, try and get Paulo again. He's being cagey, but I don't think he'd lie if he knew where Cindy was."

"Dr. Shank? If you and Mr. Turner think of anyone might be some help, find a phone and meet us back here."

"Right on it," Billy Shank said.

"Junior---"

"Shaka may..."

"Huh?" Dreamer turned to find Horace E. Temple at his shoulder. "I didn't catch it, Horace, what are you trying to say?"

"Not trying to say a thing. *She* is. Lady sittin' there stiff as a board, that's what she's saying, saying *Shaka may.* Isn't saying nothing else."

"Might be who's got that woman and the child," Turner said. "Sounds like a man'd do something like that."

Dreamer looked at the others. "Mean anything? Anyone heard the name before?"

No one had. Dreamer stood. "I'll start calling, you guys do the same. It isn't much, but it's a start.Someone's got to know something, someone's-Junior, what's wrong with you?"

"Oh, Lord..." Junior gripped the edge of the table. "Isn't any Shaka may, that isn't what it is. Mama Lucy just zapped it in my head." He stared up at Dreamer. "Isn't Shaka May, what she's sayin's *chocolate milk.* I can read it plain as day."

"Chocolate--you sure of that?"

"That's what she's putting in my head. I can *see* those fuckers, Dreamer. I know they got that little girl."

"Where, where have they got her, Junior?"

Junior looked pained. “I can see it, man. Hell, I *been* there. I been there before, but I don’t know where...!”

Diane was a fruit and veggie kid.

Diane hated chocolate milk.

Chocolate cake and chocolate pie. Chocolate chips and chocolate bars. Hersheys and Snickers and Kisses and Mars. Still, there was nothing else to eat, not a peach or a cabbage, not a veggie anywhere. Great for the roaches, terrific for the ants. She wondered if there might be rats, decided she wouldn't think of that.

The other kids stuffed themselves sick. Scarfed down zitfood until they threw up. Bunnysuit and Fairygirl ruined their pretty suits. Little Miss Muffet did it in her pants. Froggie had a fit.

Diane asked them where they came from. Everyone said "a big house." "A big house where?" Diane asked, but they didn't know that. What they *did* seem to know was each other, everyone but Diane.

They were just little kids. Five, the oldest maybe six. Real cute kids, but they weren't awfully bright. They were scared, and the goodies were *there,* so that's what they did.

Diane was scared, too. A lot more scared than the Bunnies and the Elves. She was seven, nearly eight. Her IQ was two-eighty-six. She read romances, but she knew about Stephen Hawking and Stephen King, too.

She got a PC when she was six. She was on-line in roughly an hour and a half. By noon the next day, she was privy to the darkest secrets of the Web. Diane didn't like it in there. She got away fast, but not fast enough. Not before she learned cyberland was worse than the six o'clock news.

Whatever was going on here, it wasn't any good. That's what all the chocolate was for, and the dumb costumes you had to wear. The toys and the tiny little chairs and the pictures of horsies and ducks. That, and the theme from *Cinderella,* that was rapidly driving her up the wall.

. . .

Diane was cold.

She started to shake and couldn't stop. She wanted to cry, but some of the *little* kids were bawling and she knew she'd better not.

The A/C rattled and the room smelled of mold. Bunnysuit threw up again. Clownboy curled up with an Elf. She remembered the man with the rubber Nixon head, remembered him standing by her bed. Remembered the hospital smell that made her sleep and hurt her head.

Nanny would be worried by now, but Nanny was awful dumb. Miss Alicia Fern, who came in to clean up, loved Diane and Diane loved her back. Alicia Fern was smart. But who'd ever listen to a very nice person who was black? Diane was only seven, but she knew about that.

She thought about her mother, and wondered just where she might be. Luxembourg or London, or Boca Chica Key; she never put a date on her cards, so Diane could never tell.

The bathroom was just behind the tiny tot chairs. She wanted to pee awful bad, but the Ladybug suit was real tight. The polka-dot wings got caught in the toilet and you couldn't sit right. Besides, the place was too dirty to even think about, not the kind of place she was used to at all.

. . .

"Dreamer, Dreamer," she closed her eyes and whispered, *"my good and brave knight, oh please come to me. You said you'd not forsake me, so get me out of here...!"*

. . .

Dreamer didn't come.

Instead, the door behind her opened. The bald man with shades came in. The bald man stank. Cigars and chili, beer and sour sweat.

"Hold it down," he said, "I can't hear the TV."

"I wish to go home right now," Diane said. "I don't like it here."

"Hey, I wanta go home too, I got another three hours onna shift."

Diane took a breath. "From the look of you sir, I doubt you're very heavy into reason, that or common sense. I shall try not to use hard words. Kidnapping is a federal offense. I expect you've served enough time to know that. You, and the other hooligans involved will be punished, of course. Still, it would be to your advantage to send me home now."

The bald man grinned, showing bad teeth. "Geez, you talk like a kid on TV. That show, I forget what. One of 'ems twins or somethin' they always cuttin' up?"

"You'd better listen to me---"

"Eat a cookie, eat a cake, keep your mouth shut. You *are* home, kid, okay? This is where you live."

It hit her, then, shook her real bad. It hadn't truly reached her before, but the bald man's eyes told her it had happened, it was real. They had her, whoever they were, they had her and they'd keep her, and never let her go home again.

With that, the tears began to sting and she squeezed her eyes shut. When she opened them again, the stink, was still there, but the bald man was gone...

Austin to Houston is one-hundred-sixty-three miles on the map. Junior made it in one-hundred-fourteen minutes, crossing the Harris County line going eighty-five flat. Only a driver with uncanny skills, an inborn sense of where cops like to nap behind Dairy Queen signs--that, and possible help from mystic realms--could hope to pull a stunt like that.

There was also the impetus of guilt, pure humiliation on Junior Lewis's part. He cursed himself aloud, pounded on the wheel until Dreamer made him stop.

"Whiskey and chocolate milk," Junior said, "knew that wasn't right. Bald guys in shades in a alley somewhere, middle of the night. Some fuckin' wino is praying at the van. Shepherd. Westheimer, south a little bit. North of Greenway, maybe not. Got to be east of 610, isn't far as Montrose, I'm real sure of that. Shit, man, I don't know *where* the hell it's at."

"Nobody blames you," Dreamer said, "we'll find her, all right? It'll come to you, pal."

"Yeah, right," Junior said.

. . .

Ten, twenty calls to Houston, just as many back. Dr. Billy Shank and John Turner a full half hour behind, but they were on the phone as well. Between that pair and Junior Lewis, a small but determined army was swarming over Houston long before Dreamer and Junior got to town, searching for the spot where someone was holding Diane.

Dreamer fumed over his talk to Paulo, ready to spit hot nails. Paulo was reluctant, didn't want to talk at all. Even on a cell phone, Paulo came off more distant, more cool and indistinct than when they'd talked before.

"You son of a bitch," Dreamer yelled into the phone, "you fucking wetback." Paulo called him a gringo asshole, and things got rough after that.

"Listen," Dreamer said as calmly as he could, "I've got *two* girls missing at the very same time. I don't have a clue who took the little one, but I can make a guess. The other one's maybe in Waco or Tibet. Help me here, Paulo. I don't know where to turn, man, I can't even find *up.*"

"*Compadre*, I would do anything I could," Paulo said, "I know nothing of these terrible crimes. My heart goes out to you in your time of need. I will make enquiries again."

"Fine. Fuck you," Dreamer said, and hung up.

"Something's rotten here, I'm not sure what," he told Junior Lewis. "What I'm reading is deception, falsehood and outright lies. I'm being flim-flammed, I know that."

"You and ol' Paulo been friends a long time," Junior said. "I'd say someone pushing the man or he wouldn't be doing you wrong."

Dreamer knew it was very likely so. Paulo had too much going to keep it all straight. If he wasn't lying, he was coming awful close. Only that wouldn't cut it this time. If anything happened to Cindy or Diane, Dreamer had a list. People who'd pay. It hurt him to have to add Paulo's name. He and Paulo had shared some good times.

. . .

Junior turned off of I-10, wound through the mixmaster onto Memorial Drive. He was pounding the steering wheel again, sweat beading up on his skin, on his ebony cheeks, on the brow of his Pharaoh head.

A call came from Coolie and Brim, the pair who had answered Junior's call when the *barrio* boys had discovered Cindy's Jag. Coolie thought West University--Junior said too far south. One of Billy Shank's friends saw something peculiar in the Heights, and Junior blew a fuse at that.

"Something peculiar always goin' on in the Heights, goddammit, forget about that!"

"These people are trying to help," Dreamer said.

"Yeah, I know that."

"Then take it easy, pal."

"How am I supposed to do that?"

"I don't know. I just know you should."

"What I ought to *do* is know where I was driving that night, what kind of alley I was in. Hell, if I'd even wrote it down I could look up the sheet at *Vins de Jacques.*"

Junior glanced at Dreamer, then quickly looked away. "What happened it was after midnight. Trying to get away fast. I had a woman in mind."

"You didn't have to tell me that."

"I guess I did."

"You didn't do this. You didn't carry off Diane."

"I'm not helping get her back."

"What I think is, seers ought to furnish a map. Looks like they could do that."

Junior's eyes were bright and fierce in the dark. "Getting lost is my doing. Mama Lucy's done her part."

Dreamer didn't have an answer for that.

. . .

Off down Kirby past San Felipe and Westheimer Road. Junior nearly hit a Chevy van. Dreamer gripped the seat and kept an eye out for cops.

"Don't you worry, I'm fine."

"I can see you are, friend..."

Yupon, Kipling, Marshal after that. South down Yoakum to Richmond Avenue. Dreamer prayed direct to Billy Graham, Joe Louis after that.

It was tearing him apart. He couldn't help them both at once, didn't know where to start. Hell, maybe he couldn't do a thing for either one.

Strike that, man, get it out of your head...

He still had his gear. Black shoes, black shirt, black pants. Gloves and flashlight. Big wad of fifty dollar bills. He knew exactly what he had to do. Split up. Go to Brauweiller's by himself. Maybe Lee Ann was right, maybe Gus couldn't help. Still, he had to *try,* damn it, what else was there to do?

He didn't like it, but he knew it was right. Junior had to find the place, Dreamer couldn't help. When he did, if Diane was there, Junior's troops would get her out. He could check in on the cell phones, see how things were coming off. And after they found Diane--

The phone started buzzing. Junior snatched it up at once.

"Where you at right now?" Coolie said, and Junior said, "Nowhere, man, where the hell are you?"

"I think we got something. Alley off Shepherd, back of that hardware store. Get it over here, man!"

Junior didn't answer. Junior took off. Dreamer held on tight.

"We could use that Batmobile, you going to drive like that."

Junior didn't hear him. Junior's eyes were distant, distant and intent...

. . .

The alley was dark. A few blocks away, traffic howled on 59. Seven cars and nineteen men, all of them black except Dreamer, black like Ghana, Haiti and Jamaica, every shade of coffee, cocoa and toast, all of them leery of the honky, of the Man, none of them aware that he was black inside instead of out, that he yearned for an ebony tan.

"If they get to know me, I think they'll like me fine," Dreamer said.

"Isn't time for your Eddy Murphy act right now," Junior said, "best you get back in the car."

"Wait a minute. We gotta talk."

Junior stopped. "This anything can't wait?"

"I got to go, Junior. I don't know it'll do any good, but I got to try and look for Cindy. You don't need me here, you got all the help you need. Hell, I can't stand it, taking off with that little kid's picture in my head, but I got to, okay? It's all right with you, I'll take the car, you can ride with Billy Shank. This is crazy, isn't it? Doesn't make a bit of sense, that girl's maybe in Tulsa or Iran. You think I'm wrong, don't you? Go ahead and say it. You think I ought to stay, right? You think I oughta--"

"I think you oughta shut the hell up," Junior said, "'fore you drive me nuts. Then I think you ought to do what you *want* to do, what you *feel,* man."

"You do? Serious? You're not just saying that..."

A shout from the dark up ahead. Coolie started back, Junior met him halfway.

"I got a name," Coolie said. "Davy Crockett Real Estate. That mean anything to you?"

Junior grabbed him, held him tight. "That's it, Brother, you got it--*that's* the fucking place!"

Horn felt sweat pool under his arms, felt the trickle down his ribs, felt the prickle and the sting. Horn had the A/C as high as it would go, but it didn't help at all. This wasn't sweat from the strangled summer air, from the black polluted night, from the foul percolation that swelled against the car. This was *inner* sweat, sweat from inner heat, sweat generated from sin and dark desire. What it was, Horn thought with great delight, was a manly kind of sweat, and it *smelled,* by God, smelled like the guys who lived in trailer parks. Guys in hard hats. Guys who went to sports events. Guys who only had two cars.

"If this keeps up," he said aloud, "I might not shave all day. I might start wearing dirty socks."

He parked the car a block away and walked. Houston in the summer is a swamp. He was soaked before he got across the street. The neighborhood was bad, anything could happen here. Horn felt virile, frightened and real.

He couldn't forget about the pictures, didn't hardly try. Nearly a week had gone by, they were still lurid visions in his head. God, they were sleazy, God they were fine. Girls with foxy faces, pouty little mouths. Girls with little tits and big hair. Long-legged girls in heels and white socks. Girls who had to scratch, girls who never brushed their teeth.

It was Amy's fault. Amy had driven him to sleaze. Amy smelled like peaches all the time. Amy was clean, not a blemish anywhere. Amy Horn was Best of Show, and Halloran yearned for a mutt from the pound.

A cat yowled somewhere, a dog answered back. He could scarcely see a thing. He felt along the doors, felt the ghostly numbers there: *236...238...*

Horn was ashamed of himself. Ridden with guilt, uptight, strung out, absolutely thrilled. The whole idea of SLUTTO was indecent and corrupt. No one but Mako would think up a bimbo lottery, figure how to do it, how to make a mint. And, the instant he saw those pictures, something stirred in Horn's shorts, something that Amy hadn't stirred in a year...

When Mako left the room to get a beer, Horn quickly flipped through the pictures, copied the address scribbled there.

INTERSTATE DREAMS

Knew he didn't have to write it down. Knew it was seared behind his eyes, and even lower down than that. Knew Fate had struck him in the crotch...

. . .

Horn hesitated, knocked. Ran his fingers over *240* again. It was late, maybe they were closed. Someone flipped a lock, opened up the door. Someone five-ten, slack-jawed, sleepy-eyed, stringy-haired and gaunt. T-shirt and nipples, skirt up to here, the answer to Horn's base desire.

"So?" someone said.

"Listen," Horn said, stirring up courage he didn't know he had, "I own a piece of this action, I want to come in. It wouldn't be wise to turn me down."

"You got it, babe," the woman said. "Sit-down, stand-up, regular or head? spank me, whip me, tie me to the bed?"

"Oh yes," Horn said, "that'll be fine..."

All of the cars drove off a different way. Some down Richmond, some down Main. Some down West Alabama, some down places that hardly had a name. Stopped on a dead-end backwater street full of sorrow and regret, stillborn commerce, shabby habitats. Hovels and shacks, houses afflicted with residential mange, storefronts dying of neglect. The air was a dense coagulation, hydrocarbon blight. Through dead and tangled branches, Houston pulsed beneath a septic shade of blue, beneath a veil of eerie light, a hearty greeting to the people of the night...

. . .

Junior's army flowed quickly through the dark, shadows that never made a sound. There were three cars parked on the street--two late models, one an '86. A rental down the block, junkers in front of every house.

Dreamer knew he couldn't leave now. If they'd found Diane, he had to stay. Long enough to find out. Half an hour tops. If he'd thought it would make any difference, finding where the Arab had Cindy, he would've been out of there, gone in a flash.

He crossed the street behind Junior, just behind Coolie and Brim. A sign no bigger than a calling card was taped to Number *246.* The sign read: *Davy Crockett Real Estate, Inc.*

Dreamer held his breath. Coolie shined a penlight on the door. Dreamer saw the lock, a pale taste of ginger in his head. Much too simple for any help from him. A short little guy in an Exxon cap had a pick. The lock went *snick!* Brim straightened his Bogart hat, looked at Junior and turned the knob.

An empty room, another to the right, the door open wide and full of yellow light.

Coolie stepped in the doorway, leveled a .45, grinned and said, "As you were, gents..."

Two bald men at the table playing cards. Even in the smoky light, they were both wearing wraparound shades. One said, *"Fuck!"* and snaked a hand inside his shirt. Coolie shot him in the face. In the very small room, the gun sounded like a cannon going off. The bald guy's head turned to pizza and splattered on the wall.

His buddy lost his lunch, didn't lose his hand.

"What you got?" Coolie asked.

"Pair of threes is all."

"Shit, you the winner, man."

Coolie brought his weapon down hard. The guy dropped his cards, sank to the floor.

Dreamer was already down the hall, Junior at his heels, Brim after that. Dreamer didn't want to do it, didn't want to see, didn't want to think about what he might find. He opened the door at the end of the hall. Brim pushed him roughly aside, swept a pistol around the room.

"Jesus, don't kill me, man!" The woman screamed, sprang up from the bed. Dropped her cigarette, spat out her gum.. High heels and white socks, nothing more than that.

"Where is she," Dreamer asked her, "goddamn it, there's a kid in here, tell me where she is!"

"Wuh-wuh-wuh--" the woman said, too scared to make the words come out. She pointed to the hall. Dreamer ran over Junior and bolted from the room.

Coolie was already there. Coolie and the others, jammed in the door. Dreamer made his way through. Stopped, stared at the sight, felt every hair tingle on his head.

The room was full of little kids. Fairies, Bunnies, creatures of every sort. Little kids shrieked, little kids ran in circles about the room. There was chocolate everywhere, chocolate on the walls, chocolate on the floor. Dreamer looked at every kid twice, but Diane wasn't there.

Brim picked up a Bumblebee, held the boy hard against his chest. "There you go," he said, "you be fine now, my man."

Dreamer pushed by him, jerking open doors, finding empty rooms, finding nothing there at all.

Coolie touched his arm and said, "You better come and look at this."

He'd overlooked the tiny bathroom. It didn't smell great, and no one was there.

"Couldn't have gotten out here," Coolie said, "nowhere to go."

"Uh-huh, I guess there is, too." Junior said. He nodded at the ceiling, at the watersoaked fiberboard squares. One square was gone, one slightly ajar. Pipes led up from the john. Footprints scarred the wall. Someone had stood on the sink, scooted up there in the dark.

"Get somebody up there," Junior said. "she couldn't get far."

"We don't know it was her," Dreamer said, "we don't *know* she was here. Junior, what the hell *is* this place, what's going on here?"

"Isn't any daycare center," Junior said, "I'm pretty sure of that."

. . .

There was no one on the roof. Someone had been there, they weren't there now. Coolie's people spread out to look. Dreamer talked to the hooker. The hooker's name was Amber. She didn't know a lot. Dreamer got mad. Amber remembered, she'd kinda forgot. A man had come by, she'd let the man in. The man was nice looking, if you liked the wimpy sort.

"A john. A customer," Dreamer said.

"Yeah, kinda," she said.

"Kinda what?"

"It wasn't *johns*, it was him."

"Him. Him what?"

"Just him."

"What are you talking about, girl, I haven't got *time* for this shit."

Amber didn't like to get a man upset. In the work she was in, this was not a good sign. She was there for *that* man, she said, just him. The bald guys hired her. Gave her a photograph. Said the guy would show sometime. Told her what to do when he did.

"And that was what?"

"Usual stuff. Get him stark naked, get him goin' at it, get his picture took."

"And how'd you do that?"

"Where you been, hon?" Amber rolled her eyes, wished she had some gum and cigarettes. "Fuckin' video," she said, nodding toward the ceiling, nodding at the wall. "You're on Candid Camera, man. Ever'body is."

"When was all this? What time was this guy here?"

"What *time?* When you mothers broke in, that's when. Scared the pee out of me, I'll tell ya that."

Dreamer stared. "This was just now? The guy was here? So where did he go?"

"Hey, how do I know? Son of a bitch took off. Cops break in, that's what the guys do. Say, you got a badge or anything? I'd like to see some fucking ID."

. . .

It was clear Amber knew little else. The bald guys had hired her. One was out cold, the other one was dead. Dreamer wished Coolie had left at least one in good shape, but he hated to complain about that.

Something was very wrong here. Who was the man, why was he the only john the hooker had? And what did *that* have to do with little kids? And if the guy was gone, and Diane as well...

"Has to be," Junior said, guessing Dreamer's thoughts. "Him and the kid--"

"Doesn't have to be, but I'd say it likely is. If the guy took her with him, Junior, why? Dude runs out of here naked, stops to grab a kid? That's nuts. I don't get it, man."

Junior Lewis laid a hand on his arm. "We're going to get her back, all right? That's gonna be. Take off if you want to, nothing you can do here."

"Yeah, I guess," Dreamer said. "I don't like it, but it's what I got to do."

"Can't be everywhere at once. Isn't anyone can do that." Coolie appeared as they stepped from the room, nodded, and herded them down the hall.

"Brim's got a way with kids, got a couple of his own," Coolie said. "All of 'em here's from Waifland House Number Nine. Place is a front for selling chil'ren and babies for cash."

Dreamer let out a breath. "I know what it is. It's one of Mako Binder's outfits."

"Sure enough is."

"Anything this bad, has to be him. You still got people out there, find anything?"

"You'd know about it if we did," Coolie said.

. . .

Dreamer knew about St. Sarah Jean House, and Waifland, too. They were part of the dirty secrets he'd come across, plying the recovery trade. Knowing Mako was likely responsible for Diane's being there left him with a new surge of fury, though he scarcely had room for more. Why, though? The john, the hooker and the kids. And what was Diane doing there? The other kids were orphans, unwanted children up for sale. It didn't make sense. But if Mako had a hand in it, Dreamer knew it sure as hell did...

For maybe the four-hundredth time, he asked Junior Lewis if he had the cell phone number memorized. Junior patiently said he did.

Someone had found a stack of calling cards. The cards were in Day-Glo pink and read: *Lease-A-Tot, Inc.* The name brought a chill. Something to do with the Waifland kids, but no one could think exactly what. With Mako behind it, it could be any kind of shit.

Dreamer couldn't get away. Brim wanted him to see his videos. The place was a dump, Brim said, but there were cameras everywhere.

"Isn't much," Brim said. "Man didn't have a lot fun before we busted in."

Brim was right. Dreamer could see the john was naked. The light was too bad to see his face. He hopped on Amber for a second and a half. Leaped up, darted from the room. Brim changed tapes. Snow filled the screen. There was the guy again. View from the back, tall, bony guy running bare-ass down the hall. Opened a door and the light flooded in. More snow and the screen went blank.

"That's it?" Dreamer said.

"Got about eleven cameras in the place," Brim said. "All of 'em shiny brand new. All of 'em crap."

Dreamer noticed both of the baldies were gone. Junior told him the guy who'd survived didn't know a thing at all. Coolie was certain of that. Someone hired him, told him to sit. A woman took care of the kids. Stout lady in a nurse outfit. They'd just missed her, she'd stepped out for a drink. Seeing all the traffic, she likely wouldn't come back. The Waifland kids had been there a week. The last little girl, a day and a half.

"What'd they do with the baldies," Dreamer said, "get 'em out of here?"

"Brim's uncle got a dogfood plant south of Alvin, near Crider somewhere."

"Sorry I asked."

"Be glad you don't have a dog," Junior said...

"Everybody's trying," Junior said, "nobody's giving up."

"I know that. It doesn't help much."

Dreamer stopped at the car. "Mako had Diane brought here, it couldn't be anyone else. If it hadn't been for Billy Shank's friend, we wouldn't even know she was gone. Someone got to the rest of those people at her place, made sure they kept quiet."

"Mako you're talking about."

Dreamer nodded. "Only thing I don't know is why."

What he did, at that instant, was scrawl Mako's name in black, in soot and grime and pitch, in the meanest corner of his mind, right up there ahead of Brauweiller and the raghead prince. However it all turned out--and he wouldn't even let himself think about it turning out bad--Mako's gangster clock was ticking. He was breathing, he was talking, on Dreamer's overtime.

"You got the cell phone number now. Anything happens--"

"Don't you do me that cell phone stuff again."

"I'm a little uptight."

"Uh-huh, I can see that. We find the little girl, Coolie's bunch be glad to come and help, wherever it is you end up."

"I know they would. I appreciate that."

"Black knights always ready to do a good turn."

"You got to be white to be a knight," Dreamer said, hunting for his keys in the dark. "I thought I told you that."

You told me a lot of stuff, man, a lot of it wrong, lot of it plain old shi--"

Junior had more to say than that. Something real heavy, something hard and soft, exploded at the back of his neck and shut everything off, brought him down and knocked him flat.

"Junior?"

Dreamer turned at a noise that sounded awful, sounded flat, turned and saw his friend go down, turned in time to see a demon of his own with the stench of provolone, garlic and mustard, Brut or maybe not, dropped in the same dark well where Junior Lewis had gone...

Halloran could hear them, calling to one another in the night. There had to be thousands of them, maybe more than that, swarming through the alleys and the streets. He knew from their voices they were black and he was fucking terrified. Horn didn't know a great deal about people of the colored persuasion, but he knew that they weren't the same as us. He'd read where they got to do anything they wanted to now, and surely that couldn't be right. What would they do if they caught him? He didn't want to think about that. He'd watched *ZULU* on the tube once, and stared at the ceiling all night.

A car drove by going fast, its headlights blinding white. Horn rolled in someone's flower bed, hitting something sharp.

"Hey, watch it, you 'bout kicked me in the head."

"Jesus!" Horn jumped, nearly stood up, hadn't even seen her in the dark. "Listen, kid, get out of here, quit *following* me. I do not fucking need this."

"Don't you curse at me, villain. I'll not have it," Diane said.

"I am not a villain, little girl. I'm a businessman, I'm a--" Horn lowered his voice. "Never mind what I am. It's no concern of yours. Please just go, all right?"

"You're not my daddy, I don't have to."

"Keep your voice down. A colored guy can hear you half a mile away."

"That's a racial myth. It isn't so at all."

"You think so? Take a look at *ZULU* some time."

"And cover that up. I'm too little, I don't want to see that."

"Huh? Oh, dear!"

Horn hastily grabbed his parts. Scooted away, made sure he was covered up good. Glanced at the kid, raised up and took a look around. A dog began to bark. It didn't seem close. He hoped the coloreds didn't have a dog. He'd seen it in the movies. A dog gets on your tail you're dead.

He was still in a daze, couldn't get it straight, didn't know shit. What *happened* back there? It was all a big blur, didn't make a bit of sense. He's humping the bimbo, someone's *shooting* somebody, he's *off* of the bimbo, flat out of there.

Down the hall, through the wrong door and there's *kids* everywhere. The kids start screaming. Horn is totally naked, he can understand why. He grabs at a curtain, tears it off the wall. Through another door and he's in a little john, he's trapped, there isn't anywhere to go.

He scarcely remembers climbing up the wall, punching through the ceiling, getting out of there. Over the roof, stopping at the edge. There's a Dumpster there and he jumps, rips off skin and slides down.

He's still got the curtain. Wraps it around him, ties it at the waist. Hears a sound, takes a look back. Can't believe what he's seeing back there. A little girl is climbing down the roof. Dressed in a bug suit, red polka dots.

"Beat it," he tells her in a whisper, "get out of here!"

"You can't make me, I can do anything I want."

Horn stares. The kid's just standing there, won't go away. He hears coloreds everywhere, doesn't stop to talk. Turns around and runs. Runs over old transmissions, prehistoric tires. Runs over dog shit, rocks and broken glass. Runs up a driveway, back behind a house. Someone's watching TV. William Holden, *Stalag 17,* (1953).

Stoops down low and dashes to the front. Drops to the flower bed, takes a deep breath. His heart is slamming against his chest. He doesn't know what to do next. The car's no good. It's way behind him now, and anyway he doesn't have pants so he doesn't have the keys.

At least he's maybe lost the coloreds, it seems like they're pretty far back. He has to get some clothes. Poor people hang them on a line, he's heard about that. He hopes to God they're clean. Get some clothes, use a phone. Call somebody to come and get him out of this mess. And then--

--And then the little girl he left a dozen blocks back pops up and scares him half to death...

. . .

"I don't suppose you're open to reason, little girl. What could I say that would make you go away? I don't have the cash right now, but I could send you a, ah--how does a dollar sound? A brand new one dollar bill?"

"Are you serious?" Diane pretended to yawn. "I don't think I've ever *seen* a one. Who's on the front?"

"You poor child. I suppose life's a burden for some. Ah, what exactly were you doing back there, you and all the kids?"

"What were *you* doing back there, without any clothes?"

"That's a grownup question, I don't think you'd understand."

"Try me."

"I don't have time to talk about this. I've got to leave now. You've got to stay *here.* Okay? Don't be frightened, don't be scared. Just--"

"Forget it."

"What?"

"I escaped from that foul keep once, I do not intend to be seized and taken back again. Granted, I owe you a boon for leading the way. But if you try to shed me now, I shall scream so loud that hostile horde will be on you like lice upon a duck."

"Good God." Horn was taken aback. "Wherever did you learn to talk like that?"

"Alas, my mother was a serving wench, my father is a--"

"Hush!" Horn said, and pushed her quickly down. The car stopped just across the street. Someone got out, left the parking lights on. Horn strained for a look. Let out a weary breath. It wasn't a car it was a van. The motor was running and the letters read PIZZA on the side.

Horn turned on Diane. "I am leaving now, little girl, and you're staying here. *Don't* try and follow me, you'll get in an awful lot of trouble if you do."

"Like what?"

Horn took off. Diane watched him for a second and a half.

"Fat chance," she said aloud. "I expect I can outpace a base-born lout."

The last of her wings fell off as she ran after Horn across the lawn. Horn was a pale and bony wraith, trailing a gauzy curtain in his wake...

If he answers, I won't even talk. He'll say, hey, who's this? I'll wait a second, let him stew a while. Maybe I'll say fuck you, hon, so he'll know for certain who it is. Huh-unh, I can't do that. He'll know it's me and I can't handle that...

She tried him a couple dozen times. Had a few shots, finished off the Scotch. Got in the car, took a drink with her, drove by the house. The lights were all out. It was late, but Dreamer hardly ever did that. There was always a light in the shop. One in the upstairs hall. From the street, she couldn't tell if the car was gone or not. She wasn't about to pull in and find out.

"Well shit," she said aloud, rolling down the window, shouting at the house, "what do I care if you're home or not? What do I care you got that little tart up there, you no good son of a bitch. I don't care if you fuck a herd of Waco debs!"

She threw her empty glass and it shattered on the curb. She meant what she said. She didn't give a damn about him, and every time the did part reared its ugly head she was filled with a fury, a surge of awful anger, sadness and regret.

What she wanted to do, was not feel anything at all. Her head wouldn't put up with that, and her body wouldn't help. Goddamn traitors. Any time one of the two made sense, the other caved in, surrendered on the spot. What she wanted, she decided, was a drink. A drink'd be--

--a drink'd be--

--a drink'd be fine...

A little jerk here while the film jumps off the track, a moment out of time where nothing's working right. What exactly is she doing in the car? Where has she been, where does she want to go? And what the hell happened to the drink that she had?

Eileen stopped, turned off the lights. Grabbed her hair in both hands, pulled it till it hurt. Let out a breath. Tried to see the time. Couldn't focus on her watch. Felt the tears start, felt her body start to shake and couldn't make it stop. Saw the lights behind her flash blue and red and white, wished they wouldn't do that, wished they'd fucking stop.

"Lady, you're driving in a real erratic manner, you aware of that?"

"Fuck you, pal, I'm not driving at all."

"I beg your pardon, ma'am?"

Eileen squints. A bright light shines in her face.

"Go take a leap. I'm a practicing attorney. Get that flashlight out of my eyes. Stick it up your ass."

"Ma'am, I'm going to have see your license, please."

"Fuck you are."

"All right, that's it. Step out of the car."

Eileen rolls the window up. The officer yells as he catches his hand in the glass. He opens the door, grabs her arm and pulls her out. Eileen takes a swing, misses and falls. Someone catches her before she hits the ground.

"Christ, she is somethin' else," the officer says. He rubs his wrist and makes a face. "That's my bowling hand."

"Shut up," the other man says. "Turn off her lights, get the keys. Get her purse there."

He guides Eileen to the car with flashing lights. Opens the back door, tosses her roughly in.

"Son of a--bitch," Eileen says, coming around a little now, getting a little sick. "You're in big trouble, pal."

"We'll get you some coffee," the man tell her, "fix you right up. We'll take care of you now, Eileen..."

"We're going to have go abandon this van, you know. I'll warrant the driver's calling 911 right now. He'll report his mount stolen by rogues, and they'll put out an APB. That's an All Points Bulletin, you know. I shouldn't think we'd be difficult to spot. The colors, I recall, are a sort of armor blue and meadow green. Quite distinctive, in a way, and--"

"Will you shut *up?"* Horn turned on her and glared. "I'm trying to think, I don't need any help from you. No one asked you here, you know."

"I will not suffer a vile and ignorant tongue. I thought you understood that."

Horn stared at her. The passenger seat nearly swallowed her up. Her legs swung loose above the floor.

"You're a very smart little girl. And your thinking is correct. I intend to get rid of the van, I am merely trying to figure out how."

"I've watched them wire cars on TV. It's possible I could give it a try."

"Don't be ridiculous. You're only a child."

"And you're a grown-up who's driven around the same *block* four times. May I ask the reason for that?"

"I'm sure you're mistaken."

"I'm sure I'm not."

Horn slowed and checked the street ahead, looked to the left and to the right. "What I'm going to do, little girl, I'm going to find a house that's got a light. Then I'm going to stop and let you out. Don't be afraid, just run up and knock, someone will let you in. Tell them--tell them whatever you want, I don't care what. They'll see you get home.

"Now I think that's very fair, don't you? And if *I'm* being fair, you ought to be fair, too. The way I'd like for *you* to be fair is totally forget about me. You don't know me, you never saw me before. Is that all right, can you do that for me?"

Diane rolled her eyes. "What do you take me for, an ignorant serving girl? Some poor lass with no virtue at all? No, sire, you cannot ask me to lie."

"What? Why not?"

"Because I *do* know who you are. You're Mr. Horn, and you live at

Enchanted Mesa West the same as I. I believe you live a mere three floors above. I have seen you in the elevator a number of times with your very comely wife."

Horn stared. He jerked at the wheel and nearly ran off the road. "You can't be serious, I've never seen you before in my life. I-- Why in God's name are you bringing this up now? Why didn't you say something before?"

"Well *you* didn't say anything. I thought you were simply being polite. You know, two well-born persons run into one another under an embarrassing circumstance..." Diane sniffed. "Truly, you don't recognize me, not any at *all?"*

"No, I don't. Well yes, I possibly do. I'm certain of it now."

"No you're not. That's the thing, you see. Adults are blind to the presence of a child. We are only small creatures, mostly in the way."

"I wouldn't say that. Sometimes we just--*shit*!"

Horn saw the black face appear, saw the rage, saw the anger, saw the fury in the Zulu eyes, saw the big black hands as they clawed for the door. Wrenched the wheel hard to the left. Saw the face stare right at him an instant, heard the awful thud against the van.

The little girl screamed. Horn peered in the mirror, couldn't see anything at all. Didn't have to, knew what he'd done.

"I want to go home," Diane cried, "You take me home this instant, you hear!"

How, Horn thought with a terrible chill, *how am I going to do that? How am I going to make anything work out now...?*

The next thing Dreamer smelled was feet.

Very close and big. Two big pair. One pair in jump boots, the other in black and white shoes. Wingtips circa 1946. Are these guys together? What kind of shit is this?

"Take it easy, pal, stay put. Try an' get up and I'll kick you inna teeth."

Dreamer stayed put. His head hurt a lot. Someone had given him a very hefty tap. The pickup was extra wide. The floor was full of crap. Big Mac boxes and ancient onion rings. Beer cans and girlie magazines. They bounced hard over a bump. Dreamer tasted ketchup, shrimp and kerosene. Someone ought to look at those shocks. Melissa, the goofy blonde at Billy T's All-Nite Kash n' Karry Texaco Hut, said people never thought about shocks. Melissa said--

--Aw, Junior, what did they do to you, man...

"Where is he, what'd you do to him, you son of a bitch!"

Dreamer sat up, swung at Wingtips. Jumpboots kicked him back down.

"Don't guess I know the man," Wingtips said.

"I think he's referring to the nigger, Roy Bob."

"You think?"

"I'd say he is. I don't recall hittin' anyone else."

"You sure he was a nigger? It was dark out there."

"Don't hold me to it, I'm near certain that it was."

"What'd you *do* to him," Dreamer shouted from the floor, "you answer me, pal."

"If it's who we're thinking about," Wingtips said gently, "I'm inclined to feel the dude's dead..."

Dreamer lost it. Lost it and gave out a godawful yell, kicked and found a knee, lashed out and found a crotch.

"Sheee-it," someone said, and Dreamer dropped off into the darkness again.

...

"On your feet, buster, get it outa there."

The pickup came to a stop. Someone opened the door, lifted Dreamer up by the belt and tossed him on the ground. Dreamer scraped his hands, hit his knees and rolled, came up on his back.

"Damn you, Conch, I said bring him in, I didn't say go and bust him up, you didn't hear a thing I said. If this boy's injured or maimed I will have your fuckin' head."

Brauweiller leaned over Dreamer, worry and concern in his 40-weight eyes. "You all right, boy? I got a slug of brandy here, try some of that. I get it real cheap 'cause I own a part of France."

"I'd like a glass of water if it's all the same to you."

Brauweiller made a face. "Christ, get the man some water, there's no accounting for taste."

Brauweiller stood, watched Conch run off for water and spoke to Roy Bob. Dreamer blinked and closed his eyes. Blinked and tried again. Did his very best to attach real meaning to this goofy apparition with zillionaire breath, hundred dollar brandy and Cuban cigars, a faint whiff of blueberry pie.

Brauweiller looked as if he'd just stepped out of a 1918 Army-Navy store. German airman's tunic in snappy mouse grey. High stiff collar, and a gold Blue Max. Flying jacket draped about the shoulders, Richthofen style. Goggles and helmet, shiny black boots.

None of this really worked at all. At three-forty something and sixty inches tall, Brauweiller looked very little like the Baron, more like a hog dressed up for the Kaiser's Christmas ball.

Dreamer laughed, didn't try to stop.

Brauweiller didn't care for that. "I'd control myself I was you, boy. Now get up on your feet. I hate to see a grown man lyin' on the ground."

Dreamer got to his knees, pulled himself up, keeping one eye on Roy Bob. Conch arrived with a styrofoam cup. Handed it to Dreamer with a lopsided grin.

Dreamer turned on Brauweiller. "How'd you find me? You're mixed up with that kid business too, right? You're a real asshole, but I didn't figure you for that."

"Don't know about any kids. *Listened* to you's what I did. Got you in Austin, all the way here. Isn't any secrets on the phone line any more, son." Brauweiller grinned. "Lord, I never heard so many niggers on the air at one time. You sure got a bunch of darky friends."

"Yeah, I do," Dreamer said. He thought about Junior Lewis, knew he had to put him out of his head, put his sorrow on hold, get back to it again.

His horizon was a great deal broader standing up, now he knew exactly where he was. Past the dull expanse of concrete was the brightly-lit hanger at Enchanted Mesa West. Men in white jumpsuits scurried about. Behind them, lined up neatly in a row, bright as shiny toys, were Brauweiller's Fokker D-VIIIs, wings green as lily pads, mustard-yellow noses, stubby white tails.

Brauweiller caught his wonder and smiled. "Damn, is that something to see or what? Sometimes I just bust out and cry. I don't feel it's unmanly at all. Hell, you're a flyer, son. Don't tell me it doesn't get to you."

Dreamer looked him in the eye. "Your boys here killed a friend of mine. I intend to pay 'em back in kind. That's their ticket, and you got yours. That Middle Eastern fuck's got Cindy, he's taken her off somewhere. You got her into this, mister, I hold you responsible for getting her out."

"We're talking aviation here. How the hell we get on pussy, boy?"

Dreamer went for him. Roy Bob was waiting for that, praying for the chance at a fracture or a break, a sprain, a contusion or a wrench, any sort of bodily harm.

Dreamer found himself flat on his back. Roy Bob grinned and wagged a finger in his face.

"When does this payback shit come about? I don't feel you're up to that."

Brauweiller frowned. "Roy Bob, you failed to mention any fatal incident. I do not appreciate that."

Roy Bob shrugged. "It was Conch here did it, talk to him."

"Well, thanks a fuckin' lot," Conch said, "blame everything on me."

"Out of my face," said Roy Bob.

"Make me," Conch said. He grabbed Dreamer's water, drank it, and tossed the cup down.

Brauweiller waved the pair off. "You and me have got crossways, friend. I thought we could do a little deal like decent bidnessmen. What I'm seeing is you're not my kind at all, you've got no feeling for commerce and trade. I made you a real fair offer, all you're thinking about's a goddamn gal."

Brauweiller paused and glanced across the field. "I can't have you snapping at my heels every time I turn around. I could drop you in a construction site, but I want to be fair. We'll settle this a way that's noble and good."

Brauweiller jerked a thumb in the air. "Just you and me. Up there."

Dreamer stared. "Up where?"

"Up there, boy. Men braving the skies in canvas and wood, Fokkers and Spads, screaming through the cold and fearsome air. Dawn, and a hundred engines growl, thunder over the rubble of Verdun, the stink of death rising from below..."

"You know what, old man? What you are, you are flat fucking nuts."

"Just what I'd expect from a man who's lost his nerve. I looked you up. You went down in banana-land in a heap of molten shit. Burned up all your friends. What I'm telling you is, that is not the end. Ernst Udet, he froze at the stick, you know that? Richthofen told him, 'fuck that, man, it's all inside your head.' Udet ended up with 62 kills, right behind the Baron himself.

"That's the way it happens every time. Caught in the swell of war, the coward loses heart and overcomes his fears. The brave man fills his pants and has a drink."

"That doesn't even make sense."

"'Course it doesn't, Dreamer. That's what's fun about war. No one expects it to make a lot of sense."

Brauweiller turned to Roy Bob. "Roll out Three and Four. Be sure we're gassed up."

"Forget it," Dreamer said. "I won't get in a real airplane. I sure as hell won't go up in that."

"You certain of that?"

"You bet your life, pal."

"Hey, might be you got something there."

Brauweiller looked at Conch. Conch disappeared. Dreamer heard a car door open and shut. A van pulled up from the dark. With a nod from Brauweiller, Roy Bob led Dreamer to small round window in the side.

Dreamer put his face up to the glass. Something turned over in his gut. He grabbed the van tight and held on. Eileen looked right at him. Dark shadows circled her eyes. She looked weary, cold and scared, hardly even there.

"It's a one-way," Roy Bob said. "You can see in, she can't see out."

Dreamer swung on him. Roy Bob stepped back.

"Hey," said Conch, his arm out straight, the pistol pointed right at Dreamer's head. "Try me, give me a reason, pal."

"Here's the deal," Brauweiller said. "You and me go up and have it out. You decide not, I'll have Roy Bob here gut her like a mullet on the spot. She's a fine legal mind, she's got hooters out to here, but I can live with that."

Dreamer glared. "I don't think you would."

"Not me, boy, no I never could. Him now, he don't even care."

"You son of a bitch. You make it hard to say no."

"That is real fine, son." Brauweiller gave him a fat guy grin. "I knew you'd come around. Roy Bob, get this boy suited up, I'd say a 42-long. Get a move on, now, I want to be over those trenches by dawn..."

INTERSTATE DREAMS

The wheels of the Fokker bounce twice and leave the ground. The engine howls like a gut-shot dog, and the wings begin to flap. Everything Dreamer has dreaded comes to pass--he's back in banana-land again, with the chills and the shakes and the paralytic sweats and the screaming and the dead, and the stink of crispy critters that used to be Nick and Frank and Red.

Two thousand feet above Enchanted Mesa West, he remembers the drawbacks of an open cockpit: Even if you lean real good, the vomit flies back in your face, then down your throat again.

The fear and the cold clutch his gut in their dirty fingernails but he edges them aside. Dreamer guesses it's a little after six. It's been one hellof a long night. Banking to the left, he sees Brauweiller a thousand feet below, climbing through the heavy morning air, the first hint of sunlight slanting off his wings. The "Hun in the sun" trick is what this mother has in mind, and Dreamer isn't buying that.

He kicks the rudder hard, jerks the stick to the left. Brauweiller's pushing it, gaining height fast, faster than Dreamer would have guessed. The old man knows his machine, knows what his craft can do.

Dreamer is surprised Brauweiller can actually fly. Even more surprised this tub can squeeze into an airplane at all. These cheesy little crates weren't built for persons of a grosser dimension, the chubby and the dumpy and the squat. Yet, here is Big Bratwurst himself, churning up the skies, angling on Dreamer through the wispy morning clouds. And Dreamer sees if they keep on course, his foe will be above him in eight seconds flat, not at all where Dreamer would like for him to be.

Dreamer gives the fighter a short burst of speed and sets the wing on edge, heading for the spot Brauweiller will be when he comes out of his curve. Brauweiller catches on at once, stands the Fokker on its tail, hangs there a second and a half, white tail down and yellow nose up, suspended in the air. Dreamer flashes by below, sees his mistake and knows he's very late, desperately kicks off to the right.

Twin Spandaus chatter off to port. A hail of bullets tear through Dreamer's wing. Canvas rips and shreds baring naked struts below. Dreamer bulls the stick back, jamming his foot through the floor. The little craft shudders, the engine screams and howls, twists on its back, heads for the cruel ground below. Dreamer holds his breath, fights to bring her back. The image of a moment such as this is a chilly rerun from long ago.

He levels off at three hundred feet, fights for height again, frantically searches the morning sky. The phony Hun is nowhere in sight. If Brauweiller spots him first again, flying this close to the ground...

Dreamer races for altitude, pushing the Fokker for all it's worth, banking off at random to the left and to the right, forcing back the panic, telling himself he can by God *do* this, it isn't like before, it is *not* going to happen again.

That first encounter was a fluke, he knows that he's the better man. Christ, he's flown every kind of craft there is, from a million-miler clunker in Zaire, to the Panama choppers, to the midnight killers in Iraq. If he can't beat a little fat guy, he deserves to get his ass shot down.

A thousand feet, seventeen hundred, where's the guy hiding, there isn't a cloud in the whole blue sky. Hot specks of oil fly back from the rotary engine. Dreamer wipes his goggles clean. Roy Bob and Conch said they'd kill him if he didn't wear the whole outfit--Dreamer said fine, go ahead, you won't get me in a fucking Hun suit, and neither one did.

Dreamer searches the sky again. Brauweiller has vanished, faded, melted away, he is nowhere in sight. Dreamer banks to starboard, angles off to port, and there's nothing, nothing anywhere, and then, as it happens in the air, in an instant, in a blink, his enemy is bigger than death, stronger than doggie breath. Not from below, going for the belly and the tail, not from above, like an eagle from the sun. That overstuffed sausage, that bogus Baron is coming right at him, nose to nose, playing chicken in the air.

Dreamer freezes at the stick. It has never happened, in all his flying years. He is numb, chilled, stunned and stupefied. When he tries to move his hands, he finds they're paralyzed, glacially impaired. He sees the Fokker coming, sees the flame leap from its guns--

--sees the cobalt blossom in his head, sees the moldy green explode in shards of bloody red. The colors come alive with such fury Dreamer gasps, shaken by the awesome birth of stars, by their death cry sharp as splintered glass.

And, within this incandescent glory, this cauterizing pain, he sees, once again, the phantom craft that found him on the road from Enchanted Mesa West, the ghost that stilled the night frogs and took away his breath. Out of that darkness he hears the faint voices of Junior, Cindy, Diane and Eileen, crying for his help, calling out his name, they're there and then they're gone, lost and out of sight, lost on a lonely and featureless plain...

--and squeezes the stick in both hands, snaps the Fokker in a wrenching turn to port, certain this maneuver will tear the wings apart. Not a second has passed, not the beat of a hummingbird's heart. One thing he knows about the colors in his head, they don't give a shit about clocks, never ask the time of day.

The other plane streaks by in a blur. A yard, a foot, half an inch away. Its passage leaves Dreamer's craft trembling and adrift. He rights the plane again, sees the sun disappear, sees the shadow overhead. A bright flash of yellow sears the corner of his eye. A rain of lead stitches his craft from nose to tail, *tacka-tacka-tacka-tick!*

Dreamer sees his windscreen shatter, sees a strut disappear, sees scraps of wood and canvas fall away. He jerks the plane aside, gives the throttle power, rolls the plane crazily across the empty skies.

The engine chokes, sputters and coughs, lets an oily fart and threatens to quit. Something goes *ding!* and a slug of hot metal falls into his lap. Dreamer gives a yell and sweeps it off his crotch, watches it bounce between his feet. It's half a steel bolt, sheared off the engine somewhere. Hot oil streams past his face like the Fokker's peeing black.

"Okay, goddammit," he shouts into the wind, "that's it, that's enough of this shit!"

Jerking back the stick, he kicks the D-VIII into a roll, sees Brauweiller buzz by a hundred yards below. Dreamer feints right, straightens out again. Brauweiller won't buy it, he's too smart for that. He comes up fast on Dreamer's bare belly, ready to rake him hard again.

Dreamer holds his breath, prays the engine won't quit. Four...five...six...

He wrenches the craft straight up, feels his stomach kiss his spine, hears the bullets whine by exactly where he's been, comes out of the loop and there's the motherfucker, right between his sights.

Wind screams through the braces, he aims the nose straight at the ground. Crosshairs inch up Brauweiller's tail and settle on the cockpit itself. Dreamer's twelve again, eating Fig Newtons on the porch. He's right in the middle of *G-8, Battle Aces,* page 32. Camels, Fokkers and Spads howl over the wasted battleground. The evil Baron von Knockenspielhausen leers at the Frenchy in his sights. His gloved hand squeezes the trigger. Machine guns stutter, and death spews out of the skies...

Which is fine for the Baron, only Dreamer's Spandaus don't *tacka-tick* a bit. He tries them again, and they won't do shit.

Dreamer doesn't stop. He shoves the stick forward, shrieks down on the foe. Nuts, bolts, canvas and masticated wood whine past his head. The whole plane shudders. The wings begin to shiver, the spars begin to crack.

Suddenly, Brauweiller turns and looks up. Helmet and goggles, a blur for a face. He tries to bank and run. Dreamer won't let him, Dreamer's right there. His prop shreds a rudder, bites off a tail. Brauweiller's craft begins to wobble, makes a drunken little hop.

The phony Prussian's good, Dreamer has to give him that. He struggles with the pedals and the stick and he keeps the craft aloft. Still, there's little he can do and he's losing height fast. By the time Dreamer circles, ready to make another pass, his enemy is losing it, twitching like a wounded butterfly, and the ground is a hundred feet below.

Dreamer's engine hacks and spits and there's nothing he can do about that. Brauweiller's dropping fast, but not nearly fast enough. Dreamer is fuming, sorely offended and terribly riled. Gravity will get Brauweiller, but Dreamer wants to help.

Easing down on the dying craft, Dreamer brings the stick back lightly, gives the engine a peppy little slug, then drops his heavy wheels on Brauweiller's wings.

The spars go *crick!* and then *snap!* The wings fold up, kiss one another, tear off and spin out on their own.

The Fokker drops like a brick. The belly strikes the ground with a sickening sound. Wheels shear off on either side. For a very small instant, the structure stays intact. Then, internal injury prevails, and the whole thing comes apart...

. . .

Dreamer lands quickly, bounces off the turf near Enchanted Mesa's Number Seven hole, a very tricky par 5. The plane is some two hundred yards from the hangers, and jumpsuit lackeys are rushing to the site. Dreamer reaches the spot as they're easing the pilot from the wreck.

Roy Bob steps in his path. "Hold it," he says, "you're not going anywhere, pal--"

Dreamer buries a fist in Roy Bob's gut, doesn't stop to look back.
The jumpsuits huddle by the pilot, Dreamer races for the pack.

Goddamnit, I don't want you dead, I want you alive so I can kick you in the butt...

Dreamer shoves his way through. Brauweiller's flat on his back. The first thing he sees is the bratwurst has lost a lot of weight. Down from three-something to one-one-six. A jumpsuit peels the helmet back. Dark hair spreads across the grass. Dreamer sees the old man has a very lovely nose, very full lips. *"Oh Jesus God,"* Dreamer says, and goes rigid on he spot, "what the hell you doing here, hon, you all right!"

"No, I am--not--aw'*right*," Eileen says, one eye black, the other wandering about. "Someone get me--someone ge'me a--fughing drink..."

PART THREE

Devilfish,

Morays,

and

two-legged Clams

"Don't try and talk," Dreamer said, "just lie real still, you're gonna be fine."

He lifted her head off the hard concrete. Eileen moaned and he laid her back again.

"You stupid shit--you got medica--medical training of any kind?"

"No I don't."

"Then leave me alone, oh babe, I am hurting real bad..."

She looked up at him. Mascara ran down her cheeks. He touched her gently and her eyes filled with tears. "Dreamer, why did you, what'd you--"

He could hear them now, shouting, running across the field, flashes stabbing at the dark .

"Take it easy, don't try and talk now."

"Huh-unh, listen. Don' understand, what were you doing up there? Wasn't supposed to be--"

"--Wasn't supposed to be *me,"* Dreamer finished, and the answer struck him like a fist in the gut, the answer there in the hurt, in the sorrow of her eyes, the whole thing simple and easy, cold and deadly clear.

He didn't have to ask. They'd worked it on her, same way they did with him. Showed her a video, a Polaroid shot. Dreamer out cold on the floor of the car. Go up and fight me, Brauweiller says, or I'll kill your sweetie dead.

Old man, you are pissing me off...

"They did it to us," Dreamer said. "Faked us both out. We'll have their ass for that. Minor point, babe, but I'd kinda like to hear. You could've told me you knew how to fly. I thought we were closer than that."

Eileen showed him a weary smile. "It was--kind of a surprise."

"It was all of that."

"Your big-time mogul likes to keep his people strung out to some extent. Gus said--you like the big bucks, honey, get up there and fly."

"Ah, hell, Eileen."

"Three fucking years. I threw up every time."

"You were pretty good up there."

"I wasn't--better than you."

"You were terrific. You nearly had me twice."

"You're just saying that, 'cause you think I'm going to die."

"God, Eileen, I don't think anything of the sort. You're going to be just fine!"

"I don't--think so," she said, closed her eyes and opened them again.

"Now stop it, damn it, stop doing that. "

Dreamer felt an awful sense of dread, saw all their faces, pale and ghostly white inside his head. *Eileen...Junior...Cindy...Diane...*

"Goddamn it," he shouted at the sky, "you just stop it, you hear. Leave 'em all be. Let my people go!"

"All right, " Brauweiller said, bulling his way through the lackeys and the vassals, through the minions and the serfs, "let's show a little respect, we got a wounded aviator here."

Roy Bob grinned at Dreamer, waved a pistol in his face.

Brauweiller squeezed his sizeable self into a squat, took Eileen by the hand. Pretended Dreamer wasn't there.

"You're all right," he said, "you look real good, I'd say you'll be fine."

"You asshole," Eileen said, "you fat-butt piece of crap."

Brauweiller laughed aloud. "By God, I admire your spirit, lady. Isn't she something, she something else or what? You're a big disappointment, Eileen. I expected better, I got to say that. You're no longer working for me. That means no dental plan, no future benefits.

"Roy Bob? Conch? I want this person out of here, make sure she gets proper care, make sure the bills don't come to me." Brauweiller looked at Dreamer. "That was pretty fair flying. Not a bad Immelmann, you got the roll right."

"That was real chicken shit, sending Eileen up there. You ought to get your own hands dirty some time."

"You crazy or what?" Brauweiller gave him a thoughtful look. "You are determined to cause me grief, am I right about that? I don't have time for it, son. I think I'll have to buy you some serious pain."

"You can try," Dreamer said.

"Boy, I can do more'n that."

"Keep your eyes open, old man. I don't intend to quit."

"I expect you will if I put you under a new parking lot, that ought to do the tric--"

Brauweiller's words were lost as sound, fury, chaos and distress ruled the day. A wave of heat rolled across the field as the Fokkers in the hanger brightened into fiery smithereens, blew all to hell in an orderly manner, one-two-three-four, on down the line, perky little mushrooms rising in the air, nearly as good, some said, nearly as awesome as *Die Hard Four.*

"Fug-shit-do-do," Brauweiller said as his face turned cherry red. "I'll have someone's butt for this, somebody's gonna pay, somebody's going to swing!"

Brauweiller turned on Dreamer. "I don't like your facial features, boy. What's your part in this treachery, what do you know about this?"

"I don't know a thing. I was brought here against my will."

"Yeah? How do I know you didn't trick me into that?"

Dreamer ignored him, turned back to Eileen.

Another Fokker turned to flame. Roy Bob let out a yell.

"Company, sir! Incoming!"

Roy Bob was pointing past the fire. Lights flashed and sirens wailed. Two fire engines shrieked onto the field. Both bore the crest of Enchanted Mesa West.

Brauweiller didn't look at either one. His gaze was locked on the big black Lexus, coming straight at him, coming rhino fast, as if it meant to run him down.

The Lexus didn't screech, it hummed very gently to a stop.

Lee Ann Brauweiller leaped out and headed for Gus, angry and chic in fitted jeans and a Bill Blass blouse.

"Asshole," she screamed, "son of a bitch!"

"Lee Ann," Brauweiller said, "what the hell you doin' here, you are forbidden on my field."

His eyes met hers, everything between them perfectly clear. They had loathed each other so deeply, hated each other so long, there was little they could hide, and neither one bothered to pretend.

"Your presence tells me all I need to know," Brauweiller said. "It's you who's behind all this. You destroyed my planes by incendiary means."

Lee Ann laughed. "And guess what else? There's a great deal of money missing from your accounts. I am fucking out of here, Gus, and I don't intend to write."

"Come on, Lee Ann, "what do I care? You couldn't steal enough to buy the Philippines. Those planes you burned up can't be replaced. We're talking aircraft rare as duck teeth."

"No, we are *not.*" Lee Ann faced him half an inch away. Brauweiller didn't like that, never could stand her getting close. "What we are talking about here is *Cindy,* we're talking about my sister, Gus. My own blood kin you gave to that camel-fucking sheik."

"Oh, well fine." Brauweiller threw up his arms. "Here we go with that stuff again."

"Lee Ann...Lee Ann is--that you...?"

At the sound of the voice, the color drained from Lee Ann's face. She drew a deep breath, shoved her husband aside. No easy task for a woman of normal weight and height. She stopped, then, stunned at the sight of Eileen, still and very small on the ground, face smeared with grease, hair in disarray.

"Oh God," she cried in agony and fear, "what happened to you, hon, what are you *doing* down there!"

She dropped down and held Eileen, her eyes telling Dreamer to kindly get lost. A fervent kiss, a smoothing of the hair, a whisper in Eileen's ear, and it dawned on Lee Ann that Eileen was dressed in a Hun flying suit. It took her half a second to comprehend the meaning of that.

"Oh, you bastard," she glared at Gus, "you cowardly rat, it wasn't you up there it was *her*. You sent my baby up in a crate like that!"

"So that's who it is," Brauweiller said. He looked to the sky as if God might understand. "I knew it was someone, didn't know who. My wife's a dyke and my lawyer's queer too. What did I do to merit this?"

Dreamer looked up as another siren began to wail. An ambulance wheeled past the hanger and headed toward the wreck.

"Roy Bob," Brauweiller said, "I don't see we got a need for that EMS. Take Miss Eileen and the asshole here out to where we're building that mall. Get my wife in a mental ward somewhere out of state. Vermont's fine, either that or Delaware."

Dreamer stood perfectly still. Brauweiller's lackeys were gone, making themselves useless at the fire. There was only Roy Bob and Conch. Whatever happened here, no one had to see.

"You don't want to do this," Dreamer said, "this is a serious violation of the law."

"Haw! You got a better idea? Conch, Roy Bob---"

The door of the ambulance flew open wide. Paulo stepped out. Silk Italian suit. White shirt, white tie. Five men followed in his wake. Camous and berets. Silver .38s. Paulo carried a weapon Dreamer chanced to recognize--the Steyer-Solothurn, a German sub-machine gun, 9 mm., thirty-two rounds. Originally manufactured by the Swiss in 1930, it reflected Paulo's need for exotic weapons of the past.

"Don't anybody move," Paulo said, a line that made Dreamer grin, "hands above your heads."

Roy Bob didn't move. Conch did. Paulo shot him in the knee. Conch went down and howled.

"*Senora* Brauweiller, my people will take care of your friend," Paulo said. "I suggest you ride along. You," he told Gus and Roy Bob, "get this sack of *boniga* out of here or I will shoot you both as well."

"Paulo," Brauweiller said, "your ass is grass, friend. Don't be expecting any future business from me."

"I'll take the Lexus, *Senora*, if it's all right with you."

"Thank you," Lee Ann said, "that would be fine."

"I'll take either one of you sum'bitches on," said Roy Bob, "together or one at a time."

"Shut up," Brauweiller said.

Paulo's men lifted Eileen gently on a stretcher and carried her to the waiting ambulance, Lee Ann at her side. Brauweiller shook his head. Roy Bob tried to look mean.

Eileen looked at Dreamer, showed him a faraway smile. Dreamer looked at Eileen, looked at Lee Ann. Decided there was something to think about here.

Paulo waved his weapon at Gus and Roy Bob. Brauweiller waddled off toward the burning hanger, mumbling to himself. Roy Bob slung Conch on his shoulder and trailed along behind.

The ambulance screeched off in the dark, lights ablaze and sirens whining full blast.

"I wish you didn't have a weapon," Dreamer said. "I don't trust you a lot anymore."

"Might as well, *compadre*. Like the man said, my ass is grass in this town. After tonight, I haven't got a whole lot of friends, but I might have more than you.

"Besides," he said, looking past Dreamer at the glow in the night, at the char-broiled Fokkers, at the carbonized remains, "besides, I know where that Ay-rab's got your girlfriend. You might consider that..."

Diane was sure they'd been driving all night. She didn't have a watch, but it seemed like a very long time. She was shaking, and couldn't seem to stop. The smell of the pizzas made her want to throw up.

Mr. Horn wasn't talking anymore. Ever since they'd hit the man, he'd been real quiet. Diane didn't want to think about that. It scared her every time she did. The face in the window, flat against the glass, there and then suddenly gone, and the terrible sound after that.

A scrap of some cop show flickered through her head. Nanny said don't even watch that show but that's exactly what she did. The lady stepped off the curb. The bus knocked her flat.

TV shows are what it's all about. They tell us what's good and what's not. Diane figured that one out, before she was six.

"Listen," Diane said, "you better stop, I'm going to throw up."

"You listen," Horn said, "you better not. You make a mess you'll have to clean it up."

"I'm going to urp."

"Huh-unh, don't. Don't do a thing but sit still and shut up, little girl."

"My name's not little *girl,* don't you call me that again."

"Little girl."

"Stop it."

"Little girl, little girl."

"Villain! Lout! My knight will hear of you. When he does, his hounds will track you down!"

"You're nuts. That's what you are. A nutty little kid."

"I'm going to urp," Diane said. "I'm going to urp right now."

"Jesus," Horn said.

. . .

Horn had no idea where he was. He'd been too scared to look for signs. All he cared about was losing the Zulus, getting away from there fast. The little kid was right about one thing, he had to ditch the van. Ditch the van *and* the kid. That's the part she forgot. Get another car. Get home somehow, work it out from there.

Great, he thought, how do you intend to do that? The van was a break, the keys right there. That wouldn't happen again.

He passed a street sign. Something South Main. Fine, exactly the wrong side of town. About as far as you could get from Enchanted Mesa West. He was lost. He'd run down a black guy. The kid was stinking up the car. Now what, what the hell next?

The phone rang, a shrill string of bleeps that nearly lifted Horn out of his seat. Cell phone. He didn't even know it was there. Found it there between the seats, picked it up and said "hello, who's this?" didn't even think this was not the thing to do.

"Who this is, this is the guy who's van you stole, asshole. Here. Somebody wants to talk to you."

Somebody else said, "Ah, this is officer LeBack, Houston Police Department, I want you to pull over right now, give me your street address, get out of the vehicle, sir."

"--You son of a bitch, that ain't my van, I'm responsible for that, comes out of my goddamn pay--"

Horn hung up. His hands shook. Diane said, "you better do it, you better do what he said."

"Shut up," Horn said. "Get a napkin, clean yourself up."

He looked at the phone, stared at it a second and a half. Punched in a number. Heard the phone ring.

Mako Binder said, "Hey, who the fuck is this, your interrupting breakfast, pal."

"Listen," Horn said, "I need help, Mako, I'm in a kind of bind. I'm in this van--"

"You on a cell phone?"

"What? Yes, I am. I'm in this van--"

"You simple shit. Hang up. Don't use my name. Call me from somewhere else."

"Well excuse me, all right? I just got away with my life, did I fail to mention this? There's about a thousand Zulus on my tail and they--"

"You got what, what the fuck you talking about?"

"Black persons, Negro people. I hit one, that was an accident, I doubt that'll help."

"You hit a nigger in a van."

"No. *I'm* in the van, Mako, he was in the street. I didn't even see him, I--"

"You hear me? I said don't use my name."

"Mako-Mako-Mako."

"I'm hangin' up."

"No you don't, you listen to me. This is your fault. I was at that SLUTTO place, that's when they broke in. Mako, there are *children* in there, would you like to tell me what that's all about? Little kids in dumb costumes? If I'm invested in that, I want out, I don't want any part of that."

Mako breathed into the phone. "Get out of the van. Dump it somewhere. Get a fucking cab."

"Are you serious? I'm out on the highway somewhere, I'm not even in town." Horn glanced at Diane. Cupped his hand over the phone. "I can't just leave the little kid out here, she knows who I am, for Christ's sake, she--"

"What, what are you talkin' about, what kid is that?"

"The one that *followed* me, Mako, don't you listen to anything I say? She knows who I am, she lives three floors down from *me.* Can you believe that? Don't ask me how *that* happened, I don't have the faintest idea."

Mako was silent.Horn thought he was gone, but the whisper of the line was still there.

"Look at the signs, Horn. You got a sign there somewhere, what does it say?"

Horn said he didn't see a sign anywhere. Mako said wait and you will, and Horn did. Half a minute later, Horn said, "I'm on 90 A. Says if I want to turn off, I'll hit Post Oak next."

"Good. Do that. Wait right there."

"What are you going to do?"

"What do you think? You stepped in the shit, I gotta fix that."

"I appreciate it," Horn said, "I--"

Mako was gone. Horn put down the phone. He looked at Diane. Diane had rolled up in a ball and gone to sleep.

He felt the ache between his shoulders go away. He could get out of this, everything would be fine. There was no one in the world he despised more than Mako Binder. He was scared of the man half the time. But if Mako said he would handle something, then he would. Handling things, fixing things up, was what Mako Binder did best...

"Where, damn it," Dreamer said, "where *is* she, you taco-eating spic. You tell me now."

Dreamer came at Paulo with anger in his heart, with incandescent eyes, with a hostile attitude, a man clearly bent on mischief and murderous intent.

"Hold it," Paulo said, bringing his deadly Steyr-Solothurn to bear. "I am overlooking the racial slur because I know you're out of sorts. You want to get your girl? Get your gringo ass in the car and do not pull this crap on me again."

Dreamer got in. There seemed little else to do. The Lexus came to life. Paulo raced down the long runway, as if he might decide to fly. In less than a minute, he left Brauweiller and his vassals and the fiery hanger behind.

"I don't know what you're up to," Dreamer said, "right now I don't care. Wherever she is, I intend to get her back. Nepal or Shanghai, it's all the same to me. I'll go to Prague or Labrador. I'll even--"

"Houston," Paulo said.

"Huh?"

"She is right here in Houston, *compadre,* the Arab never took her out of town."

"Jesus. Where?"

"Top of The Prick. They've got three floors. Abd-el-Yusuf's been holed up there having raghead fun since he found out Fort Worth wasn't for sale."

Dreamer looked Paulo straight on. "How long you known about this? It better not be real long."

"Not before today. And don't start pushing me, *amigo.* You are pissed off, fine, but I won't put up with that."

"Hold off on the *amigo* crap. You and me aren't in love again yet. Just get us there. Fast."

Dreamer grabbed Paulo's cell phone, punched a number in.

Coolie said, "Who are you, what you want, get offa this line."

"It's me," Dreamer said.

Coolie took a breath and said, "What the fuck happen to you, where you been, man?"

"It's a real long story, I got taken against my will. Coolie, I'd be grateful if you'd take care of Junior Lewis till I can get there myself. Junior had specific plans for his journey to the afterlife. I won't go into details on the phone. You know anything at all? Tell me you've got a line on Diane."

Silence from Coolie, noise from outer space.

"Hello," Dreamer said, "you there?"

"I am *here,* man, I'm not real sure about you. What's with the afterlife shit, what we talking 'bout here? I haven't got Junior Lewis, you saying he's not with you?"

Dreamer's chest tightened in a knot. "You haven't found him? He's dead, Coolie. They killed him when they kidnapped me. Oh my God, he's just lyin' out there!"

Static, Coolie fading in and out. Coolie sounding white on the cell phone, like everybody did. You bounce off the satellite, swim back down through the sub-atomic shit. It comes out coated with an echo and a twang, with a jangle and a quack.

"I am way across town," Coolie said, drifting back in, "I'll get someone over there quick as I can. You far from there, man?"

"You won't believe this, I got to rescue another one now. This one's in the hands of a Middle East prince."

"You do this full time?"

"Not if I can help it. Let me give you this number. Keep in touch, man."

Dreamer gave him Paulo's number, hung up.

Get her back, whoever you are up there, she's just a little kid...

"I'm sorry about the girl. I know this has happened. I know nothing else. I would help you if I could."

Dreamer looked at him. "And you just found out about Cindy today? I'm going to believe you, Paulo. We'll start over with that."

In the light of passing cars, Paulo looked like a dashing Latin star, like a Gilbert Roland or an Anthony Quinn, if either of the two had been ugly and short.

"Things happen, *amigo.* I got client heavy, somewhat over my head. I have worked for the Japanese tuna people and the 'save the dolphins' bunch. I have worked for the Israelis and Iraq. Greenpeace and Exxon and Shell. Ford and GM. Castro, the CIA, and the Mob. I am in great demand, I have the very much *popularidad.* People come to Paulo because he is good, because Paulo is the best. Paulo is like a priest, he will not betray your trust."

He glanced at Dreamer then, to see if he cared to challenge that.

"This is where integrity has brought me. Honesty has put me in very deep shit. My clients often clash. I find it difficult to fairly serve everyone at once."

"I could've told you that. I did, but you were too drunk to recall."

Paulo looked hurt. "Paulo's mind is as sharp as the steel of Toledo, as sharp as the *espada* that kills the bulls. There is nothing I forget.

"I have not betrayed you in spite of what you think, Dreamer. Certainly never with intent."

"That makes it all right?"

"It pains me to tell you my phones have been bugged for some time. So have yours, *compadre.* Not every call, not all the time. Enough to do damage to us all. I am the master of the bugging trade, but to my great shame I have learned there is someone better than I."

"You got an idea who?"

"Some part of this I know. Not all. The moment I discover this treacherous act, I reverse the situation and listen in to *them.* I find out some, some I do not. One thing I learn is where they have the girl. Another thing I learn, they do *not* know about Lee Ann."

"Lee Ann. Lee Ann Brauweiller."

"*Señora* Brauweiller has been a client of mine for some time. Not an easy thing, since Gus was a valued customer as well. Since Lee Ann's sister was taken, I have done all I could to find her and bring her back."

"And you couldn't tell any of this to me. You had to leave me out in the cold."

"The shit I referred to was getting very deep."

"Uh-huh. This bugging business. Let me guess. Gus Brauweiller himself."

"Most astute, my friend. And you are at least half right, because *el gordo* is not alone in this. He is often in league with other mogul types. I expect he has even dealt with Mako Binder at times. And Halloran Horn. They all get together to fuck each other out of pennies and dimes. It gets very complicated. Sometimes, they even fuck themselves."

"And all of them--Horn, Binder and both Brauweillers are clients of yours."

"Were," Paulo sighed. "Yes, to my great sorrow this is so."

"Jesus," Dreamer said.

. . .

Paulo looked weary. As well he should, Dreamer thought. A man who has tangled himself in an impossible web should be thoroughly spent, done in and tuckered out. Greatly fatigued at best.

Driving south on 45, Dreamer studied the awesome spectacle of Houston's downtown. There were many great buildings there, but rising far above the rest was the city's tallest structure, the great Prick itself. At one hundred eleven stories, The Prick was higher than the World Trade Center's twin towers. Architect Newton Fielder Forbes didn't try to top Chicago's monument to Sears. Forbes liked Chicago, but he hated New York.

It wasn't officially The Prick, it was Brauweiller Tower. Forbes claimed the engorged upper quarter was semi-Persian with a pinch of Burmese. Even those who didn't know Gus knew better than that.

Hang on, babe, I'm coming for you, I'm on my way now...

. . .

"I would have helped you if I could. This is *not* an apology, friend, Paulo does not apologize. But I will tell you I regret not closing down the business before I did."

"I know what you regret. What you *regret* is your high wire broke and fucked up your act."

Paulo hesitated. "I see I must tell you the rest. It was Lee Ann who brought me to my senses. She is my conscience, she is my heart, *mi corazon."*

"She's your what?"

Paulo wouldn't face him, Paulo looked at the road. "You think I am foolish, and surely you are right. But I love her, Dreamer. I know she is pussy inclined, that she can never be mine. I am nothing but a straight wetback in her eyes, but I worship her all the same. When her sister was taken, I had to make a choice. Devotion to my goddess, or great financial loss."

"I can't believe I'm hearing this," Dreamer said, though he knew full well he could. He also knew this was not the moment to discuss his out-of-body lust with Lee Ann.

"Believe it. What the movies tell you is true. A Latin is a great and generous lover, but he is also a fool. I became enchanted the first time I saw her, when she came to me to squeeze her husband dry. His obsession with early aviation showed me how. A simple variation of the 'Lost Squadron' scam. A very fine con, begun by C.I. Knickerhazen of Cold Bridge, Indiana, a man who made remarkable replicas of Camels and Spads, Fokkers and Halberstadts. It is now in the hands of his great-grandsons.

"The Fokkers cost Gus around thirty million-five. Lee Ann came out with ten of that, I came out with six. Brauweiller made an ass of himself, and Lee Ann was greatly satisfied. She gave me a kiss, Dreamer. Not on the mouth, of course, I could not expect that."

Paulo caught the look on Dreamer's face. "We are *friends,* Dreamer, at least I hope we are. I have shared my whiskey and take-out Indian food with you, and now I have shared my dreams. I have also done a great deal more this day, such as saving your fucking life. I hope you appreciate that."

"I do, Paulo. And I trust you appreciate the fact that I am not yet sure that I will beat you senseless and leave you in an alley somewhere. I haven't decided yet. When I do, you'll be the first to know..."

Ahmad Alam was born in Fasa, Iran, which is south and west of Niriz, not that far from Lake Bakhtegan. He had not been home since he was twelve. He did not intend to go back. Fate had led him to the service of Abd-el-Yusuf, which, to a lad from Fasa, was a bird nest on the ground.

He did not like Houston, which was humid as a swamp, not at all like the dry desert air. What he liked, though, was working for the prince in this wonderful land of big cars, Big Macs, big and lovely girls, and the lovely Dennis Franz on TV.

At the moment, he stood on the loading dock at Brauweiller Tower, sweating in the fierce morning heat. He hated the guise of security guard, a post of great humiliation for a person of his class. Still, he would suffer through it for his prince, the Hand of God, the Lord of many Tents, Abd-el-Yusuf. If he got off at six, there would be fine bowling on the cable TV.

. . .

In spite of his discomfort, Ahmad kept his eyes on the truck unloading goods for the prince. The driver worked in a steady, orderly manner. First, he rolled out cases of Coca-Cola, Pepsi, Sprite and Mr. Pib, and set them near the freight elevator. Then he brought boxes of salted cashews, a favorite of the prince. Finally, the driver loaded several cases of 25-year-old single malt scotch--a treat contrary to Islamic law, but Abd-el-Yusuf was a law unto himself. This, Ahmad knew, was not the only deviation practiced by the prince. Deviations which included unclad cuties, breaded pork chops, and a near obsession with Barry Manilow.

All is in order, thought Ahmad, as the driver stacked his goods in the freight elevator. The prince's guards above would carefully search each case, but his job here was done.

--At least he thought it was, until the driver went back and brought another item out.

Alarms went off in Ahmad's head. This load was not like the others. This was not a case of anything, this was a very large box. A wooden box a meter square and nearly two meters tall. The box was not labeled at all--more than that, the driver seemed excessively strained as he rolled it down the dock.

Ahmad stepped into the driver's path. The driver smiled and thrust a clipboard in his face.

"You want to sign for this, *amigo?* You authorized?"

Ahmed bristled at that. "I am authorized fully to do the signing of any sort. What is this you are having in the box?"

"This box."

"Yes. Indeed this very box."

"This box here."

"Have we not established that? Are we not agreeing this is the box we are speaking about?"

"I have no idea."

"What is that?"

"I said, I have no idea. The manifest says 'box.' You want to take a look, here."

Ahmad frowned in the general direction of the form. He could not read the language of Iran, much less the squiggles written there. Besides, he did not like this man who, though his face was as dark as his own, was not of his people at all. He was surely of the Mediterranean persuasion, Italian or some other mongrel race, and likely a Christian besides.

"I ask of you again," Ahmad said, "what is being in the box?"

"And I am telling you again, I don't know what's in the box. I drive the truck, I am not responsible for the box."

"Is it possible, then," Ahmad asked, deftly sliding a hand behind his back, "that there could be an assassin in the box?"

"A what?"

"An assassin person. This is a box of adequate size to conceal such a person inside."

"There is no one in the box."

"Ah, this we shall see."

Ahmad swiftly brought his hand from his back, a hand that had slipped beneath his coat and slid a pistol from his belt. Without further word, he emptied seven rounds from the semi-silenced weapon into the wooden box, creating a pattern from left to right.

"There," Ahmad said, "if there was in the box a person, I am sure he is of little purpose now."

"Dios," the driver said, "I wish you hadn't done that."

"Now," Ahmad said, pointing the weapon directly between the driver's eyes, "we shall be opening this very box and see."

"I don't guess we will," Dreamer said, suddenly rising out of cases of scotch, which were not really cases at all. He sapped the guard solidly on the back of the neck. Ahmad rolled his eyes and sank to the elevator floor.

"Very nice," Paulo said, and spoke a single word into the button of his shirt. "I don't believe he's dead, but I doubt he'll trouble us again."

Five very short, stocky young Hispanic men, lightweight contenders from Houston, San Marcos and Chihuahua, Mexico, emerged from the truck into the elevator. All carried silenced 9mm automatics and Israeli combat knives. Without a word, they dragged Ahmad behind the many cases, and concealed themselves there.

Dreamer stepped out of his fake stack of scotch. While the guard had been intent on the decoy box, Dreamer scanned the elevator and its shaft, searching for crimson tigers and bright yellow snakes, TV monitors, lasers and gimmicks of every sort. He found a single listening device, but that was out of whack. Cost: $159.98. Disgusting, Dreamer thought. The sheik would spend eight-hundred grand on a jazzy sports car, but he bought his equipment in an alley somewhere.

Paulo looked at Dreamer. Dreamer said "Go." The elevator jerked and whined. One of Paulo's men gave him Ahmad's uniform and Paulo slipped it on.

"This weapon is a find," he told Dreamer, inspecting Ahmad's gun. "This is a Browning 7.62 automatic pistol, made in 1903 by Husqvarna in Sweden. It is the legitimate item, *amigo,* not one of the cheap, Chinese ripoffs manufactured at the time."

"Fine," Dreamer said, "I'm happy for you, man."

He watched the lights above the door. It seemed to take an hour to get up to fifty, and that was only halfway there. A queasy feeling had settled in his stomach, starting as a flutter and rising to a twitch, growing to a fist that seemed to have a good grip. It happened a lot these days, and he knew the reason why. It was fear, uncertainty, the knowledge that he was as vulnerable and naked as anyone else. That his weirdo talents were of little value here. His enemies were not electrons, tigers he could tame. They were men with large guns who would shoot him in the head, and scatter his colors everywhere.

It was the question he'd asked from the start: When's it going to be there, when's it going to quit? Terrific with locks, lasers and alarms. Bells, buzzers, traps of every sort. It let him take it easy, slip among the indigos and midnight blues, drift with the fine black souls. Kept him from the screaming bloody reds sometimes. Sent him out on Out-of-Body fun.

Didn't warn him what would happen to Cindy and Diane. Didn't bother to mention Roy Bob and Conch. Showed him the phantom Fokker, all right—didn't tell him he and Eileen would try to murder each other in the early morning light. Dreamer knew he wasn't Mama Lucy, didn't want to be. Thought it would be nice if the goddamn pellet in his head would give him a clue sometimes.

"You okay?" Paulo said, "you all right, man?"

"I'm fine," Dreamer said. "Fine as I can be."

"Good. I am pleased to hear this. I suggest you stay down low. Let us handle this."

"I can help out, I don't have to hide."

"I am not concerned with your courage. I don't want you in the way."

"Oh."

Dreamer looked at the elevator ceiling, trying to imagine what they'd find.

"You know what the guy was playing, I talked to on the phone? Zamfir, for Christ's sake. You believe that? This is Coolie I'm talking to, the dude's *black.*"

"I would believe most anything today," Paulo said, "even that..."

103...

104...

105...

Dreamer waited, crouched behind a case of Mr. Pib. The young man beside him had a fighter's scar above his eyes. He looked at Dreamer and grinned.

"No problema," he said, and Dreamer wasn't sure about that.

Paulo stood with his back to the door. Ahmad's uniform was long and the sleeves were too short. Paulo didn't seem to mind.

106...

107...

108...

There were locks on the three floors above. Locks on safes, locks on cabinets and doors. There were faxes, phones and intruder alarms. TVs, radios and VCRs. They were all still there, but Dreamer had given them a sedative and put them all to bed.

The elevator doors slid apart. Three men in Nikes and bedouin wear. Rolex watches and AR-15s.

"Ahmad?" said one, followed by gabble no one understood.

Paulo turned, sprayed them with his sub-machine gun. The weapon made little sound at all. The three slammed back against the wall. Paulo's men flowed into the corridor, three to the left, two after Paulo to the right. Dreamer remembered why he'd always felt safer in the air—at least until the shitstorm over banana-land.

He followed the sound of gunfire to his right. Everyone's weapon went *phhht! phhht! phhht!* No one made a lot of noise. Paulo's gunmen and the Arabs were polite.

The hallway was scattered with canned goods, cookies, video tapes and Hershey bars. Coffee beans and tins of sardines. Russian hand grenades and Tanquery gin.

One of the sheik's men was sprawled on the floor. Dreamer stepped over him, smelled something good. Possibly mutton, heavy with spice. He stuck his head through a door. Lead plunked the wall and stung his eyes.

"Idiota!" Paulo grabbed his legs and pulled him down. Bullets peppered the wall again. Dreamer saw they were in a large kitchen, up against a refrigerator door.

"You want to get killed, do it somewhere else. I thought you'd been in war before."

"We never flew as low as this."

Paulo raised up and loosed a volley. Ducked his head again.

The weapon shuddered and brass flew everywhere. Pots and pans clattered. Someone fired back. Dreamer and Paulo were covered in a black and gooey mess.

Paulo wiped a finger on his shirt, stuck it in his mouth.

"Perdicion! That's caviar. The very best beluga. That son of a bitch is a barbarian."

Paulo tossed an empty clip aside, loaded up again. Before he could fire, a whistle came from across the room.

"Miguel's got him. We're clear."

Dreamer followed. The kitchen had become a war zone. The floor was slippery with food and broken glass. Red sauce and pasta dripped from the walls.

Paulo was in a huddle with Miguel. Dreamer saw the man who'd murdered fine caviar. He was silent, paying for his sins.

"This floor's secure," Paulo said. "Chavez and Bruto have got the stairwell. We're heading up to one-ten."

"You think they've got Cindy there?"

"No. The big shot always takes the whole top floor. There's a private elevator, but you took care of that."

Paulo showed him a knowing smile. "You have many cute tricks, my friend. It is kind of you to share them with us now."

"*No problema*," Dreamer said, and didn't add anything to that.

"Stay close. These people are *loco.* We're going to have to take them down." He caught Dreamer's look. "You got another way, let's hear it now."

"I'm just thinking about her. When we start up there."

"Don't," Paulo said. "Thinking will get you dead here."

. . .

One-ten was thick with cordite, enough to sting the throat. Chavez, Bruto and a skinny boxer named Cubano had cleared the way, leaving havoc in their wake. The floors here were marble and the walls were watered silk. Now there were chips in the floor and the walls were stitched with lead.

There was little left to do. Paulo's men had struck with fury and surprise, everyone had fled. They were making their stand on the very top floor, and there was nowhere to go after that.

A boy named Carlos had been grazed in the head. His brother, Benito, tried to help. Carlos shrugged him off, saying his wife could shoot straighter than that.

It was clear that one-ten had been a barracks, playroom, brothel, sandbox and sports arena for Abd-el-Yusuf's men. In a very short time, they had turned the place into a sewer. Girlie pictures on the walls. Cook fires on the marble floors. A dozen dead chickens hanging from a crystal chandelier.

For a moment, after the floor was secured, female screams caused some alarm. Then Bruto found a covey of harlots locked in a closet by the stairs. Bruto wanted to call a break, Paulo said absolutely no.

"The rest of this could get a little hairy," Paulo said. "Depends on whether these *zonzos* care to die for the cause."

Dreamer shook his head. "There are facets to your character I hadn't imagined before. The wizard of finance runs a small army on the side. No wonder you've got such terrific business clout."

"I take great offense," Paulo said. "Your words are an affront. A man likes to keep his facets to himself. You will remember this, if it should come to mind again."

They had blocked the doors at the top of the stairs, and piled up stacks of antiques. A dab of plastique took care of that. The door had been built for privacy, not to keep invaders out. The prince had not expected a siege of contenders from Austin, Lubbock and Veracruz. It's hard to anticipate a thing like that.

Dreamer followed Paulo, weaving through the shattered and the broken and the cracked, 18th-century chairs from France, Czarist pornography and Degas pastels. Slipping through the chipped and the splintered and the smashed. Chinese art and Federal beds. Baccarat crystal and Turkish comic books. And all the while *phhht! phhht! phhht!* from the bullets overhead.

Cindy, Cindy, hang on...Dreamer's coming, babe!

A shout from Carlos, a warning from somebody else. Arabs streamed through a door no one had checked out. Paulo's men beat a hasty retreat. Dreamer sprawled behind a genuine Colonial chest. Bullets chunked pioneer wood, saving Dreamer's ass.

Paulo rattled something in Spanish, *"Despues de banarme, halle que tenia un calcetin!"* After bathing, I found that I had one sock!

Dreamer was certain he'd said something else, but he couldn't tell what. He answered with a cry of *"Rabano! cebolla! Carne de puerco,* men!"

His words seemed to rally the troops. Everyone shouted, and drove the Arabs back.

Paulo kicked in a door and sprayed the place with lead. A Florentine mirror vanished in a million shards of glass. Dreamer paused to look. It was a lavish bedroom, done in lavender and red.

Someone cried out. Dreamer raced down the hall. Bruto was down, writhing and jerking about. Blood ran down his sleeve.

Dreamer tore a piece of Bruto's shirt, wadded it up and pressed it against the wound.

"Hold that. Tight. You'll be all right. *Bueno?* Uh, no *usted hurto* too much?"

"Por nada," Bruto said, "I'm cool, man."

Dreamer nodded and grabbed up Bruto's weapon. Cautiously, he peered around the corner. A long hallway. Three or four doors. No one in sight, but someone had brought Bruto down.

A marble-top table stood just across the hall. The legs were exquisitely carved, ending in the fierce claws of lions. Dreamer risked another look, then dashed for the other side.

The Arab appeared out of nowhere at all. Short and very dark. Lime-colored suit, blue shirt and tie. No shoes or socks. He held the little shotgun tight against his waist. Didn't shoot at once. Stopped to look at Dreamer, caught in the middle of the hall. Paused to slick his hair. Paused to give a chill desert yell.

Instead of being dead, Dreamer had ample time to fire. He squeezed the trigger twice. Missed both times. The Arab stared at Dreamer, clearly petrified. Dreamer fired and missed again. The Arab dropped his weapon and fled. Dreamer fired and this time he hit. A bullet creased the man's butt. He stumbled and howled, scrambled through a door.

Dreamer picked up the shotgun and made his quickly down the hall.

Someone ripped off a clip. For the most part it was quiet. Four doors ahead, two things to do: Stay under cover, wait for the rest. Or take a chance on the doors.

"El Fucko," Dreamer said, "let's get it over with."

Two steps to the door. Carefully turn the knob, push it open quickly with the gun. A big hand slammed him in the chest, jerked the weapon from his grasp.

Dreamer stumbled back fast. The man was the largest, possibly the ugliest, human he'd had ever seen. He was bald and he was mean. All he wore was a dirty jock strap and a bad attitude. He danced toward Dreamer on tiny little feet, massive fists flailing at the air.

"Shitto," Dreamer said, and turned around and ran.

The giant was faster than light. He grabbed Dreamer's collar, picked him off the floor and threw him at the wall.

Dreamer tasted blood, knew his nose was flat. Tried to move, too late for that. A big hand lifted him again, held him up close. An awesome view of warts. Tooth decay and zits. Extremely bad breath. Dreamer knew the man was eating snakes.

Everything began to go red. One second, two, he'd be out of it for good. Found a hand that worked. Made a paralytic fist, rammed it up the giant's nose.

The monster roared, shook Dreamer hard and tossed him to the ground. Dreamer didn't wait for pain, knew he didn't have the time. Dodged past a big sequoia leg, went for the shotgun just inside the door. Grabbed it, slid on his back, turned around and fired.

The 12-gauge jerked and made a lot of noise. The giant stared at his hand. Two fingers left, the rest was burger meat. Blood fountained like a Pepsi opened in the sun. The man poked his hand into his gut, cutting off the flow in an ample roll of fat. Dreamer fired again. The shotgun went *chink!* but nothing came out.

The big man laughed. In spite of his shattered hand, he came at Dreamer fast. Dreamer was running out of hall. He bolted for a door but the giant had figured that. He took one step, used his hammer like a fist, nailed Dreamer's head.

Picked him up, held him close. The breath went out of Dreamer's lungs. His head filled with pink and purple glass.

Two seconds, three, then **ZAP!***you're done for, pal... just do it, man, even if you hate it, do it right now...*

The giant began to howl. Dreamer held on, though his hand was horrified. His hand didn't care, his hand wasn't bound by any moral law.

Something broke, something squished, something crunched with a terrible sound. The giant squealed, grabbed his crotch, rolled his eyes and did a header to the ground.

Dreamer gasped for breath. Stared in wonder at his hand. Knew he could never ever use it, never get it clean again.

To his left, bare feet stuck out of the door. The feet were attached to a lime-green suit. The man was breathing softly, a bloody crease across his ass. Dreamer leaned down and reached beneath the lime coat. Came up with a .32 Beretta Brevet, chrome finish, 1953.

Everything was quiet. He checked behind him once. Looked in the door to his right. Empty, no one there at all. Opened the door to his left. The room was full of broad-tailed sheep, *Ovis laticauda,* he recalled, a common variety found in Egypt and many Asian lands.

Abn-el-Yusuf was crouched on a red velvet bed, his back against the wall. Spike heels, fishnet hose. White tennis dress.

"You cannot be harming my person," he said, "I am diplomat."

"Anyone can see that," Dreamer said. "Get down from there. Where's Cindy? Goddamn you, don't fool with me."

The prince gave him a look of contempt. "You will call my embassy. I am diplomat. I am to be treated with respect."

"You got it," Dreamer said. He took careful aim, and shot the prince in the foot.

Abn-el-Yusuf tumbled to the floor, grabbed his foot and howled.

"What you are," Dreamer said, "you're a ruthless, greedy, camel-breath son of a bitch. I don't like you at all. Talk to me nice or I'll shoot you in the head. *Where is Cindy, you fuckin' freak!"*

Paulo, Carlos and Miguel appeared in the doorway, weapons sweeping the room.

"*Jefe*," Carlos said, there are *oveja* everywhere."

"Paulo, kindly get out," Dreamer said, "I am having a discussion in here."

"Miguel, do not harm the creatures," Paulo said. "Animals are not responsible for their acts. *Dios,* this is not a pretty sight. I would not care to guess what may have occurred in here. Carlos, leave something for the authorities to find. The Klan, the Israelis, you pick. Get the live ones out. All except this *insecto,* he will stay here."

With scarcely a glance at the prince, Paulo emptied half a clip in the man. Abn-el-Yusuf twitched and lay still.

"Aw, shit, man." Dreamer stared at Paulo. "You crazy bastard, I want Cindy back, I don't want him!"

"I have saved you the dishonor of talking to him, *amigo.* The girl is safe, she has not been harmed."

"Why the hell didn't you say so?"

"I cannot think of everything at once."

Carlos nodded at Dreamer. Dreamer followed, sprinting down the ruined hallway, past the fallen giant, past the scattered bones of antiques. Carlos led him to a dead-end hall. Opened a door and stepped aside.

Dreamer walked in. A small bedroom. A single bed, a dresser and a chair. A bathroom off to one side. A tray of food untouched. Coffee, half a donut. Dreamer picked up a bathtowel from the bed. He could smell her, the spice of her flesh, the scent of her hair. He could feel her very presence, he could almost touch her hand.

Dreamer turned on Carlos. "What is this, where is she, man!"

Carlos blinked. "She is here, where you are standing, only a moment ago, *señor.* I do not know what—"

Dreamer turned and ran. Checked every room on the floor. Started down the stairs, stopped at the elevator. Stared at the numbers going down.

99...

98...

97...

96...

He pulled out his cell phone, punched in Coolie's number.

"Uhuh, what?" Coolie said.

"Anything? Anything at all on Diane?"

Nothing, man. And Junior Lewis isn't where you said. If that dude's dead, someone come and hauled him off."

Dreamer felt a lump of ice in his chest. "Where are you, I'll be right there."

Coolie told him, and Dreamer rang off.

He could go after Cindy, try every floor, try and track her down. But he knew she wouldn't be there, knew he wouldn't find her, knew that she was gone...

"What are we supposed to be doing," Diane said, "I don't see *anything* here."

"Just walk around, don't go anywhere," Horn said, "We'll be here a while."

"What for?"

"Because I said so. Don't start asking a bunch of dumb questions, little girl."

"Don't call me little—"

"Shut up, okay? Go sit in the van."

"Well excuse *me.* What'd *I* do?"

"Go on, get inside."

"It's smelly urp in there."

"Well who the hell is responsible for that?"

Diane didn't answer. She walked a few feet down the road. Stayed in the center, not on the side. There were dead weeds there, and weeds meant snakes. Outside in the summer, snakes are everywhere. One of her nannies said that. Alicia Fern, the one who was black, the only one she liked at all. She wished she was with Alicia now, instead of on a scary road with Mr. Horn.

She'd liked him some at the start. Not really, not a lot, but she sure didn't like him any now. Didn't like *any*one who got all crabby and cross, and that's what Mr. Horn did. He was real irritated, like grownups get. He'd started being mean when he talked on the phone. When she looked at him now, he'd look the other way. It gave her the jitters when he started doing that.

The access road was hot from the merciless sun. The heat came up through her shoes. It was late and there weren't a lot of cars. Now and then a semi strained up the interstate, the sound whining high then howling back down.

Dreamer, Dreamer, my beautiful knight...you're late, my love, come and get me out of here—

"Little girl..."

"Whuuu-huh!"

Diane nearly jumped out of her skin. When she turned he wasn't half an inch away. Squatting down, his face next to hers, man-sweat, bad breath, a dusty kind of mouse-in-the-attic kind of smell that she didn't like at all.

"You *scared* me, you creep, don't ever do that."

"I'm sorry, I didn't mean to. I just wanted to, you know, kind of talk."

"Talk about what?"

"I never did anything bad to you, little girl, did I? I wouldn't, I wouldn't ever do that."

"You better not. I have noble friends at court. You do me harm, your arse will be in a sling."

"See, that's just it. I *wouldn't* do anything. I'm—I think, a basically decent person. I'm a businessman. I have a company that does a lot of science things, you're too young to understand that. I have a wife, she's a very nice lady, you'd like her a lot. Very lovely, not too bright. I think I—I'm sorry, where was I? Yes. All this—all these *events* that have somehow happened tonight, I don't know what it's all about. I know that—because of our convergence, our encounter, so to speak, certain things have to be—fixed. Personally, I don't see that. I don't see why we can't just..."

Horn seemed to run down. His face looked awful. White as milk in the middle of the night, moon on the bedroom wall. He seemed to get smaller, sag like a rag-tag worn out clown that you wound up with a key. He smelled just awful, like a sick old aunt. Looked so bad that he scared her half to death.

"What, may I ask, is the *matter* with you," Diane said, backing away, one step then another, as far as she could go. "I want to leave, Mr. Horn, I want to go home right now."

"That's the, uh, thing," Horn said, "that's what I wanted to say. I'm going to walk up the road for a minute, you stay here."

Diane went cold. "Huh-unh, you can't leave me here."

"Just stay right there, don't follow me," Horn said, walking the other way. "Someone'll come in just a little while, little girl, now you go with him."

"What? What are you *talking* about? I don't want to go wi—"

"Someone's already here..." someone said.

Diane screamed. Someone came at her, someone picked her up, held her in the air. Too fast to see him, too quick to tell. Then someone was gone, and she was on the ground again, down on the warm asphalt, down in the middle of the road. Something frightful was happening, something very bad, something too terrible to hear. She clapped her hands very tightly to her ears, but that didn't help, and the sound was still there.

She shouted as loud as she could, prayed that when the someone finally got to her, she wouldn't even hear it, she wouldn't hear anything at all...

Nothing pisses Mako off more than changing stuff around. Mako likes a little starch in his shirts. A little, that's it. He don't like a lot. You make an egg sandwich, you got to put pepper in twice. Some of the pepper floats off in the grease, so you got to do it twice.

What he doesn't like most is being out of town. Being out of town is a pain in the ass. Your pillow's not right. You got some bimbo don't know what you like. Still, it's what you got to do sometimes. A lot of shit is going down, you don't want to be around.

Mako figures he isn't doing bad, considering the mess everything got in. All he's been doing for three weeks now is putting out fires, cleaning up everybody's crap, keeping his bidness intact.

One thing that's going okay is the Brauweiller deal. Gus's wife is pissed because Gus gave her sister away, she's taking him for everything he's got. Gus is fighting back, but he's lost a lot of heart since his toys burned up.

Mako's playing wait and see. When a cow like Brauweiller, Inc. goes belly up, there's plenty of ways to pick the carcass clean. What Gus and Lee Ann don't know, they got no way to find out, is Mako's stolen a chunk of the company already through phony deals without putting in a cent. This is because Mako follows the Family Bidness Rule Number Six: The best way to fuck somebody is start at the top and work down. Which is why Mako came to an understanding, some time ago, with a couple of big ticket lawyers work for Gus. One has a serious problem with any drug that's white. The other collects gym suits from Czech hockey teams.

Mako is glad to see Gus go down. Gus is a stubborn son of a bitch. Mako tells him something, Gus does something else. Mako says, "that's a bad idea. Don't give the ay-rab your sister-in-law, give him somebody else." So what does Gus do?

Then Mako says, "You got Dreamer on your ass. Here's how to get him off. Tell him you'll fight him a duel up there. He wins, he gets the chick back. Send some dummy up there to shoot him down."

Great. Gus sends up this hot-shot lawyer who is fucking Dreamer, who is also, by the way, sometimes fucking Gus's wife. Mako doesn't like this at all. He bought the firm where Eileen works, and figured he could use her sometime. So Dreamer shoots *her* down instead, and now he's really pissed off.

It doesn't help Mako's attitude he finds out Roy Bob and Conch, bozos work for Gus that Mako's paying off too, they're the ones pick up Dreamer, they don't bother to pass this shit along.

Halloran Horn is something else. Mako gets nervous when he thinks about Horn. The SLUTTO setup was fine. He knew Horn would show up sometime, he'd get some shots the guy wouldn't want to share with anyone, especially Mrs. Horn. So Mako puts the SLUTTO babe in a spare room at Lease-a-Tot. Hey, you got a room, why waste it? You get a shot of Horn, close the place down.

Meanwhile, Mako's holding the little girl with the Lease-a-Tot kids. As soon as he finds out the kid knows Dreamer, he sends a guy out to bring her in. Mako's got the kid, he figures Dreamer will tell him how he gets in and out of places no one else can do. This is insurance. Mako likes insurance a lot.

So who's going to figure, in a thousand years, Dreamer and a bunch of niggers are going to *find* the place while Horn is there humping the help? What are the odds on that?

On top of all that, where's Horn and the kid? Mako takes time to drive out and save the guy's ass, do what has to be done which Horn can't possibly do. And when he gets there, somebody's been there first. The van's not there, and somebody lost a little blood. Horn or the kid or maybe both. What's *that* all about? You got a serial nut, he beats you there and does them both in?

Mako doesn't want to know. He doesn't wait to find out. He's got a couple lawyers in the firm handles Horn Life Engineering, Inc. One of them drinks, the other's married to a goat, something like that. It isn't any trouble to find a body that's a little like Horn, some guy in a wreck. Add some ID. The widow Amy Horn is dense, but she's vaguely aware that she's rich, and the flow of recreational drugs hasn't really slowed a bit.

Mako can now take a bigger bite out of Horn Life Engineering, Inc. Get the science guys back on the Product again, which Horn never did.

With new financial clout from Brauweiller and Horn, Mako figures he can take on anyone now. Including those fucks in Miami and New York, who think he's getting too big for the Family and would like knock him off.

There's only one thing he's got to do, one loose end to tie up, everything will be fine. He knows Dreamer's trying to find him. He knows the guy won't give up until he takes Mako down. Dreamer's not going to forget about the kid. He doesn't even know that Mako, in a way, had a hand in messing with the other broads as well. What he's gotta do is take Dreamer out, get him off his back. This is what he's got to handle now.

. . .

What he'd like to do is forget the whole thing for a while and get some sleep. It's late and he hasn't been to bed. His eyes are hurting and the whiskey doesn't help. He hasn't got—what, a couple hours in three fucking weeks.

A lot of shit's been going down, but that isn't all, and he can't tell anyone that. He can't go to sleep because every time he tries there's an old nigger lady in his head. He closes his eyes, there she is. She's screaming, she's yakking all the time, she's spouting from the bible, she's driving him nuts.

And, if he can't tell anyone *that,* he sure can't tell them she's not just there when he tries to go to sleep. That he's starting to smell dead flies and barbecue, starting to see her when he's still awake...

"I bet I said it a hundred times," said Betty the Crush. "Someone ask me, girlfriend, what's more fun than stickin' your tits in a fan? I say, what it is, you sit in a car in a alley somewhere? Want to make sure it's a hundred an' ten, want to be sure you got the A/C off. *Gotta* make sure you got some gnats. Don't get a date goin' to take you out to dinner somewhere. Get some fucker won't let you do nothin', won't even let you *smoke.* Fucker don't want to be touching your parts, sure don't want you touching his. Man, that is what *I* call fun."

"Will you hush?" Asher said. "We're not going to be here long, just try and hold it down."

"That's what you saying last night."

"All right."

"Night before that..."

"Well I am saying it again, all right? You gotta understand this here is official business, hon. Business isn't fun. Most of the time, business is stuff like this."

"Maybe your business isn't. Mine is."

Betty crossed her legs, a motion that sounded like satin and silk, like a whisper, like a sigh. Avery Asher felt a chill. She could do that to him, shake him up at will. Anytime she moved, anytime she caught his eye, Avery felt he was eighty years old, either that or twenty-one.

He was truly smitten, taken with her charms. Betty was the fever in his soul, Betty was his passion and desire. And, if he died, if he croaked, in the fury of her love sometime, that was just fine, that was how he'd like to go.

The only thing he wished she wouldn't do, something that she did without meaning any harm, was remind him that she did enjoy the business she was in. Even though Asher wasn't paying anymore—they'd gotten past that—she still had a horde, a throng, a multitude, of clients eager to test their mettle against the legend of Betty the Crush.

"What the hell the matter with you?" Betty said, the one time he'd dared to bring it up. "Business is business. My social life is somethin' else."

Asher knew he could never see it like that, not the way he loved her, not the way he cared. Still, he never brought it up again, and kept his misery to himself.

. . .

"You could tell me what we're doing here, hon. Long as we got to do it, don't see the harm in that."

"I told you," Asher said, "If I knew, then I would. I don't know if it's anything at all."

"Uhuh. We're sweatin' like pigs, you don't know why."

"That's right."

"Can't even have a cigarette, keep the bugs off."

"I'd like to have one too."

"You got any problem with a mint?"

"With a what?"

"Can I eat a Lifesaver, hon? I got half a pack here. Isn't any New York Strip comes out on a iron plate, sizzlin' with butter on top. Boy comes around says 'you care for fresh ground pepper, ma'am? You want some hot bread?' Know I'm not about to get that, sittin' out here in your fuckin' sweat lodge, so I'm thinking mint. I'm partial to the cherry and the orange. I'd save the limes for you. If that isn't breakin' any rules, babe."

"Thanks," Asher said, "that helps, that really helps a lot."

Betty sighed. "I'm sorry, love, I keep forgetting myself. I'm not a law enforcement officer, I haven't had all the training like you. I can't sit around do nothin' all the time."

"Just try. I promise we'll go in a while, just try."

Betty tried. She was still for a minute and a half. "You want me to do something, babe? Something maybe ease your tension, take off the strain? At the same time keepin' real quiet, you don't have to get up or do a thing..."

"Jesus, Betty!"

He slapped at his leg like a bug was in his pants. His pulse shot up to one-twenty-two.

"You know I can't do that and do something else too. Two things at once, that doesn't work for me."

"Works for me, hon."

"Well I'm not you. I'm just a plain ol—" Asher stopped, squeezed her hand and let it go. "Goddamn, what's that?"

Something moved by the big pecan tree, the one at the side of the house. Moved, slid out of sight. In spite of the bright lights Dreamer had ringed around the house, whoever was there managed to stay under cover somehow. Whoever was there was damn good. Avery Asher had only caught a piece of him twice.

"Stay here," Asher said, "stay cool and don't get out."

Betty stared, nodded 'okay.' She didn't have anything to say this time.

Asher got his Sig-Sauer from under the seat and slipped out of the car. The door lights were permanently taped, he never had to think about that.

He squatted low and started through the trees. It was times like this when he knew he was truly getting old. This, and other combat situations, like a nooner with Betty, or the special at Juan's.

Asher waited, Asher didn't move. Whoever was there was good at waiting too. The intruder had the advantage. Somehow, he'd managed to get very close to the house without being spotted, slipping through the harsh cone of lights. Asher had to stay where he was, hidden in the dark at the back of the yard. If he stood up now, the prowler would spot him. A goddamn overweight deer, standing in the middle of the road. And half a second after that—

"Shit!" Asher gave a start, like the man had somehow looked inside his head, listened to his thoughts. Something went *phhhht! phhhht! phhhht!* quick as that, and Asher knew at once what it was. He had a suppressor just like it himself. The soft sound of glass followed that. Then all three lights at the back of the house went out, leaving Asher, and whoever else was there, in the tree-shrouded dark...

"I do not care for this," Eileen said. "If I'm going to be a paralyzed lawyer, I can do it fine at home."

"You're not paralyzed," Dreamer told her, "quit saying that. You're out of action for a while. You are dancing impaired."

"I'm a bitch who can't walk, hon. Don't you tell me what I am."

"Well you quit saying what you're not. Couple months you'll be on your feet again. Dr. Watters—"

"Dreamer? Will you look at me?"

Eileen wheeled around to face him. Two little stitches at the corner of her mouth. When she crashed, the goggles struck her face, leaving raccoon rings around her eyes.

"Every time I say something, you turn away. Stop, I mean it now."

"I'm stopped."

"You're stopped, you're not looking, you got to do that too."

"Okay."

"All right. I don't want to be here. I don't want to be at *your* place, I want to be at mine. I want to be *home.* Is there some way I can make that clear?"

"You need to be here."

"I *need* to be home!"

"You need someone to do stuff for you. While you're in the chair."

"They got nurses for that. They're better at it than you."

"I don't think you understand," Dreamer said. "There's chivalry involved, I got to think of that. When a flyer downs a foe, he's honor-bound to help, get 'em back on their feet. That's the airman's code."

"Jesus." Eileen wheeled a little closer. Dreamer had to back off. "Pardon me for asking, is there something else here? Like something of a personal nature? If that's what you're doing, just quit. I believe our relationship, what there was of it, has really turned to shit."

"I wouldn't say it's bad as that."

"I would."

"We used to like each other fine. Maybe I'm harking back to that."

"Harking back. That *is* what this is all about, then? You are harking back? Goddamn it, Dreamer, don't. I cannot handle harking, I cannot handle this..."

She quickly turned away. But not before he saw her, not before her eyes began to blur, not before her mouth got that funny little twitch.

He didn't know what to do then, didn't know what to say. He said, "Listen, you want another drink?"

"No."

"I think I might," he said.

"Good. You do that."

He took his drink, which he didn't want at all, walked to the window, pulled the curtains slightly aside, peered out at the night. After everything that happened—Junior, Cindy, Diane, Eileen, God, what else, the Arabs and the Brauweiller mess—he'd put in some outside lights. It looked like a Federal pen around the house. Not a pleasant summer night, more like a mall somewhere. It pissed him off that he had to do that. It wasn't over, wouldn't ever be, not until he found the bastard, not until it was done. He wasn't any closer than he was at the start, and the strain was beginning to tell. Maybe no one else saw it, but Dreamer could feel it, knew it was there.

. . .

They were in the little entry off the shop. A couch and a table with old magazines. The fish motors hummed, and the bubbles did their Lawrence Welk act. He missed having Dinh. Not that he ever did anything, but at least he was there.

He'd set up a room he never used downstairs. A room that they used to call a parlor, when parlors were in. Downstairs, because Eileen was in the wheelchair and couldn't go up.

He glanced back at her across the room. She'd changed her mind, fixed another drink. He didn't know what else to say. What he'd said was true. They'd liked each other, they'd been pretty close. What was wrong with that?

When they let her out of the hospital, she'd been too weak to complain. As a matter of fact, she'd been real nice. He really liked that. Taking care of her, bringing her soup. Eileen sleeping a lot, not talking back. Now, she was getting her strength back. Acting like Eileen again.

Eileen was Eileen, but Dreamer didn't feel like himself anymore. Not some*body* else, not like that, just not exactly him. A Dreamer that didn't feel right, a Dreamer that didn't fit.

It wasn't the little piece of tin and the colors that shifted through his head. All that was still there, still out of whack sometimes, like a TV that's got a bad wire. Sometimes it works. Sometimes it doesn't do shit.

What it was, he knew, was something down deep, something inside. Something way down in the cellar, behind the other crap. It's always hard to look at that stuff, because the one that's looking is you. How can you trust somebody you know as well as that?

He looked at Eileen. Eileen was still holding her drink, still looking at the wall. He didn't say a thing, but she knew he was there.

"I think I've given too much of myself. I think I ought to slow down."

"I think that's a good idea," Dreamer said.

"Lee Ann wants me to go with her to France."

Dreamer was glad she couldn't see him, glad she was looking the other way.

"You think you will?"

"Well I can't do a whole lot now, can I? Not till I get out of this chair."

She wheeled around then, not looking at him, looking at her hands, looking at her glass.

"This isn't your business, Dreamer, I'm not bringing it up because it is. I'm just saying, that wasn't any big thing, me and Lee Ann. It was more like friends. Lee Ann's good people. She's a real nice person's what she is."

"I know she is."

"You don't even know her."

"She was at the airport, Eileen. I've seen her at the hospital since."

Eileen nodded, looked at him then. "Anyway, I don't know why I'm talking to you about this. It wouldn't make any difference if I did go off to France."

"Is that a question, you asking me that?"

Eileen looked annoyed. "It isn't anything. I just said, is all."

"What I think you ought to do is what's best for you. I wouldn't know what that is. I don't know what *I'm* doing, what I'm going to do. My lifestyle's been slightly askew, I don't have to tell you that. Everything that's happened to everyone I know. Junior and Diane. Cindy. You and I coming close to killing each other, for Christ's sake. Losing Mama Lucy on top of all that."

Eileen's face softened. "She was a very old lady, Dreamer. I know her passing hurt you something awful, but she had a good life. You think about that."

Dreamer didn't answer. People you love go and die, that's a personal affront. All the platitudes won't bring them back. He thought about Mama Lucy, wondered where she was right now. Maybe she was having ribs with Moses. Drinking a Nehi with Martin Luther King. Maybe she was fixing Jesus fries and onion rings.

He looked at Eileen. She still slept a lot and she'd dozed off in her chair. He went over quietly and took away her drink. She looked real fine, just the way she ought to be. Like everyone else, newborns and oldsters, devils and saints, sleep faded every waking role, stripped all the masks away.

"I hope you change your mind about France," he told her. "Lee Ann's a good person, I like her a lot. But I don't want you and her doing that. What I'd like, is you keep doing that kind of stuff with me. Whether we irritate each other or not, we don't all the time. You ought to think about that. Sometimes we do all right, even when we're standing up."

He couldn't think of anything else. He didn't know how he felt or what, couldn't take it any further than that. He knew, though, if she wanted to go home tomorrow, he'd think of some way to make her stay. The same as he'd tried to do today.

He was standing looking at her, getting sleepy himself. The knock on the door was very light, hardly a touch, but it brought him up at once. The clock said after five. Too late for night, too early for morning to come. He looked through the door and then opened it quick, his heart nearly coming to a stop.

"Hi there, hon," Cindy said, "I hope I didn't get you up..."

Dreamer stared for a moment, then laughed, ran and took her in his arms, kissed her, held her tight.

"God, I been worried sick. What happened, where you been? Why'd you run off like that?"

He held her away, then brought her to him again. She rested her head on his chest.

"How'd you get here," he said, looking past her, "where's your car?"

"I parked up the street, Dreamer. She hesitated, drew away a little, looked at the ground. "I'm not staying, love. I'm kinda moving on."

"Cindy—?"

She stopped him with a finger to his lips. "Listen to me, okay? This is real hard, but you've got to understand. You and me are bound to each other. We got a cosmic link and it can't be broke, we're paired in sweet eternal bliss. The only thing is, it's not for *now,* hon. We're just not ready, that's for another time. I can't say when, that's not for us to comprehend. All I know is the Fates, in their ever mysterious ways, some day they're going to step in, then you and me..."

"Yeah, I know," Dreamer said, startled, possibly dazed, possibly stunned to hear the words come out, surprised that they came out of *him,* and, an instant after that, not surprised at all.

Cindy drew a little breath. Looked at Dreamer, looked at him again with silver angel eyes, looked deep and deeper still. Then, with no warning at all, broke into a laugh so sweet, so absolutely fine.

"Oh, Dreamer, you *do* know, don't you," she said, holding him close, squeezing him tight. "You know, I can tell. I'm so very, very glad, I never, ever wanted to break your heart."

"Yeah," Dreamer said, still lost in her eyes, "I guess I do. I didn't know I did."

And Dreamer truly did. Knew his ache and his wonder and his need was a package so pretty you didn't want to open it at all, a package you could open too late or too soon, and lose whatever's inside. And, if he'd thought about cosmic links instead of cheerleader thighs and silver angel eyes, he would've known the two of them really didn't fit, might sometime, but not yet.

"You going to be all right," Cindy said, "you okay with this?"

"I'm fine," Dreamer said. "I'm still a little dizzy is all. Where do you get all this? Jesus fax you or what?"

"Mama Lucy did."

"When was all this? Before or after she joined up with the hereafter gang? Cindy, I can't keep up with your angel routine. I don't know how you work things out."

"I don't think that's what I am," she said.

"You don't think. You don't know?"

Cindy looked past him. "I've got to go, love, I really do."

"You, going to be—you know, what you were doing, you going back to that?"

"You mean hook? Oh my no, I don't have to do *that* anymore. I'm thinking science this time. That quantum stuff has a lot of appeal."

She came up on her toes, wound her arms around his neck, kissed him soundly on the mouth. Stepped back and smiled, walked off in the trees.

"You and me and this bliss," he said, "when you figure that'll be?"

She was gone, then, lost in the dark. Softness still pressed against his chest. The scent of her hair still lingered in the night.

She was absolutely right. He'd loved her forever. Loved her a minute and a half. It was over and done. And, with any luck at all, they could start all over, do it all again...

Asher moved quickly, blinded by the change from light to dark. Didn't even try to be quiet. He was fifty-two, tipping in at three-oh-eight. The guy had to know he was there, fuck him if he couldn't take a joke.

Asher stopped. Went to his knees, weapon out stiff in both hands, supercop stance. He was getting used to the dark. Light reflected from the city through the trees, lights from the front, dimly outlining the house.

His heart slammed hard against his chest. The bozo out there, every squirrel on the block, could hear him gasping for breath.

Okay, asshole, here I am, take your best shot...

Nothing. Not a motion, not a sound. Someone walked up the street, got in a car and drove off. Avery didn't look at his watch. Guessed it was half past five. Daylight in an hour and half. All this shit would be over by then. Maybe he'd be having breakfast with Betty, maybe not.

Somebody moved, somebody slipped through the shadows by the house. Sweat stung his eyes. Asher blinked, squinted at the dark. Something wasn't right, something was *wrong* over there. The shadow didn't move, but something else *did.*

Asher sucked in a breath. One of the shadows seemed to hum, seemed to waver, seemed to move in a dazzle in a blur, move in a manner the eye wasn't fashioned to see.

Asher's hair began to tingle, cold raced up his back. He could smell the stink of fear, taste the anger in the air. Then someone moved, came right at him, didn't make a sound.

"Stop right where you are," Asher said. "I'll blow your fuckin' head off, friend."

The figure stopped. Asher shifted his weapon to the left hand, drew his heavy flash with the right. Shined it at the shadow's head. Bright moon face with tiny ears, hair shaved down to the skull. Black pajamas and B.B. eyes. Buddha, if you really pissed him off, Buddha on a really bad day.

"Dinh, what the hell you doing out here, you want to tell me that, it's the middle of the night."

"Work here," Dinh said. "Take care of fish."

"Huh-unh. Dreamer said you quit."

"Quit over now. Comin' back. Take care of goddamn fish."

"Well there isn't any fish out here. Step aside easy, boy, don't try any Oriental shit on me. Now who else is with you, who's back there?"

"Bugalah," Dinh said. "Come back, findin' bugalah breakin' in."

"Findin' what?"

"Bugalah. Criminah bugalah your job, Asher, not mine. I pay fucking tax."

"Oh, that's real cute. Go sit down where I can see you, don't go anywhere."

Asher stepped away from Dinh, pointed the pistol and the flash toward the house. He saw the figure at once. Stopped, drew in a breath. For the second time that night, the hairs stood up on his neck.

"Holy shit," he said, squatted down and looked back at Dinh, but Dinh was already gone out of sight...

He closed the door quietly. Eileen was still asleep. The touch of Cindy's skin, the spice of her hair came with him in the house. Came in this time, it seemed, without any guilt, without any sorrow or regret. Bringing all the good stuff in, leaving the bad parts out.

Dreamer had to flinch at that. It sounded like the goodies his mother used to sew and hang on the wall. Happy little sayings. Homey sermons that seldom worked out in real life. Still, a lot of things didn't look the same as they had just a few weeks before, so think about that.

Like me, for a start. Why he didn't feel like himself. Why he wasn't the standard issue Dreamer anymore. (l) He didn't think the colors in his head had much to do with that. That was just something that happened, something that was there, and this was something else.

(2) Maybe he was wrong about that. Maybe it was the other way around. The colors, the gift from that ugly hunk of slag in his head, were not quite the same. Now—though he couldn't say why—when he closed his eyes and let them drift into life, they seemed to have a deeper, richer hue. The reds not so bloody, the greens not so bold. He sensed they could still open locks, scream like lunatic prophets now and then, but it wasn't the same, wasn't like it had been anymore.

So maybe *I* changed *them*, he decided. Maybe these wise and cheery colors are reflecting the new, improved Dreamer, who will see deeper aspects of life, wear clean ties and act reasonably refined.

He liked the sound of that. Thought about it twice. Decided it was happy bullshit. More of mom's samplers on the wall. Still, it felt good and made him want to smile.

"What's the matter with you, I miss a joke or what?"

Dreamer looked up. "I thought you were asleep."

"I know you did but I'm not."

"You feel okay, can I get you anything?"

"What time is it, I forgot my watch."

"Close to six."

"Christ, in the a.m., right? I *hate* this thing, I absolutely loathe being stuck like this. A couple of your lights went out in back. You better get 'em fixed."

"I'll do that today."

"This was while you were outside, friend."

He didn't need to look, knew she was looking at him.

"Cindy was here. Came to say goodbye."

"Goodbye."

"She's not staying in Austin, she's going somewhere."

"Well, I'm glad she's all right."

"Yeah, me too. Eileen..."

"You don't have to, Dreamer. I've heard all your sly orations before. Even the ones where you mean it, like I feel you do now. You have been a rude, selfish, uncaring son of a bitch. You're sorry, and you wouldn't cause me hurt for anything. What happened is, you had a high school hard-on for a while. You weren't even thinking straight, you can't imagine how that came about. I expect you'll take me out somewhere that doesn't have a burger on the sign."

"That's a lot better than I could've done it, Eileen, but I truly mean every word you said."

"Uh-huh, maybe." Eileen looked down at her hands. "I was awake before you went out. I know you're not aware of that. I heard how we irritate each other, how we don't all the time. How sometimes we do all right."

"Oh boy," Dreamer said.

Eileen shook her head. "What do you think is the matter with us? I got to be drunk to say nice stuff to you. You got to wait till you think I'm asleep. What kind of shit is that? We keep telling each other, hey, we're good *out* of bed, too, like that's some awesome fucking deal. Lots of normal folks do that. We do it, we get to feeling proud."

Dreamer walked over, scooted up a chair and sat down where his knees touched hers. "I get this funny feeling sometimes when we, you know, let go and let ourselves be us."

"What kind of feeling, hon?"

"Like I want to throw up."

"That's nice."

"No, I mean that in a very positive way. What I'm saying is, when it happens, I think I ought to, what? Back off, get the hell out of there."

Eileen tried to speak but Dreamer cut her off. "You said the other day I didn't care about you. You said it pissed you off when you thought about that. What I think is, you're not any different than me. I think this is a two-way deal. I think you get up and run just as quick as I do."

"I know I do."

"What?"

"I know I do," she said. She reached out and took his hand. "This is the straightest answer you'll likely ever get, Dreamer, so listen to it good. I'm a flat-out coward, and so are you. Every day, I get up scared I'm going to lose. Lose all my money, lose it in bed. Lose to some fat asshole in a sweaty courtroom. I expect you get scared when you—when you go out and steal stuff, whatever the hell you do, which I don't even want to talk about, Jesus, how did I get on that?"

"We going to just go on, keep doing this?"

"What? Getting scared? Drinking crying getting scared again? I don't know, hon. I wouldn't know how to start on doing something else."

"I do."

"What?"

"First thing we do, you don't go to France with Lee Ann."

"Then what?"

"Then we see what happens next. You and I make a plan, we're going to really fuck it up..."

Mako looked bad. Mako looked like a sack of chicken bones. Asher had no idea what secret Asian arts Dinh knew. All he could recall was Kung pao and Mu shu. This one seemed to center on eye, ear, crotch and kidney blows.

"Don't stand there doing nothing," Mako said, "gimmie a hand here."

"I don't think you ought to move," Asher said. "You don't look good to me."

"Fuck what you think. Fuck you, pal."

Mako groaned, made a face and stuck out his hand. Asher grabbed it, Mako held on. Pulled himself up, stumbled, staggered, closed his eyes in pain.

"I think you ought to sit. You might've busted something inside."

"That fuckin' slope, that's who's gonna get busted inside. Bastards comin' over here, taking good jobs from white guys. Aw, *shit,* man."

Mako blinked, wiped a string of blood from his mouth. One ear was swollen, one eye was black. He wore a black shirt, buttoned at the top. Black pants, wingtip shoes. Asher saw the S&W 9mm in his belt, saw the long suppressor on the barrel's end. Saw Mako looking right at him with little septic eyes.

"I know you. I seen you before. You're Asher, you're a cop. What the fuck you doin' here?"

"Mr. Binder, I was about to ask you the same thing."

"You know me. That's good. We don't have to waste any time. I got bidness here. I haven't got time to fuck with you. If you know Mako Binder, you gotta know you don't want to mess with me. Am I getting through, you see where I'm going, friend?"

"Yes, sir, I do."

"Good. I'm pleased to hear that." Mako drew in a painful breath. "I ain't feeling so hot. What you want to do is go. I'm doing you a favor here. I'm forgetting I saw you, you're forgetting you saw me. Somethin'll come in the mail. A thank you note from me. You got any problem with that?"

"No, I don't," Asher said. "Frankly, I'm getting too old for this shit.

I'm not looking for trouble anymore. Not from you or anybody else."

"Good. That's smart." Mako nodded, braced one hand against a tree. "Not get the fuck out of here." He looked at Asher, turned and stumbled off in the dark.

"Mr. Binder..."

Mako stopped.

"Turn around," Asher said, "spread your legs put your hands up don't try anything funny this is the police don't make a move you're under arrest stop or I'll shoot you dago son of a bitch."

. . .

"Where you been?" Betty said. "Christ, Avery, what kind of date is this?"

"Don't ask a bunch of questions," Asher said, "I'm about all talked out. Pop the trunk, hon, let's get somethin' to eat..."

INTERSTATE DREAMS

The new guy looks funny, he drags one leg and he walks with a hop. His face has been hit, fractured and broken, shattered and split. He's purple and blue and he hasn't healed up. His lip is cut open and his jaw is out of whack. He jerks his head and twitches like a bird.

This is a guy, thinks Wallace Pailey Marshall, who is flat out of luck. This is a guy very much like Marshall himself.

"I know you or what?" Marshall says.

"Whuuugh," the guy says.

The guy looks familiar to Marshall, but so does everybody else.

"I know where we can maybe get a drink," Marshall says. "But you gotta act right. You gotta walk straight, you can't go wobblin' about. Listen, what the fuck's the matter with you, pal?"

"Whuugh," the guy says.

"You musta done something. Anybody want to mess you up like that."

The new guy thought about that. "Drivin' inna car."

"So?"

"Out inna dark."

"Uhuh."

"Pretty li'l girl."

"Well, shit, no wonder," Marshall says.

The new guy doesn't say a thing. He stares at the freeway, at all the bright lights, at the yellows and the golds and the greens flashing by. He remembers he had a fine car, maybe three or four. He remembers he had a nice suit, shoes that didn't hurt. He can't remember where or even when. What he's doing here, where he's ever been. Another thing he can't recall is who he is. All he remembers is he hurts, he hurts real bad all the time.

Later, Wallace Pailey Marshall sleeps. The new guy stares at the cars for a while, then falls asleep as well. He sleeps, but the pain is still there.

Wallace Pailey Marshall has a dream about Amy. The new guy dreams about her too. In both of their dreams, Amy bakes in a white bikini in the sun. Amy sweat and baby oil slides down her breasts, down her lovely thighs. They can't remember that Amy doesn't know about nouns. That she doesn't do letters past "F." All they remember are the lovely Amy parts.

They vaguely recall the taste of whiskey, the smell of new cars. One of them thinks about lobster, one of them thinks about steak. One of them thinks about tennis, one of them thinks about golf.

Both of them think about what they haven't got. They think about the finest, most precious gift of all, those deep, wondrous silver straws that suck chilled air from the frozen lake at the center of the earth...

"I had a bad dream," Diane said. "They came and got me and snitched me off again."

"No one coming to get you, hon. Isn't anyone goin' to do that."

Junior sat on the edge of Dreamer's bed in the big bedroom upstairs. The wind came up and it rattled the branches in the trees. He heard Dreamer talking to Eileen for a while, then everything was quiet.

"Am I going to have to go back? Do I get to stay here?"

"Why don't you tell me what you want to do."

"I wish to stay with you and Dreamer. I feel good here. I'm not real frightened anymore."

"That's what me and Dreamer were thinking. We think that'd be good too."

Diane reached up and squeezed his hand.

"You saved me, noble sire. If I wasn't pledged to Dreamer, I would pledge myself to you."

Junior Lewis felt his heart swell. "That was the good Lord himself did the saving part, hon. I was just there, doing his will. Man hits me on the head. Another one tries to run me down. All I did was hang on by my fingernails, babe, wait for that fool to quit drivin' around."

"You did more than *that*," Diane said. "I owe you my life, and you'll always be my black knight."

"There's historical precedent for that. Old Tamerlane, back in thirteen-something, I forget. He was overrunning Persia, invading Samarkand? Best horse soldiers he had, the most fearsome of all, those fellas were black. Mean mutha— Hard-fighting men. Dreamer thinks he knows everything, he doesn't know that."

"Will you tell me the story sometime? About Tamerlane's knights?"

"Anytime you like, darling. You get to sleep now."

Diane sighed, looked out at the moon and the trees in the dark.

"These are evil times, sire. We are plagued by base and lowborn men. Sometimes I grieve for this kingdom of ours."

"It's bad, all right," Junior Lewis said, "isn't any question of that. I'm thinking, though, it's gotta get better sometime..."

If you were going to change me, what would you do? How would you want me to be?"

"You think I'm nuts? I wouldn't dare answer that."

"Come on, Dreamer. Not for real, just suppose."

"Just suppose."

"Right."

"I can't think of anything at all."

"Shoot. You're scared."

"You said suppose."

"Just suppose, is all."

"Huh-unh. You're fine the way you are."

"You coward. I know what it'd be."

"What?"

"You'd like me better if I was black. You'd like that just fine."

"Oh, for Christ's sake, Eileen."

"You would. Admit that you would."

"I won't because it isn't true at all. Any way you look at that remark, it's a racist thing to say."

"I wish you weren't such a chicken. I think we'd have a better chance in this new, improved relationship if you'd be honest with me."

"I'm honest with you. I just don't have anything to say."

"You do but you won't."

"No I don't."

"Yes you do."

"No I don't, okay?"

"One thing."

"What?"

"One thing. Even if it isn't a real big thing, just tell me what it is."

"Let's get off of this."

"Come on."

"You won't like it."

"You don't know if I will or not."

"It's no big thing."

"You said that, go ahead. It doesn't have to be."

"I like about everything about you. Even the stuff I <u>don't</u> like, I like just fine. I think I probably love you. I'm not sure, but I think that's right. The only thing—"

"What?"

"Listen, it's not anything at all."

"Go on. Say it."

"I don't think I should."

"Dreamer—"

"All right, okay. Like I said, it isn't important, it doesn't mean a thing. I just wish you weren't a fucking lawyer, Eileen. I sure could do without that..."